HorrorScope

A Zodiac Anthology
Volume IV

Edited by
H. Everend

Copyright © 2024 by January Ember Press
Artwork Copyright © by
"image: Freepik.com". This cover has been designed using assets from Freepik.com
Cover Design by GetCovers

Authors hold copyrights to individual works.

All rights reserved. No part of this book may be reproduced or transmitted in any form or by any means, electronic or mechanical, including photocopying, recording, or by any information storage or retrieval system without the written consent of the publisher except where permitted, by law. For more information, address: harrieteverend@gmail.com

These are works of fiction. Names, characters, places, and incidents either are the product of the author's imagination or are used fictitiously. Any resemblance to actual persons, living or dead, events, or locales is entirely coincidental.

I WANT TO DEDICATE THIS FINAL VOLUME TO EVERYONE WHO SUUBMITTED THEIR PIECES FOR NOT ONLY THIS COLLECTION, BUT FOR ALL THE PREVIOUS ONES TOO. WITHOUT ALL OF YOU, THIS WOULDN'T HAVE BEEN POSSIBLE. THANK YOU SO MUCH FROM THE BOTTOM OF MY HEART:

A.D. Jones
A.S.C.
A.W. Mason
Aiden E. Messer
Alana K. Drex
Alex Penuelas
Alex Tilley
Alexander Michael
Alice Stone
Allison Hillier
Alyssa Milani
Alyssa Stadnyk
Amanda Jaeger
Amanda Worthington
Amber Hathaway
Andrew Jackson
Angel Krause
Anthony Taylor
AP Vrdoljak
Arabella K. Federico
Ashe Woodward
Ashleigh Hatter
Ashley Nestler
Ashley Scheller
Becca Joan
Bethany Russo
Briana Morgan
Brianna Malotke
Brooklynn Dean
Bryce Johle
Byron Griffin
Caitlin Marceau
Caleb J. Pecue
Caleb James K.
Chaz Williams
Chris Steele
Christian Francis
Christopher La Vigna

Christopher Robertson
Damien Casey
Dan B. Fierce
Daphinie Cramsie
Dave Musson
David Royce
David Washburn
Delliom Ellidom
Devon Talbott
Dominic Rascati
Dorian J. Sinnott
Dylan Colon
Elias Chase
Elliot Ason
Emma Jamieson
Eric Woods
Gillian Church
Greta T. Bates
Hayden Robinson
Hayley Anderton
Ivan Lopez
J. Rocky Colavito
Jack Finn
Jasmine de la Paz
Jason A. Jones
Jay Parker
Jelena Vuksanović
Jena Glover
Jenna Dietzer
Jessica Huntley
Josh Hanson
Julia C. Lewis
Kassidy VanGundy
Kay Hanifen
Kerry E.B. Black
Kirsten Aucoin
Konn Lavery
Kyra R. Torres

L. Pine
L. Stephenson
Lanie Mores
LaShane Arnett
Lennox Rex
Loki J. DeWitt
Lucy Grainger
Lylith & Herne
M. Rook Grimsley
Marilyn Young
Marissa Yarrow
Marshall Gunness III
Morgan Chalfant
Nadine Stewart
Nico Bell
Nikki Kossaris
Nina Tolstoy
R.E. Sohl
Rachel M. Shannon
Rose Whittaker
Ryan Meyer
S.C. Fisher
S.L. Shearhart
Sabrina Voerman
Samantha Arthurs
Samuel M. Hallam
Scott McGregor
Shantel Brunton
Shawnna Deresch
Skye Myers
Stormi Lewis
Taylor Pawley
Torrence Bryan
Wendy Dalrymple
Wesley Winters
Willie R. Heredia
Zach Swasta
Zary Fekete

TABLE OF CONTENTS

Aries
The Elements of Eldritch – *Lylith & Herne*
The Wardrobe – *Rose Whittaker*
Fireproof – *A.D. Jones*

Taurus
Man O'Gold - *Alex Penuelas*
Just Missing One – *Alyssa Milani*
Til Death - *Jena Glover*

Gemini
Twin Telepathy – *Kerry E.B. Black*
A House with Two Front Doors – *Jenna Dietzer*
Hole of Darkness – *Alyssa Stadnyk*

Cancer
Love on the Shore – *Alexander Michael*
You and Your Cancer – *Ashe Woodward*
Control – *Anthony Taylor*

Leo
Leona – *Hayden Robinson*
Sins of the Flesh – *Emma Jamieson*
The Burning Night – *Lucy Grainger*

Virgo
Immaculate – *H. Everend*
Beneath the Archives – *Jack Finn*
Immortal Virgo – *Allison Hillier*

Libra

By The Scales – *Elliot Ason*
Just ~*Libra*~ Things - *Kassidy VanGundy*
Lord of Death - *Sabrina Voerman*

Scorpio

Scorpio in Dreams - *Morgan Chalfant*
A Cold Winter's Call - *Alex Tilley*
Venom of God - *Byron Griffin*

Sagittarius

Dark Arrow – *Jelena Vuksanović*
Rosalind – *Ashley Scheller*
Bog Hag – *Caleb James K.*

Capricorn

I've Come for the Master - *A.S.C.*
The Capricorn Man – *Lanie Mores*
Fair Share – *Daphinie Cramsie*

Aquarius

Underwater – *AP Vrdoljak*
Pale Sister – *Skye Myers*
An Unusual Agreement – *Brianna Malotke*

Pisces

This is My Weight to Bear - *Caitlin Marceau*
A Gift of Pearls – *S.C. Fisher*
Lady Fish - *LaShane Arnett*

The Elements of Eldritch
-Lylith & Herne-

There were more of us when we started, and my thoughts were on my fallen brothers and sisters as we prepare for the final task. It's taken so long to get here. It feels like years, but as far as I can calculate, it's been five months since we embarked on this journey—this quest. Five months since I first met the group, that was to become closer to me than anyone else has for a long time.

Returning to that first meeting in the tavern, the details are hazy. I know there was a lot of laughter as we all agreed to band together and undertake what none of us knew would be the most brutal quest any of us had ever faced, but I don't remember any of the words we spoke. I don't remember any awkward first meeting small talk, although it must have been there. I don't even fully remember who gave us the task, who gave us the instructions that would lead so many to their deaths. All I remember are the faces of my comrades as they were. Everything else in my mind is shrouded in fog, except for the name we gave the quest—The Elements of Eldritch. It was not very original, but it was definitely fitting, as our quest was in the realm of Eldritch and involved recovering the Five Elemental Tokens from the beings that now guarded them. Only when they were together again and returned to their rightful home could Eldritch be free from the crawling terror it had borne for far too long.

Many had tried before us—all had fallen and failed. But we were the ones. We were the chosen ones. We believed it. We were veterans of many previous campaigns, although this would be the first we had done together. There were twelve of us at the start. Three of each class: Elves, Mages, Thieves, and Warriors. We thought that would be enough. It may still prove to be, but I'm no longer so sure.

We are down to just the two of us now. Myself and the Elf, Morgana. Will we overcome the Demon that holds the Fire, The Old God himself, Aries? It sounds impossible, but we have learned that numbers do not matter; all that matters are wits, courage, and a willingness to sacrifice everything you hold dear. So as we stand here, Aries, I tell you, "Beware! Death has come, vengeance has come, victory has come, and we will reclaim the Ram's Skull you stole."

I know it's important to prepare myself fully, to remember that I am the most powerful Warrior left in the realm, but I can't help but feel a little terror at the task to come. I remember all too well the fate that befell ten of my original companions, and in doing so, my testicles shrivel and contract, reminding me that I am flesh and blood—I am mortal.

We started with what we thought would be the easy task: The Blood of the Earth. The task was straightforward. Kill the Vampire and retrieve the flask that contained the blood of the firstborn, Lilith of Eldritch. We knew where the Vampire dwelled; the journey to reach him would only take a week or so to complete, and we knew that, like all Vampires, this one had no magic beyond the power to influence thought. Our plan was simple: when we reached the Castle, we would send in our best Thief, Gerald, along with two of our Mages, William and

Julia. William would be tasked with casting a spell to reveal where the beast was hidden, Julia would counter any mind tricks the Vampire could throw, and Gerald would sneak close enough to plunge a stake through his foul heart as he lay helpless during the Sun God's time.

The journey to the Castle was uneventful, beyond one meeting with a Cave Troll, but this just reminded us how strong we were, as I, Tom and Miriam—the three Warriors—despatched the giant beast with ease.

When we reached the Castle, we immediately felt the influence of the Vampire. We all felt a dread fall over our hearts and doubt enter our minds where before there had just been confidence and determination. Julia tried casting a counter spell, but it didn't seem to work. She said it was because we were not inside the walls of the Castle. The three who would confront the Vampire prepared themselves as the rest of us made camp and tried to ignore the growing sense of unease and discontentment. As time wore on, William and Gerald seemed to be affected more than the rest of us, and eventually, they were at the point where if they didn't go now, they could never raise the courage to start. Julia wanted to wait, but Gerald persuaded her. They set off with only a few hours left before Luna took sway over the earth, and the Vampire would be reborn. The worst possible time to start this task. We watched them go and prayed that we would see them again.

Sol died, and Luna had shone her radiance over the land for five long hours before we felt the dread flee from our hearts, and we knew the Three had completed their quest. We who had remained behind rejoiced and awaited the return of our conquering heroes. At least, we rejoiced until we heard the weeping. It seemed to be coming from just outside the campfire's range of light and was the most heartbreaking sound any of us had ever heard. Morgana and I went to investigate and found Julia lying on the earth, her head buried in her arms, hiding her face. I picked her up and carried her back to camp, where she eventually showed us the Flask of Lilith. She also told us of the fate that befell William and Gerald.

Julia had cast her magic, and the fear of the Vampire had retreated from Gerald and William. William said the words of revealing, and the Vampire was uncloaked and visible to Gerald. He moved with the sly speed of his profession and was beside the Vampire before the others could react. Just as he was about to deal the death blow, the Vampire's eyes snapped open, and Gerald was lost. As the Vampire's curse had laid over us, the journey to the Castle had taken the Three friends longer than they realised, and night had now arrived. Before our Mages could react, the Vampire had crushed Gerald's windpipe with one long-boned hand. William changed his spell from revealing to immobilisation, but it wasn't strong enough to stop the Old Beast. He turned the full force of his mind tricks onto William, and courage fled from the Mage's heart. His words faded, and the beast was free to destroy him with a swift bite to the neck. He had underestimated Julia, though, as many had before. She snatched the stake from Gerald's dead hand and plunged it through the Vampire's back, piercing his foul heart. The deed cost her dear, and she was forever lost to darkness. It took all her strength to retrieve and return the flask to us, but she was never the same again. We had completed one task, but at what price? Losing two of our companions shocked us to the core, and poor, dear, beautiful Julia was now just a shell of her former self.

The next task was to find the Kraken that held the Tears of Pisces, the charm that represented Water. We knew the journey would be long, so it proved, and this time, the travelling was not so easy. We met a band of robbers after fourteen hard days' journey, and Julia was taken from us at their hands. We avenged and mourned her, but we were now down to Nine.

I will not relate everything the Kraken did to us before we recovered the Tears; the memory is still too foul for me to speak of it. However, this task marked a turning point. At that point, we understood exactly how far the Guardians of the Tokens would go to protect them and inflict horrors on all who came to challenge them. I will tell of the fall of Miriam, so you understand why we spent so long hacking the Kraken with blades before we dealt the killing blow, but I will not speak of any other horrors we witnessed in that place. Prepare yourselves.

We were all helpless in the dungeons of the Kraken, held naked and tormented by his minions for a time beyond measure before he appeared. The pool in the centre of the floor bubbled like boiling water, and then a tentacle appeared, followed by another, and then more. They snaked out of that water, dripping slime and filling our nostrils with a stench beyond anything we had imagined in our worst nightmares. The tentacles made straight for Miriam, and we could only watch in horror as two of them wrapped around her ankles and pulled her legs wide apart. Another tentacle slowly climbed up her leg and over her hip, leaving a trail of slime on her stomach as the tip of it reached her breast and caressed her nipple. Miriam opened her mouth to shout in disgust, but before a sound could leave her, another tentacle had entered her mouth and was now being forced down her throat. Her eyes were wide with shock, then pain, as the tentacle at her breast seemed to use its suckers to attach to her nipple and pull back, stretching the nipple away from her breast, finally pulling it free, leaving tendrils of hanging flesh and streams of blood flowing over the underside of her breast and down her stomach. With shocking speed and much thicker than the others, another tentacle came out of the water and speared into the opening between Miriam's legs. It seemed to pause, then fucked her with unrelenting force and speed. After a time, it came entirely out of her and waited a few inches from her vagina. We thought it would retreat into the water, but it didn't. Instead, it plunged back into her. At the same time, the tentacle in her mouth shoved itself down, seeming to try to meet the one invading her pussy. Miriam died soon after as the thick, slimy shafts tore her apart from the inside.

I will not tell any more of the struggles we endured before defeating that vile beast and claiming our second Token beyond stating that we were reduced to Six, Tom and Glenda both having been taken by the Kraken in the same manner that Miriam fell.

We took some time to recover after that encounter, making camp and staying there for more than a week, doing little other than arguing whether we should continue the quest. None of us had ever seen anything like this on any previous adventure. We had all seen death more times than we could remember, but never such savage, explicit sexual violence and torture. We knew that we had signed up for the most challenging quest any had ever undertaken, but we were not ready for this. The rules, it appeared, had changed.

We decided we had invested too much to quit and tried our best to recover our courage and wits as we headed off to our next task, but the Horror of Eldritch had invaded our minds now, and we would never again be free of it. The third task, the Twins of The Air, was another shock to our rapidly deteriorating mental courage as the Dragon took another of us with shockingly casual brutality. Mark, the most courageous of us, volunteered to enter the Dragon's Lair and slay the beast. We watched him depart; we heard his screams; we saw his dismembered body; we reached that state that only comrades who have suffered so much can go to—and the Dagon felt the full force of our wrath.

We had completed three of the five tasks, but now our band was just five, and Pauline was wavering between life and death, having been struck by the Dragon's claws during that last fight. We debated the merits of resting to allow her to heal, but the growing unsettlement that had invaded our minds was at work, and the debate turned into an argument, and then the argument turned into a fight. We reduced our own numbers from five to three that fateful night. Pauline died, raving and ranting as the Horror of Eldritch overcame her mind, and John died at the hands of Morgana.

John had always had an eye on her, and I could understand that, as Morgana was the most beautiful thing we had ever seen, and her spirit only enhanced that beauty. She is strong. She is powerful and confident. She is dangerous. Most of us recognised this and worshipped her at a distance, but that night John showed his true nature, and during the physical altercation, he tried to rape her. His actions stopped the fight between myself and Ash, as we saw our comrade having her clothing torn away and fighting to prevent John from forcibly entering her. We turned all our aggression and rage onto John. We pulled him off Morgana and held him down, allowing her to have her revenge. She meted out punishment in kind, and John died with blood and faeces running down his legs underneath a tree with a jagged stump, where a branch had been violently torn off by Morgana.

The remaining three of us were filled with rage and determination to complete the final two tasks and end the quest, but we were also heavily infected with the Horror of Eldritch, and our minds and judgment were clouded and in tatters. The fourth task was the breaking point for us, and Morgana and I lost our remaining sanity. To complete the Judgement of Spirit, we had to choose one of us to become a sacrifice. What being could conceive of such a horror? How could we determine which of us would fall? Ash took the choice out of our hands when his mind finally broke utterly, and we awoke from sleep to find him gone. We searched for him for many long days but never found a trace of him. We are curious to know if he simply abandoned the quest or succumbed to the Horror of Eldritch. All we know is that we now had four of the five Tokens and were a team of two. Myself and Morgana. We would have to face the final task banded together or fail utterly.

So now we are here. We only need the Stolen Ram Skull of Fire to complete the quest and free Eldritch. We only need to kill Aries. Now, we begin...

"Holy fucking shit, you two! I can't fucking believe you've got this far!" said Duncan. "When we met in the pub, and you chose me as Dungeon Master, I knew it would be an epic game, but fuck me, after all these weeks, you guys have done us proud!"

The ten friends eliminated during the previous sessions sat around the big table, looking at the two remaining players with admiration and concern.

"Are you two ok?" asked Pauline. "You're looking strange, Morg. You too, Adam."

Morg and Adam, the final two players, didn't reply. They just looked at each other with blank stares and then turned their gaze back to Duncan. The look they gave him wasn't encouraging, but in his excitement, Duncan didn't notice.

Realising that Adam and Morg were about to embark on the final game battle, the ten friends, now without snacks or drinks, retreated to the kitchen to prepare. They also needed a break from the tension that they could feel was building in the room. No one wanted to discuss the strange and unnerving vibes Adam and Morg were giving off that made them all feel uneasy.

"Ready for the final boss?" Duncan asked. "No one has ever got to Aries before. It's insane that you managed it, but I don't think you've got what it takes to defeat him." Duncan laughed nervously and turned his concentration to the books and dice in front of him on the table. He didn't notice Morg rise from her chair and linger around the table; neither did he notice Adam pull the knife from his pocket and move in the opposite direction to Morg.

From the refuge of the kitchen, the other players were unaware that anything was wrong until they heard Duncan's screams of agony crying out from the gaming room. Leaving their snacks and drinks behind, the friends nervously made their way towards the desperate pleas for help from their Dungeon Master.

So ends Aries, speared by my blade and rendered unmanned by Morgana's teeth. Ultimately, all you had was mind tricks, disguising yourself as an ordinary man speaking words we didn't understand to deflect and confuse us. We were disappointed in you, Aries; you were supposed to be the God of War but fell so easily. Or is it over? Was this all a trick? The horror is still on us, and I see our dead companions coming towards us out of the mist; Morgana sees them, too, so I know it's not just in my mind. Aries is a trickster, and this must be his final test for us. I look at Morgana and see the resolve in her eyes as we walk forward to meet the evil spirits of our dead companions, our blades drawn and ready to slay...

THE WARDROBE
-Rose Whittaker-

I open the door and search through pressed white shirts,
Their cotton like snow, cold and stiff,
My hand plunges deeper, touching ice and freezing in a drift beyond,
I go on.

Pine trees hang from a night sky, their branches flat, their leaves starched in place,
and I go on.
A raven atop the lamppost watches me as I stalk familiar tracks, his eye glittering,
and I go on.
The fawn is alone in thick tawny trousers and a proud white crest -
I leave no scarlet pool,
no shriek pierces our heart,
no tools are needed for my transformation.

I pick my way back through the tracks, cloven feet in snowy gloves,
My deer old clothes don't pinch or rub, they cling as if I were born this way.

The pressed pines huddle together but I slip through their crowd with ease,
emerging from the
shirts anew,
My trophy skin just like a soul, its eyes glittering.

FIREPROOF
-A. D. Jones-

I was born a bit different. That's what they told me anyway, when I was seven and they explained to me, once again, why I couldn't go outside and play with the other children.

"I know it's hard," Father said as he gave me that look of pity that he had perfected for these talks. "Your skin isn't like the other children's. Thirty seconds out there in the sun and you will blister and burn. I can't see my little girl suffer like that."

I shed some tears, obviously, but knew that would be the outcome of the conversation before it even began. Seven years old and already fully resigned to the fact that it was unlikely I'd ever see the outside of this house.

This prison.

This beautiful stately home with its huge bedrooms, each equipped with grandiose four-poster beds, its exuberant playrooms and expansive library. A home many would absolutely dream of for certain, but just like you can provide all the trees and scenery you like for that majestic lion, a cage is still a cage.

My name is Freya. I have long blonde hair, the colour of wheat grain with sporadic darker strands throughout, that if I catch myself just right between the rays of sunlight and my mirror, glow like honey dripping through my wavy locks. My eyes are the grey of impending rain clouds, and my skin is pale and unblemished except for the freckle on my right eyelid, my little smudge of Dutch cocoa. These things I note as I sit day after day in front of the ornate gilded mirror and look at myself. My skin doesn't look any different from the other children.

For as long as I can remember, I haven't left this house. My education has been the undertaking of both my parents in unison. Father was at the forefront of things, as I think he loved the sound of his own voice. Mother was excellent with numbers and the sciences. Apparently, this is what's called homeschooling. I didn't know for a long time that children all went to school together in big buildings specially built for such purposes. Once I got a little older and the wealth of extra education, I could find collected like treasures in the books of the library were unlocked to me. I learned about a lot of things my parents had kept from me. I devoured those books with a fervour I couldn't measure, and they were my secret little trips to the outside. I travelled the world with Dickens, went on adventures with Don Quixote, fell madly in love with Heathcliff in Wuthering Heights and wept openly with Frankenstein's creation. I travelled far and wide and even though they were in my head, the sights I saw.

With a whole world of adventures at my fingertips, I was able to remove myself from this smothering house for short periods of time, but the greatest tragedy for me wasn't the locations I was missing, nor the adventures themselves, it was the friends made along the way.

I have never had a friend to call my own. Well, not in a proper sense, anyway. I have an imaginary friend. Her name is Barbara, and she is my only friend. She's tall and beautiful and has blonde hair flecked with honey, just like I do. She is older than me, somewhere closer to my parents' age, I think, and smells like lilac, charred wood, and a sweet, sickly fragrance that I can't place. Barbara visits me most days and recommends good books for me to read and tells me about the world outside. I'm not allowed to tell my parents about her, or she will have to go away, so it's our little secret.

As I got older, Barbara hasn't changed at all. Such is the way of a person born of imagination, but she talks to me more like an adult now and teaches me things that I find fascinating. It is a simple task, for instance, to gather easily accessible herbs and leaves collected in a fabric pouch and place them at an open window to entice a cat to come be your friend. Barbara calls it a familiar, but I have named him ragamuffin. He brings me dead things which I find a little disgusting, but Barbara says they will come in handy in the future. Something else she plans to teach me, I suppose.

It was a relatively cloudy day, and my parents were both out of the house, a thing that was seldom known to me and, being now a restless teenager, I was struggling largely with boredom. It would be fair to say that the playrooms of my younger years were void of any appeal and left to the past under a layer of dust, and so I decided today was the day to test my skin.

I was too young to remember the burning and blistering my parents would still recount to me any time I pressed them to let me try again, so I was going to see for myself. The clouds above were grey, and the sun wasn't visible in the sky, so I could step out just enough that I could quickly dart back in should I begin to burn.

I found myself stood at the open back door, literally wavering on my first steps into the outside world, an odd sense of fear and excitement mixed as I rocked on my feet in the kitchen. Even in the warmth of August, the clouds in the sky were dense and heavy, creating the perfect day to experiment with my condition. I would skip just to the end of the garden and back.

Realising that I had been holding my breath for probably thirty seconds without noticing, I exhaled and took a step forward out of the kitchen door. I had no time to react to the heat from the paving on my barefoot before someone forcefully pulled me back into the house.

"What in the hells are playing at?" The look on my mother's face was both a look of rage and abject horror as she pulled me back and, in a fluid move, spun me into a waiting chair at the dining table.

"Is this what it's come to?" she spat. "We can't even leave you alone for an afternoon without you casting yourself into harm's way?" there were tears in both our eyes already.

I pleaded with her to calm down and to at least see it from my point of view, but it was to no avail. Apparently, there didn't need to be any consideration for what I was missing out on as long as she was around.

In what I believe was an attempt to soften the blow of the bolts and locks that were now placed on the doors and windows throughout our homestead, Father brought home a new book for me, the latest work of Charles Dickens, Little Dorrit. I am honestly unsure if this was an oversight on his part or if there was some intentional malice. Little Dorrit, the story of a girl born and raised in prison. The irony was not lost on me for a second and I will confess it caused a rage within me I hadn't felt before.

Barbara said that this was a good thing and that I could harness that anger and make use of it moving forward. She has shown me how to make a small flickering flame in the palm of my hand using only a pinch of soot. At first, I was scared because I obviously didn't want to burn my hand, but she assured me it would be okay. It seemed that the women in my family had some kind of protection from fire, although I wasn't sure what she was referring to.

It was such an odd thing to sit and focus on the little pile of soot that sat in my palm and imagine the flames in my mind, the sensation of warmth building in my hand and an almost dizzying feeling throughout the rest of my body, akin to the moment before a shiver runs down your spine.

With Barbara's guidance, I gradually improved my skills as I repeatedly snuffed out and relit the flame. She says that I am a natural, and it makes me happy to see her beam with pride as I take to her tutelage. If I am being honest with myself, I am sure now that she isn't a creation of my own mind at all, though I'm not ready to approach that conversation just yet. The way she tilts her head and smiles softly when I do well with her teachings makes me think there is something more to her, and truthfully as I am growing into my body and my features are sharpening, I can see a likeness between us taking shape.

I made my parents ill. It was just an experiment, and not something lasting or dangerous, a little malady to see them bedbound for some days with lethargy and fever. Thanks to my partner in crime, who I am now almost sure is a spirit of some kind, it was a simple matter of taking some herbs and ground animal bones, courtesy of Ragamuffin, and focusing my will on them in a binding spell. The results, it seems, were swift acting and rather more potent than I had expected, but it shall pass quickly, and it is yet another piece of my arsenal that I shall take with me going forward.

I couldn't suppress my curiosity any longer, and I began questioning Barbara relentlessly, like water bursting through a dam. I've come to realise that my imaginary friend is actually the ghost of my grandmother, who passed away many decades ago. It's as if she's still here, making sure her wisdom lives on. The menfolk, it seems, don't carry the gift and so Father has been passed over in this instance.

When I asked her about my supposed 'condition', her expression conveyed more than the response, confirming what I have always believed - that I do not suffer from it. I can feel the surge of rage inside me, pushing aside any thoughts of concern.

I sit peacefully in my room as I prepare for what is coming next. I have laid out all my treasures before me and find them calming. I position many velvet herb pouches specifically around the animal bones. I arrange the bones before me in the shape of a V, with intricate curls at its tips. The shape resembles the ram's skull that I have copied from memory many times on paper. The more I look at it, the more I can see how it also resembles the female reproductive organs, and I wonder if that is in part where the power that it seems to imbue me with comes from.

I place two fingers into the small bowl of soot before me and trace black patterns across my face, first running down the bridge of my nose and then along my cheekbones. After that, I draw a sequence of sigils in the black residue across my chest and then stroke my hands together, transferring as much of the soot as possible across both my hands.

It was late now, and the moonlight was slowly creeping along the floor of my room as I readied myself to head downstairs, Barbara standing at my side, her hand resting on my shoulder in a delicate and maternal manner.

With her help, I have pushed the limits of my abilities far beyond that which I considered feasible, though in truth I may have been holding myself back all this time. I waited until long into nightfall before taking it upon myself to ignite not just my palms, but everything within my proximity. I sat cross-legged in the parlour and channelled all my rage and emotions into the spell, and watched as the fires burst into life around me, dancing like small spirits of flame on every surface.

Grandmother was right in her much earlier declaration. The flames danced gleefully around me with little more than a gentle warmth. No harm would fall unto me by fire, a gift from her she sadly couldn't afford to herself. The fires spread out across the room, and I watched as they climbed the curtains and lick at the ceiling before engulfing the room entirely.

There weren't any screams or cries that I could discern, and to this day, I am not sure if I consider that to be a blessing or not. I waited quietly and patiently for the entire house to become a raging inferno before I stood up from my position in the parlour and made my way to the front door. Standing on what would be the precipice of a new life, I turned to take in a full view of the burning building before looking back to the now heat buckled wood of the door to the house. I extended both my hands out in front of me, palms towards the door, and focused hard. I swear I could feel Grandmother's hands on my shoulders as she stood behind me and willed me to concentrate.

A shockwave of vibrations ripped through my body and outwards from my palms, sending a blast of power into the door and splintering it like brittle kindling, the pieces flying away as if struck by some unseen force. I stepped, for the first time, out into the cool night air and breathed in the gentle breeze as I walked down the long path from the house, the blaze of the building illuminating everything around me in its glow.

Grandmother had seen that she would be the last of us to ever burn. Through her strength, she also made sure that she would not be the last of us to exist. Just as the moon will rise every evening and the skies will fill with thunder, there will always be witches.

Man O' Gold
-Alex Penuelas-

"Once there was a man with a body made o' gold,
His smile was timeless, and he ne'er grew old,
This be the tale me father foretold,
Of the poor man with a body made o' gold.

"Friends were aplenty, and enemies too:
One stole his hat, another his shoe!
The poor man wept, his tears pure azure:
His enemies, and friends, stole these too!

"One night, the man o' gold wept no more.
The townsmen found 'em on a Plutonian shore.
His eyes obsidian as they ne'er were before:
The poor man o' gold wept no more.

"His body then crumbled into fragments of gold,
its wealth was timeless, and ne'er grew old,
This be the tale me father foretold,
Of how the poor man's sufferin' struck us gold!"

Just Missing One
-Alyssa Milani-

I know walking in the woods at night isn't the smartest thing to do, but it's the fastest way home. I can take the long way and get caught in the rain, or I take the shortcut and make it home a whole twenty minutes sooner. So, I take the shortcut.

Unfortunately, the rain started as soon as I stepped onto the path in the forest, but the rain isn't that bad. Drizzling for now. Plus, I've been walking for a good ten minutes. There's no use in turning back now.

It's eerily silent tonight, the pitter-patter of rain falling on the leaves is calming. But the fog and chill crawling up my spine is not.

After the week I had, I just want to get home and face plant onto my bed. I manage the local apothecary shop. There's a Zodiac Sign theme this week. It's plastered all over the shop. I have every sign memorized in case a customer asks…they don't. I chose to work the night shift so my days can be free. It's a fun job, except for this part. Leaving work alone at night is not my idea of fun.

A twig snaps behind me causing everything in my body to freeze. My heart is in my throat, my hands are shaking at my sides, the fucking tempo of the blood pumping through my veins is alive and wild in my ears.

Slowly, I turn to look back even though my instinct is to run. My damn curiosity needs to know what that sound was. My mind must be playing tricks on me. There are shadows, moving slowly in and out of trees in unnatural ways. Shadows spanning almost as high as the trees, climbing, disturbing. And yet, my feet are firmly planted as I watch my eyes feast on my impending doom.

Another twig snaps to my left, closer than the first. Too close.

I whimper, taking a step back as the shadows continue to sway, a soft chat moves through the silence. And that's my cue to run.

I take in as much air as I can and charge in the direction I was headed, feet pounding on the uneven ground.

The chanting grows louder, shadows surrounding me. But I press on. I'm so close to the end of the path. So fucking close.

Sweat forms and drips from my brow, getting lost in the pouring rain that grows heavier the louder the chanting becomes. I glance back, seeing the shadows of the creatures crawling toward me. Shadows, so many of them following me, surrounding me.

I pump my legs harder, the fear clawing at my neck. Scratching its way as heat rises and clouds my vision with tears.

The stench of rot fills the air, closing my windpipes from allowing any air in.

I start coughing, gagging really. But I can't stop. Not now. Not when I'm so close—

I trip and slap the ground with an oof; wet leaves and muck stick to me. I spin my head around, looking behind me. But I see nothing but darkness. The light of the moon giving enough shine to show me there's nothing but my psychosis fucking with me.

No shadow.
No chanting.
Silence.

I suck in a rush of air and start laughing. "You're going crazy, Melanie. Fucking crazy."

I push myself up and dust off the decaying leaves from my chest. "Crazy," I tell myself with another chuckle.

But I hear it. Faint, but it's there. Another twig snaps to my right, another shadow climbing the tree. Another soundless scream.

I don't bother looking around, I push forward, running as the sounds of a thousand screams belt out behind me.

My heart skips, my breathing wavers, and my entire body trembles, yet I push forward. The road is right there. My house is a block and a half from it.

I'm going to make it.

I glance back again, those shadows reaching out for me, fingers long and pointy, unnaturally shaped.

They won't get me.

I'm going to make it.

I'm going to make it.

All the air is sucked out of my lungs, leaving me gasping as I body check into someone.

I fly backward, thudding to the ground and coughing. Bile rises, stinging my throat as I try to cough out my ability to breathe normally again.

My muscles screamed as I try to stand, legs wobbling, arms too weak to support me. The ache that crawls up my spine feels like the unnatural fingers running along my skin.

The man I ran into doesn't move. He's standing like a statue, arms folded across his chest, hood low on his eyes. His nostrils huff out breaths every five seconds. Heavy breaths that sound like they're coming from an animal.

"There's s-something in the woods," I say, my voice trembling.

He doesn't move.

A fucking statue that didn't even budge when I ran into him. I don't like this. Fear is a quiet killer, attacking the heart, the soul, and playing tricks on the mind.

I saw the shadows.

Heard the chants. The screams.

I'm getting away from this damning forest. Away from this lunatic. I'm going to make it.

By God, I will make it.

He huffs again, slowly uncrossing his brute arms.

I gulp down the burning in my throat, looking back at the deafening silence other than the rain. There's nothing there.

Nothing.

Whatever was after me is gone.

Maybe there was never anything after me. Maybe I'm losing my mind. I work too damn much.

I clench and unclench my fists, determination to continue through the end of the path, home.

I turn back to the man and he's gone. My breathing shakes when I see no trace of him ever being there. No footprints in the mud, no snapping twigs nearby.

Nothing.

I take a step, then another, and I buck it for the exit. Forcing my aching legs to get me home.

The street lamps are out, the roads are quiet. It's just me and my heavy breathing moving through the night.

Work the night shift, I said.

You'll get more sleep, I said.

Like the stupid bitch I am, I walk to work instead of driving. All for nothing now.

The rain lets up as soon as I cross the street and head for my house. One more block and I'm safe. Just one more block.

I pump my legs harder, keeping my focus in front of me even though something flickers in my peripherals.

When I round the corner and see my house, I glance back and see the shadows again.

They're following me.

They're surrounding me like an auditorium and I'm on stage, front and center.

I grit and bare my teeth. "Fuck! Leave me alone!"

Chants start again, quiet this time. Enough to send that impeding shiver up my spine again, rising the hair on the back of my neck.

Then I see him. The statue of a man standing on my front porch, arms folded across his chest, breath clouding around him in heavy huffs.

I'm not going to make it.

I skid to a stop, looking back to see the shadows have stopped, too.

"What the fuck do you want?" I shout so loudly my voice cracks.

The man slowly uncrosses his arms, and as quiet as a mouse, he steps off the porch, his moves so calculated and precise.

I whimper as I take a step back, looking at the house across the street from me. They have a dog, if I get closer to their property, the dog will go wild and set off some nosy neighbors.

I take a step back, then another, until I'm walking quickly to the fenced-in property.

The man follows, slowly, face still covered, breaths still heavy and releasing every five seconds.

But the dog's not barking. *C'mon, Roscoe, fucking bark!*

I turn my head to get a look at the doghouse, everything zooming in on it. Roscoe can't bark. His fucking head is missing.

A scream climbs up my throat, rolling to the tip of my tongue, but when I turn to release it, the man is standing before me. Huffing his breath in my face.

I whimper, looking at the shadows as they sway slowly from side to side.

What is this?

Why the fuck is this happening to me?

The man slowly raises a hand, touching my wet hair and curling a strand around his finger. "Perfect," his deep, guttural voice says.

"What do you want?" I manage through a whisper.

He steps back, huffing again, and turning to the shadows. They start moving, coming closer to me. My will to live jumps out of me and I shove the man, making no attempt at moving him, but it allows me to charge in the opposite direction of the shadows. Maybe if I can outrun them, I can whip around I get back to my house. Safety between four walls.

Or wake up from this fucking nightmare.

I don't make it more than three steps when the brute giant grabs me by the hair and yanks me back, holding me up as my legs dangle.

I scream, flailing around with kicks and scratches at his wrist. He doesn't seem to care because he doesn't move. Doesn't react, he holds me still.

He lifts his head, the moon shining onto his face and showing me that toothy grin. "Don't be scared, little lamb, we won't hurt you yet."

"What the fuck do you want?" I yell, still trying to kick myself free. But with every kick, he absorbs like some fucked up punching bag.

His hood slides off a bit when he looks up at me, eyes as dark as the night sky, and a gold piercing dangles from his nose. "To have some fun, isn't that the whole point?"

He sets me down and brings me closer to him, looming over me by at least a foot and a half. "We're all here to play."

I glance over his shoulder, the shadows have become people, grotesque-looking people with contorted smiles and stares that are blank. Eyes so pale they look like the moon.

"I don't want to fucking play," I growl and punch as hard as I can.

But he absorbs it, that smile forming on him. "Oh, little lamb, when I'm done with you, all you'll want to do is play."

I scream and yank out of his grip, some of my hair remaining in his fist. "No!"

He chuckles. It's so evil and cynic, a cry slips free from my parted lips. I stare at the decaying bodies following him, limbs missing, eyes white and staring ahead at nothing with contorted smiles all aimed at me. But each of the ten creatures trying to get at me has a symbol carved into their forehead.

A zodiac sign.

The man slowly removes his hood, a Leo sign scarred on his forehead.

My eyes do a round of the crowd in front of me. Eleven signs, but there are twelve zodiac signs.

He's missing one.

He's missing *me*.

Tears slide down my cheeks as I meet his gaze again, he hasn't moved, he's sizing me up. Studying me, claiming me. "Taurus. All you're missing is a Taurus."

He nods, a blade sliding into his hand. "Ready to play a game, Melanie?"

"Go fuck yourself," I spit and grit my teeth.

He laughs, cracking the bones in his neck. "If I have time, we just might."

As fast as he grabs me before, I'm pushed onto the ground and his body is pressing down on me, constricting my breathing. I'm paralyzed. My limbs are locked at my sides, my ability to scream is trapped. I'm at a standstill.

It's useless to fight anymore.

To understand what the hell this is.

It's useless when my screams are silenced by his blade carving my zodiac sign into my forehead.

"Perfect," he breathes, licking the wound, and rising. The gold piercing is no longer dangling from his nose. "Just perfect."

I don't move as the rain begins to pour again, falling on me in mean and bitter drops, washing away all madness.

He stands over me, watching as I get lost in the dark sky as a cloud eats up the moon.

A cool metal pierces my skin, that gold ring falling onto my upper lip. A scream rises again but doesn't slip free. It's consumed. He's consumed it.

He's complete.

He watches me as my eyes continue to stare blankly at the nothingness and his enormity lowers again, touching my face.

Making me one of them.

TIL DEATH
-Jena Glover-

June 17

    I breathed deep, expanding my lungs and belly with the force of my long inhale. Summertime was always my favorite, with its warm sunshine and clear blue skies, and I was lucky to have a strong, allergy-free body. While pollen face-fucked every friend I had, I could enjoy the fresh summer air in peace.

    As I exhaled, turning to smile at my wife, I felt a tickle in my throat and coughed it away. She furrowed her brows and cocked her head at me, concern filling those honey-filled brown eyes of hers. My Lacey looked every inch the fretful housewife, but she was truly just a worrywart.

    "Should I call the doctor on Monday, Vic?" she asked, fingers fluttering over the apron tied around her waist.

    "Save my money, Lace," I grumbled, fighting back another cough. "I just need some water. Some spit went down the wrong pipe."

    She nodded at me, but I saw the doubt in her eyes that had me clenching my jaw. Damn woman worried over me like I was a baby; it never ceased to infuriate me.

    "I have some cough drops in the house if you need it." And then she went back to talking to the neighbor woman, Stephanie, about the best time to do different things in the garden.

    Walking into the house, I rubbed at my neck, that feeling of a cough building still hovering in my throat. *Just a cough, Vic*, I told myself. *Just a cough.*

July 21

    "That's it. I'm calling the doctor, and you're going to go!" Lacey snapped, yanking the book out of my hands.

    "No," I said simply, reaching for my book.

    I hadn't even been in my recliner for thirty minutes when the woman started nagging me. *More cough drops?* this and *Still coughing?* that. It was driving me nuts.

    "Vic, you've been coughing since the block party. That was more than a month ago. I'm worried about you."

    "Worried about me, or worried that the moneymaker might not be able to keep you comfortable?"

    I knew it was a low blow, but her constant nagging was like a hammer pounding at the back of my head, the pain radiating upwards. For the past week, our home had been filled with tension as she anxiously fussed over me for having a simple cough. But if she knew I was still smoking, she'd nag me harder. So, I wisely kept my trap shut and needled her away from even heading down that path.

    Her eyes welled up with tears as she gazed at me, her lower lip quivering. Once upon a time, the sight would have broken me, made me beg for forgiveness.

But ten years of marriage had shown me that Lacey only cried to manipulate me. I stubbornly refused to give her that much power over me ever again.

"How can you say that?" she finally asked, wiping at the tears that had slipped out. "You *know* how much I love you, how much I've sacrificed to be with you."

"You call choosing me over some screaming brats a sacrifice? Grow up, Lacey. I work hard so you can stay here, gardening and cooking and getting your hair and nails done." I lurched out of my recliner, holding back another cough that left my voice gravelly. "I'm the one working my ass off to keep a roof over our heads and food in our bellies. Don't talk to me about sacrifice."

"You're an ass," she sobbed out, tossing my book at my chest. "And you're too damn stubborn to see that I'm worried because I love you like crazy."

Catching the book, I glared at her. "You're worried that you'll have to take care of me if I'm sick."

"Go to hell!" She pushed past me, her footsteps echoing as she ran up the stairs and slammed the bedroom door, the sound of her sobs seeping through.

I settled back into my recliner, the navy blue upholstery soft and the cushions plush and comforting. My body was starting to ache from too many long days and not enough peace in my house. Age was settling in as middle age approached, and my joints reminded me more often than not that I was no longer the same twenty-five-year-old man I'd been when Lacey and I had first met. Refusing to be ashamed of my harsh words, I didn't let myself look toward the stairs or think about how hurt my wife must have been.

Her anger and upset were her problems, not mine. If she'd just quit nagging...

September 1

My lunchbox no longer contained the same loving notes Lacey used to tuck inside them, and I rolled my eyes at her petty behavior. In place of the note was a plastic bag filled with cough drops.

The week before, she'd started sleeping in the guest bedroom, claiming that my coughing would wake her up. But did I *ever* complain about her incessant snoring? No. No, I did not.

I was a far better husband than she was a wife.

The ham and Swiss cheese sandwich with spicy mustard and homemade mayonnaise was my favorite, and Lacey had even added a baggie of beef jerky to my lunch. Maybe she was trying to apologize? I wasn't sure, but the sight of the beef jerky was enough to warm my heart toward her. But just a little.

Damn woman worries too much, I thought, removing the sandwich from the plastic bag.

"What'd your old lady send ya with today, Vic?" John, the assistance supervisor, asked me as he tossed his own brown paper bag onto the table in the lunchroom.

"A couple of my favorite things," I replied, eyeing him.

John was a mess. His unkempt, long hair and grimy nails gave him a sloppy appearance at best. But all the girls in the office giggled over him. And with the way he bragged, I didn't doubt he'd taken at least one of them out behind the shop for a quickie.

I tried to take a deep breath to refocus, but my lungs felt like they stopped before I could inhale even halfway. *Damn cigarettes,* I thought, patting at the pack in my breast pocket.

"You good, man? You're looking a little pale." John cocked his head to the side.

"I'm fine." I *was,* damn it. Perfectly fine.

However, my trembling fingers went into my pocket and retrieved the cigarettes. I only indulged in smoking while on my work breaks, concealing this habit from Lacey and her worrying. After my emergency bypass surgery the year before, she had made me promise to quit smoking. I'd tried my hardest, but the best I could do was hide it from her.

What she didn't know couldn't hurt her.

The rest of the day, I kept trying to suck in deeper and deeper breaths, becoming lightheaded with the effort. My coworkers steered clear of me, giving me concerned looks whenever I swore. After my fifth attempt at a deep breathing exercise, I dissolved into a coughing fit, my lungs squeezing and squeezing with each desperate attempt to clear my lungs.

Taking the handkerchief out of my pants pocket, I coughed heavily into it, my stomach pushing upward to help my lungs expel whatever was in them. Mucus, dark and tarry, hit my cloth-covered palm. Blood speckled the cloth as well, and I felt some trickle from my nose just before it plopped onto the handkerchief, too, bright and morbid.

"Yo, man, you good?" That came from Charlie, my supervisor. He was close to retirement age and a strict, no-nonsense type of guy. I respected him a lot, normally, but I wanted him to shut the fuck up at that moment.

"I'm fine," I bit out, voice low and angry. "Just need to get some more tissues."

Charlie nodded, the only sign that I could leave the shop floor. Irritated that I was definitely getting a cold, I hurried to the one-man bathroom at the opposite end of the shop, cutting around machinery and coworkers without looking at anything or anybody. Pressing my handkerchief to my nose, I stopped the blood from pouring down my face, though I could feel the warm, sticky wetness spreading over the cloth.

Once I had taken care of the bloody nose and cleaned my handkerchief, I felt slightly more at ease. Breathing still sucked a little bit, but I didn't feel like I had to cough again and my nose didn't feel like it would bleed any time soon. Charlie was waiting for me outside the bathroom, one eyebrow raised and his arms crossed over his burly chest.

Concern filled his deep brown eyes, and his mustache pulled down with the force of his frown. "Vic, I think you should take the rest of the day."

"What? No. I'm fine."

Charlie shook his head. "You should go see a doctor. You're coughing all the time, irritable, and now you've given yourself a bloody nose. What does Lacey think?"

I rolled my eyes. "Lacey is a woman. She worries and she nags and she won't stop pushing."

"We're concerned for you, too, Vic. It's not just her."

"Charlie, I'm good. I just want to get my work done, and then I can go home."

"I called in Mike. He's going to take over your station. You're going home." When I opened my mouth to protest, Charlie hardened his voice to say, "That's final. Go home."

Bunch of fucking nags, I thought, shoving the damp handkerchief into my pants' pocket.

When I got to my truck outside, I couldn't help but smile at the sight of the tackle box in the bed, as if my irritated prayers had been answered. Charlie told me to go home, but Lacey wouldn't be expecting me for another four hours. I had plenty of time to relax by my local fishing spot and enjoy the fresh air.

That's what I needed: fresh air. Not the stuffy, stale air inside the factory. Nope. Good, clean, fresh oxygen would definitely help.

And as I sat in a lawn chair thirty minutes later, feet crossed at the ankles with a fishing pole in my right hand and soda in the other, I thanked Charlie for being "concerned" enough to send me "home."

September 15

The loogie I spat into the sink was bright red, so much blood filling the mucus that it was all I could see. I'd woken up dizzy from coughing, the alarm clock reading just past three in the morning. My lungs hurt, a deep ache that turned sharp and stabbing every so often.

My sleep had been getting worse over the past few weeks, but it was the first time I'd felt like I was drowning in my phlegm. Dragged from a dream where a man with a knife had stabbed me in the back before chasing after me, knife held high over his head and a maniacal grin on his face, I had rolled over to cough into a tissue.

The floors in the hallway behind me creaked, the sound echoing in the room thanks to the fact that my wife was cleaning all the carpets we typically placed on the hardwood floors to muffle sounds. Without turning around, I knew Lacey was standing just outside the bedroom door, waiting for me to turn around.

"Go away, Lace," I muttered, barely loud enough for her to hear me.

I wanted to cough up the shit in my lungs in peace. Tar, blood, mucus, and spit weighed them down; I just had to put some real force into coughing it all up. To do that, I needed to not have a woman hovering over me like a mother hen.

"Why won't you let me be worried about you?" she whispered, pushing the bathroom door open a little wider.

Our eyes met in the mirror over the sink. Dark purple shadows marred the delicate skin under her eyes, evidence of her sleep deprivation. She looked noticeably thinner than she had just a few months ago, her daisy-yellow nightgown hanging loosely on her frame.

My heart thumped hard in my chest, and I swallowed around the sudden lump in my throat. Here was my wife, the woman I'd loved for years, losing sleep over me. I could handle a little cough; I couldn't handle her looking at me like she was terrified I was going to leave.

Slowly, I turned on the faucet and let the water wash away the evidence of what was coming out of me. Once it was gone, I turned to face her, leaning against the edge of the sink and opening my arms to her.

"Come here."

Like she was under a spell, she walked until her toes were nudging mine, leaning forward to allow me to wrap her in my arms. With my cheek pressed against the top of her head, I sighed.

"You've lost weight. Are you really that worried?" The words came out gruffer than I wanted them to, but I couldn't take them or the tone of my voice back.

"Of course I am. The man I love has been coughing nonstop for three months." She pulled her head back to look up at me. There was no pity, no contempt, no anger in her gaze.

Just love and fear.

"It's just a cough. If I get any other symptoms, I'll go to the doctor." Not.

"You promise?"

I nodded, smiling gently at her.

And then she opened up her mouth to spike my temper. "You're looking a little pale and skinny. Is that another symptom, or are your coworkers stealing food again?"

"I'm not looking skinny. I'm just as strong as I've always been."

"Okay. Well, you should get some sleep. You have to work later." She smiled gently at me and rose to her tippy toes to press a kiss to my cheek. "I'll make you a roast beef and provolone sandwich with that spicy mustard you like for your lunch."

"Can you put some pickles in the bag, too?"

Lacey patted my cheek before taking my hand to lead me back to our bedroom. "Sure can. Do you want some beef stew with homemade sourdough for dinner?"

My stomach growled in answer, and she laughed. Here was my wife, the loving, kind, patient, understanding woman I'd married. Maybe she was finally understanding that I was okay.

But the thought of the blood in the sink kept me awake for another hour as I clutched her to me. My arms tightened around her as I willed sleep to take me again.

October 29

The scale told me that I'd lost another ten pounds in two weeks. My lungs still ached like I'd slept with a twenty-five pound weight on my chest, and my legs and arms refused to work as well as they had for most of my life. Each movement felt like slugging through water at the bottom of the Mariana Trench. The pressure caused a weakness that I'd never experienced.

I shook my head. Maybe Lacey had switched to that keto shit again without telling me. The likelihood was low because I'd spit it out and refused to eat it the last time, but I'd been working overtime for the past month due to a supply chain issue, so the lack of sleep could've altered my taste buds.

Downstairs, I heard her singing along to the radio, her voice a little too high and off-key to be considered good. On one particularly high note, I winced, stepping off the scale.

The mirror in front of me told me nothing good. Shadows took over my collarbones, showing that the muscle there was wasting away. My cheeks were thinner, though I'd grown my beard longer to conceal it as much as I could. Small bruises dotted my abdomen and ribs, their origins unknown.

Lacey's music changed, the song that came on an old country tune that told of how he decided to live like he was dying. The words clanged around in my brain as I twisted side to side, examining every visible inch of flesh.

Am I dying?

If I was, I didn't look too terrible. Sure, I had lost weight and had bruises, but my smile was still straight and white, my eyes were still the same sparkling blue, and my abs looked more defined than ever. Even as I struggled for each breath, I was vain enough to think the weight loss looked good enough that I shouldn't truly be concerned.

Grabbing my boxers from where they were folded on the sink, I tugged them on. They slipped a little over my hips, the dropped waist drawing attention to the V on my hips.

Yep, still got it, I thought, smirking.

I was fine. One hundred percent totally, completely fine.

My jeans were loose, too, and I made sure to notch my belt a little tighter to make sure they wouldn't fall down while I was working. The red and black flannel shirt I tossed over my black cotton t-shirt didn't quite hug my shoulders the way it had before, but it made movement easier.

In the bedroom, I sat on my bed and pulled my steel-toe boots to me. But when I bent forward to tug them on my feet, my lungs constricted painfully and my vision swam. Flashes of light against the blackness told me I hadn't passed out, but I was close. Oxygen refused to enter my lungs no matter how much I tried pulling it in, my lungs painfully tight in my chest.

"Lacey!" I choked out, the words barely more than a whisper.

She continued to sing, her voice swirling through the melody of the actual song. The words spun through my head, a whisper in the shadows as I tumbled into the darkness. They were all I heard before my body met the ground, only a thud breaking the noises from downstairs.

When I woke, it was to a large brute of a man shouting, "Take her away!" as his hands pressed agonizingly against my chest. My heart felt fluttery and weak, beating too quickly and too faint for me to feel my pulse anywhere else but its painful constrictions under the man's hands.

"We've got a pulse! Time to move!" he shouted.

And then I was lifted into the air, my mind finally realizing that a hard piece of plastic was under my body. Straps were tightened quickly as the two men raced me down the hall, down the stairs, and outside into the waiting ambulance. The second I was secured inside of it, the piercing cry of the sirens broke through the morning air and we were off, my body swaying side to side as we hit every bump known to man.

"How," I gasped out, my ribs and lungs aching, "much.." another attempt at a deep inhale, "will…this…cost…me?"

The paramedic looked down at me, grimacing. "Sir, worry about that later. You didn't have a pulse for nearly three minutes."

And then he was strapping a blood pressure cuff on my arm, concentrating over his stethoscope. A pulse oximeter — I was surprised I remembered the name of it — was placed on my pointer finger. His eyes went wide, and he slapped the front of the space to get the driver's attention.

"Faster," he commanded quietly.

That was how I knew I was going to die. The quiet urgency of a man trained to take care of the injured and dying ricocheted through my brain.

At the hospital, the men in the ambulance moved quickly, getting me to the emergency room where a doctor, an older woman with frizzy blonde curls and wrinkles around her chestnut eyes—a pity, really, because I was sure she was a stunner in her youth—started barking out orders.

"Heart attack?" she called out, looking at the paramedic who had brought me back.

"His lungs sound like shit, so I can't be sure. Heart stopped, though."

"Got it. Thanks, Jeffries."

And then I was being checked out, test after test being proposed until a portable x-ray was brought into the room. So many doctors shuffled around me, poking and prodding, their faces stone in the face of whatever had brought me into their sterile abode. After a few minutes of positioning me, most of them left except for the blonde doctor, her brown eyes shrewd. She wore a blue vest, its thickness clearly designed for protection against radiation.

When she was done, she ushered the others back in to help her whisk the machine and the pictures she'd taken with it away from me. Then she stripped the vest off, tossed it to the side, and began her examination. Cool hands touched over me, lifting my shirt to reveal the bruises and see just how hard my lungs were working to gasp in air.

"Pam, get in here," she called, looking toward the door.

An even older woman popped into the room, her graying hair falling around her shoulders, blue eyes wide. "Yeah, doc?"

"Get the oncologist and a phlebotomist. I need some tests run."

My blood froze in my veins, and I felt my heart thud thickly in my chest.

"No," I wheezed out, still feeling the horrific crush of my lungs as I tried and failed to inhale.

Something like pity flashed in both women's eyes, but Pam simply nodded and dashed out of the room.

"My name is Dr. Warren," the blonde said, sitting slowly in a chair next to me. "The notes the paramedics left said you were down for three minutes. You have a couple of broken ribs from the CPR, but your lungs, to be blunt, sound like they're full of fluid. You have bruising on your neck, abdomen, arms, and hands—and that's just what I can see. Jeffries, the paramedic who brought you back, told us that your wife found tissues full of blood and mucus, saw that you were eating less, and that you've had a cough since June."

"No...sy...bi...tch," I retorted. "I'm," another painful attempt at inhaling, "fine."

"Your blood oxygen is eighty-eight percent. Frankly, I'm surprised you're still conscious."

So matter of fact, this devil of a woman.

"Not...can...cer." My protest was weak.

"We'll see," Dr. Warren responded, frowning.

Lacey burst into the room, accompanied by another nurse. Tears were dripping down her cheeks, her hands wringing together. The worry lined her eyes.

"Vic, are you okay?" she cried out, coming to stand next to me. The nurse who'd brought her in gently maneuvered around her to start hooking me up to different machines.

"Get him started on oxygen right away," the doctor ordered.

"What's going on?" Lacey demanded, squeezing my hand. "Did he have a heart attack?"

The nurse and the doctor exchanged a look, but I shook my wife's hand, drawing her attention to me. "They...think....can...cer. I...don't."

Fresh tears welled in her eyes, and she pressed a soft kiss to my forehead. "It can't be cancer, baby. It just can't."

But it was. When the bloodwork and x-rays came back three hours later, the diagnosis was confirmed. End-stage lung cancer.

The dawning horror grew frighteningly stark as the oncologist, a Dr. Myer, and Dr. Warren laid out their findings. Lacey's hand trembled in mine, and I held it as limply as I could. She cried silent tears; the water slipping down her pale cheeks as she dutifully listened.

It pissed me off. Thoughts of chemo, losing my hair, losing weight, vomiting, and more filled my head. I would no longer be a good-looking man in the prime of his life. My life savings would be drained to fix my stupid lungs, and I'd lose my only source of income.

"What treatments?" Lacey asked.

"I am so sorry," Dr. Myer replied quietly. "It is too advanced. We can make him comfortable."

"Not...dy...ing."

But three pairs of eyes looked at me with pity.

"Get...out..."

"No, baby, we can–"

"Get...out!" I used as much force as I could, the effort a monumental task.

Lacey's lip trembled. "But–"

"We'll give you two a moment."

And then we were alone. The once beautiful woman I had married was gone, replaced with someone who pitied me. She was already accepting my death.

Well, I wasn't.

"Leave."

"Vic–"

"I…don't…want…you…here!" I pulled my hand from hers with the little strength I had left. The fractures to my ribs did not help the fact that I could barely breathe to begin with, and I wanted to scream.

The pain was rising, a tidal wave threatening to drown me.

"I'll go," she whispered, hurt written over every last millimeter of her face. "But I will be back tomorrow."

October 30

My husband, Vic, died last night. Stubborn, selfish, vain, and clinging to the idea that he was right until the very last minute, he died alone. The nurse who'd called me to tell me had tried to comb his hair, make him look better than he had when he'd been taken in. They'd tried to take care of him as he struggled for his last breaths, shunning the love I had always tried to give him.

Sitting at the table in our kitchen, I ran my fingers over the pages of the will he'd kept in the safe for the past five years. He'd left everything to me, of course. We'd drafted the will as a birthday present for him, his birthday forever immortalized on the scrap of paper that was the last page. April 29, clear as day.

It was a little ironic that he'd died on my birthday. We'd said that our birth dates being exactly six months apart had been a sign. I hadn't known what the sign had meant until I got the phone call, though.

It was early still, the sun just barely edging over the horizon. It was beautiful in a way I couldn't remember a sunrise being beautiful in the past ten or so years. Of course, it was hard to find beauty when you were dismissed and trivialized at every turn, held to impossible standards by a man who didn't give two fucks about you beyond what you could do for him.

The sun's rays hit my rose bush, capturing the beauty of the reds and pinks to turn them majestic. And then they hit the mound of dirt directly in front of the bush, bringing a soft smile to my face. Because what I had buried there would never be found, would never direct attention back to me.

The last pack of Vic's horrid cigarettes were buried several inches deep in the ground, surrounded by freshly tilled soil for other plants I would grow the following year. Sealed in four layers of plastic bags, no one would ever know the lengths I had gone in order to ensure that the asbestos I'd laced the cancer sticks with had sped up the process.

I was free. And my husband had only his own bull-headed bullshit to blame.

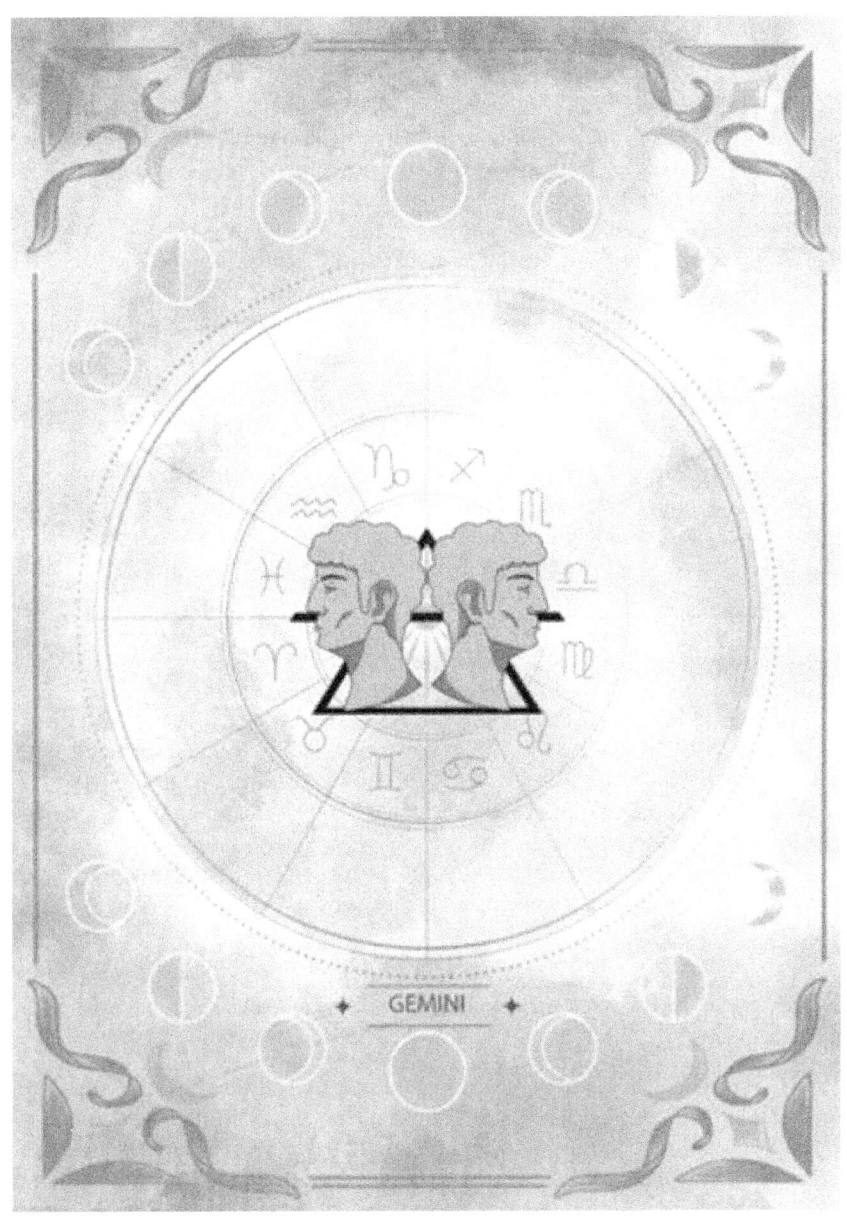

Twin Telepathy
Kerry E. B. Black

Becky and Christine weren't really twins, but everyone thought they were. In fact, the girls weren't even sisters. They were cousins, sharing not only the same age but also resembling each other with their matching heights, builds, and striking black hair. What really made them seem so alike, however, was an unspoken agreement between the young girls that Becky be the queen and Christine her loyal subject.

This dynamic, with Becky as ruler and Christine her mostly mute subject, kept their friendship viable from their earliest childhood and through the tragedy that saw an orphaned Becky installed as a permanent, adopted resident at Christine's house.

The pair needed no other friends. They had each other.

Becky chose their activities, assertive to the point of imperiousness. The girls went on long hikes into the surrounding hills or skipped rocks off of the Allegheny River. They fed visiting Canadian geese on their journey south for the winter and caught bunnies in clever traps of Becky's devising. They ground every yellow flower they discovered beneath their matching sequin 'Dorothy' shoes.

If Christine ever objected, Becky's anger flared bright as a Beltane fire, loud and unending until Christine backed down.

Christine overheard her parents' concern one evening when she couldn't sleep. She settled on the floor outside the living room, where their discussion rose in volume.

Her father began. "She runs rough-shod over our daughter. When was the last time Chrissie asked for something on her own? Everything is filtered through Becky. I don't think it's healthy."

"Honey," her mother reasoned. "That poor girl lost both of her parents not long ago. We need to be patient."

"I think we need to keep an eye on things. That's what I'm saying."

Christine's mother sighed, her voice weary. "I hear you, but we need to give it some time."

"And that's another thing. Did the police ever find out how they were poisoned?"

"It was a mix-up. The rodent poison and the sugar look just about the same."

His voice rumbled. "That's some messed up 'Shirley Jackson' shit there."

Christine startled when Becky touched her shoulder. Putting a finger to her cousin's lips to insist on quiet, the girls spied on the adults' conversation. Becky balled her hands into white-knuckled fists. Her nostrils flared like they were ready to spew smoke, but she remained quiet, and so did Christine.

The next morning, Becky remained abed longer than usual. Christine brought a bowl of cereal to her on a tray.

"I don't want any." Becky turned away to face the wall.

Christine chewed her lip, forehead knotted with concern. "Aren't you feeling well?"

"No. I feel like an unwanted orphan."

"Please don't say that," Christine said as she climbed into Becky's bed, enveloping her in a hug from behind. "What can I do to make you feel better?"

Becky said nothing for a while, and Christine wondered if she'd fallen back to sleep until Becky rolled to face her.

"Let's surprise Auntie and Uncle. We can clean the house."
Christine grimaced. "Why?"

Becky shrugged, her eyes downcast. She mumbled, "Maybe then Uncle will like me."

They started in their shared bedroom, making the beds and tidying the toys. They wiped the doorknobs and dusted the baseboards.

Becky pointed to the stairs. "Get the yellow cleaning stuff in the cabinet. I'll take the dirty clothes to the laundry." She scooped up the laundry basket. "And don't let your mom know what we're doing, okay?"

They met after, Becky holding a white gallon jug with a blue lid, Christine a yellow container of ammonia. "Why don't you wipe down the sink and I'll tidy Auntie and Uncle's bedroom.

"I can't clean the toilet. Mom won't let me use the cleanser."

Becky shrugged. "Just wipe out the sink and tub."

When Christine threw the antiseptic wipe into the trash can, Becky smiled at her. "I'll vacuum. You clean out your dad's CPAP machine."

"How do I do that?"

"I think you put a little of that," she pointed to the ammonia, "into the machine's water. Then when it's turned on, it cleans out the hoses."

"Makes sense."

"When I run the vacuum, Auntie will know what we're doing, so we better hurry to finish."

Christine sprinted into her parents' bedroom to splash the cleanser into the CPAP reservoir before the vacuum roared into life. She fluffed the pillows on her parents' bed and pushed a dresser drawer closed. Everything looked perfect, but the cleaner smelled strong, which made her dizzy. She spritzed a bit of her mother's perfume to improve the scent in the room when Becky pushed the machine along the carpet.

They nodded at their work, twin smiles on their faces. Christine threw her arms around Becky. "They're gonna love it!"

Becky's cheeks burned, and she felt uncharacteristically sheepish. "I hope so."

Christine squeezed her hand and made a bold and atypical suggestion. "Let's go to the park to play."

Becky and Christine skipped hand in hand to engage in private games of sorcerers and outer space. When the streetlights flickered on, they hurried home for dinner. The usual schedule included Christine's dad returning from work, taking a nap before dinner, and the family sitting for a meal when the streetlights lit their spring-wich street.

On their return after an afternoon of sunshine and games, Auntie greeted them at the door. "Did you have fun?"

They smiled widely. "Yes."

"Good. Go wash up. I made stuffed chicken breasts and creamed peas for supper."

The girls' plump cheeks dimpled. "Yum!" As they turned to hurry to the washroom, she added, "And Chrissie, wake your daddy, please."

"Yes, Momma."

Feet pounding on the hardwood floors, they raced to the washroom, giggling as they soaped each other's hands, careful to rehang the hand towel they'd used.

"Do you think they noticed the cleaning we did?"

Christine shrugged. "I guess so. It sure smells cleaner."

Becky lingered in the washroom doorway, watching as Christine knocked and entered her father's room. "Wake up," she said. "Dinner's ready." A pause. "Daddy, it's time to get up." Another pause. "Daddy?" Louder. "Daddy!" Christine appeared in the bedroom doorway, face drained of color. "He's not waking up, even when I shake him!"

"I'll get Auntie!" Becky exclaimed and ran to tell. After a hurried exchange, Becky and her aunt ran to Christine. The three shook her uncle, calling to him, increasing their volume and the force of their movements. Auntie dialed 9-1-1, and as they waited for an ambulance, Christine clung to her father, tears streaming down her face. Becky carefully removed the CPAP mask and gently placed it back on the machine, its soft hum filling the room. She moved it nearer to the window and opened the sash to ward off the antiseptic smell, which was giving her a headache.

Flashing lights and a mournful siren announced the ambulance. "Might be a heart attack," the older of the E.M.T.'s said to the other as they strapped Christine's father to a gurney. Although they didn't stretch a white sheet over him, they'd stopped trying to resuscitate.

Christine clung to her mother, burying her bawling face in her clothing when the ambulance pulled away. Becky rubbed her back as the lights receded from view. No siren needed for the trip.

Auntie knelt to address her daughter and niece. "I have to go to the hospital, but you two keep each other company while I'm gone." She swallowed hard and offered a wobbly smile. "I'll be back soon. I love you both." She embraced the girls, rubbing their backs before departing.

When the door clicked shut, Becky slapped the side of her thigh. "Guess we should eat."

Christine's tear-swollen face reddened. "I can't eat. My Daddy's dead."

Becky took her hand and tugged toward the dining room. "You have to eat or you'll be dead, too." She shrugged. "Besides, your mom put a lot of work into making this dinner, and we love stuffed chicken breast."

Christine pulled away. "I'm not hungry." She ran to their shared room and slammed the door.

Becky ate two portions, tidied away the meal in plastic containers, and washed the dishes. When she tried to get into their bedroom, she found the door locked.

Christine never locked the door, especially not with Becky around. She furrowed her brow and knocked. "Open the door, Christine. I think you bumped the lock."

Christine didn't answer or open the door.

"Are you okay?"

No reply.

Becky lifted a heavy bronze statue of a mother cuddling a child from the hallway table and returned to the door. "Christine?"

Still no response.

"I'm coming in. I need to know you're not hurt." She raised the statue over her head with both hands, like a sacrifice on an Aztec temple, and slammed it into the knob. Metal on metal. Dings, dents. After three strikes, the handle fell to the hardwood, scuffing the polish and leaving a divot.

Christine huddled near the furthest bedpost, clutching a stuffed bear from her days in the crib. From her wide eyes streamed tears. "You broke the door?"

Becky ignored the question and approached with the slow and steady care of someone in the presence of a skittish colt. "Why didn't you open up?"

Christine's chin wobbled, and she narrowed her eyes. "My daddy's dead."

"I know. He was my uncle." She slid onto the bottom of Christine's bed and stretched out, belly down. She rested her chin on her clasped hands and sighed. "I know you're sad."

Christine collapsed around her teddy bear, sobbing into its worn, tan fur.

"Please don't cry, Christine. Now he's with my parents. They're together."

When Christine showed no sign of calming, Becky curled into a fetal position at her feet. "I'm here, Christine. I'll always be here."

Becky tried to guide Christine through their usual nighttime rituals, but Christine wouldn't budge from her perch at the top of her bed. Becky washed her would-be twin's face and hands, carefully brushed her hair, and pushed her under the covers. She kissed Christine's forehead, surprised by the warmth radiating from her skin.

The sun set long before Christine's mother returned. The quiet click of the front door lock announced her return.

Becky found her leaning against the door, coat unbuttoned, purse dangling from a loose grasp. Her vacant expression glided like a ghost, taking in nothing.

"Auntie, I think Christine might be sick. She feels warm." Becky licked her chapping lips. "Maybe she has a fever."

Christine's mother gazed at her niece, deep in thought. She walked mechanically towards her daughter, briefly pausing at the broken door. She lay on the bed and curled around the bundle of blankets that cocooned Christine.

Becky chewed her lip, perplexed. "What did they say at the hospital?"

Her aunt's shoulders quivered, and she buried her face in the downy marigold of Christine's duvet.

Becky tiptoed to her bed, collected her blanket, and gently draped it around her aunt, ensuring she was warm and cozy. Silent as a cat, she tunneled beneath the cover and rested at their feet.

After the sun had set, Auntie cleared her throat and sat up, her hand still resting on Christine's slight shoulder. "Girls, a police officer will be by, maybe even in a little while."

Becky sat up, the cover falling from her. "The police? Why?"

"Just to ask some questions." Auntie rubbed a circle on Christine's shoulder. Christine didn't move.

"Nothing to worry about. Just part of the procedure. But we should clean ourselves up and try to look presentable in case they show up tonight." She leaned over and kissed the top of Christine's head where tufts of her hair peeked from beneath the blanket. She started toward Becky but stuttered, her cheeks flushing, before brushing a kiss on Becky's cheek.

Becky followed her aunt to her bedroom.

Auntie wrapped her arms around herself and rubbed away the risen gooseflesh. "Why's this window open?" she mused to herself, unaware of Becky lingering in the doorway. After she closed it and turned off the CPAP machine, she turned to leave the room and jumped back, hand to chest, with a little yelp.

"Becky, you startled me!"

"Sorry, Auntie." She tipped her head to the right and considered the room. "Do you want me to change the sheets?"

Auntie's chin wobbled. "No, honey. I'll take care of things."

The doorbell announced visitors.

Auntie's eyes clouded with misery. "Please get the door."

Becky remained rooted in place. "It's probably the neighbors bringing casseroles and covered dishes. That's what they do when there's been a death."

"Or it might be the police." Auntie stared at her niece. "Answer the door, please."

"Ok."

When Becky pulled the door open, two uniformed police officers loomed. "Are you Becky?"

She nodded.

"Can we come in? We have some things we'd like to discuss."

"With me?" When they nodded, "Why?"

The officers, Baker and Reese, pushed by and motioned for Becky to take a seat on the sofa. They asked about the recent loss of her parents. Becky felt heat seep over her skin as she answered. "I already told the other police about that, though."

Baker nodded, and Reese named the officers who investigated her parents' deaths. Baker wandered out of the room, and Becky heard the low rumble of conversation from there. She didn't need to worry. Her aunt loved and defended her, and her cousin was her twin, the shadow of her glowing brilliance. Every light cast a shadow, after all. So why, Becky wondered, did her chest feel so tight?

The stairs groaned beneath the assent of two people, one heavier than the other. Becky stood to follow.

"Please take your seat, Becky." Officer Reese's tone bore none of the politeness of the words. In fact, beneath their intonations rumbled what could only be a threat. "I have some more questions."

Becky's heart raced ahead of the presumed accusation. "I'm just a kid. Shouldn't my aunt be here?"

"It was your aunt who asked us to speak with you."

Heat blazed over her face with the betrayal. Auntie protected. She didn't accuse.

"About what? What do you want from me?" She forced tears through desert-dry ducts and contorted her face in a rictus of grief. She shaped her voice into the tremble of a younger girl. "Did I do something wrong?"

The officer studied her, impassive as a gargoyle. "Nobody's saying you did anything wrong."

"Then why are you asking me so many questions?"

"Becky, I hear you're a smart young lady."

Becky wiped the tears from her flaming cheeks and stuck out her chin with a nod. She was smart.

"You get good grades?"

Another nod.

"Especially science? Chemistry?"

Self-possession replaced the girlish voice. "I'm in advanced classes."

"Bet a smart girl like you would know if you mix certain household compounds. It makes a poison."

She froze, snared by the words.

Officer Baker joined them. Christine and her mother huddled together near the stairs. He dipped his chin toward his chest while maintaining eye contact with Officer Reese. Clutched in his hands were the yellow bottle and the now empty white gallon jug, remnants of Becky and Christine's earlier cleaning session. Officer Reese filled his cheeks with a puff of air, which he slowly exhaled.

Becky furrowed her brow, eyes wide and blinking with confused innocence. "I think I've heard that. About the poisons." She turned to regard her aunt and cousin. "Did something happen?" She spun back to the officers, innocence incarnate. She gasped, quiet, and the color drained from her cheeks. "Oh, no."

She wheeled back to look at her cousin. "Christine, when we were cleaning, you didn't do anything with Uncle's CPAP machine, did you?"

Christine's mouth dropped agape. Her voice trembled with fear. "You told me to pour some of that," she pointed to the ammonia in Officer Baker's hand, "into Daddy's machine."

"No, I didn't, Christine. Remember, I told you I would clean his CPAP, and I did." She fluttered her long lashes, sweet as a fawn. "I wanted to help."

"So you poured bleach into the reservoir, didn't you?"

She nodded, then her eyes widened even further, a look of terror crossing her face. "Christine, please tell me you didn't put ammonia in Uncle's machine!" She exclaimed, her voice filled with panic. "Mixing bleach and ammonia…" She turned her attention to the officers. "Oh god, please tell me that's not what killed my uncle!"

Christine broke down, sobbing uncontrollably.

A House with Two Front Doors
~ Jenna Dietzer ~

Cora averted her eyes from the spiderwebs dangling above the threshold and pinched back an urge to judge. The duplex was like an Impressionist painting—dreamy from a distance, with its cottage blue siding and red doors. But up close, it was a mess. Cracked sidewalk, crooked mailbox, and a dead, forgotten yard. The two front doors were placed uncomfortably close at the center, inches from each other. The windows were barred.

When the landlord, a thick man with chest hair that peeked from his shirt collar, opened the front door, the citrusy smell of bug spray overwhelmed Cora. She coughed into her sleeve.

"What do you think?" he asked. He waddled to the center of the room and raised his hands in a grand gesture that exposed his drenched armpits.

Cora knew it didn't matter what she thought. The duplex was her only option. Teal walls and a shag carpet so blood red she could feel a gag surfacing in her throat. The window unit sat idle—or worse, it was dead—which explained why the room felt smothering despite its brightness.

She chewed the inside of her cheek and offered a pained smile. "Can I see the rest of it?" she asked, gesturing down the hall. Cora knew she'd be signing paperwork regardless of what the other rooms revealed. But she still wanted to pretend she had a choice, just for a few more moments.

"Suit yourself." He shrugged and marched down the hallway. At the bedroom, he stepped aside so she could peek in. Here, the walls were whitewashed and pockmarked with holes of various sizes. A gray rug covered the bare concrete floor. But it was still more inviting, with its matching single bed and desk below the window. Shadows from the window bars made stripes that stretched along the floor.

"Then there's the bathroom," the landlord chimed in. She followed him to the end of the hall. "Tub probably needs refinishing. We'll tackle that later this year." He scratched at his belly as she glanced around. "So, how long you plan on staying?"

Cora winced. "Well, I … um …" She couldn't stop staring at the blue toothpaste streaks cemented to the sink edges.

"We can do month-to-month. Most people can't commit to a full year. I get it."

Then Cora saw, along the wall that separated the duplex, something tall and hidden behind a bath towel. "What's that?" she asked.

The landlord turned around and chuckled. "Just a gift from the previous tenant."

One of Cora's eyebrows raised. "Gift?" Anyone renting this place couldn't afford to leave gifts.

When the landlord turned toward her again, his expression was flat. "It's a full-length mirror. Has a few scratches on it, but it's nice enough I covered it while we repainted the place. If you find you don't like it, just leave it outside on the steps. Someone'll pick it up."

The chitchat ended there, and the landlord went to grab the paperwork. Her hand felt so heavy as she passed him the cash for the first month's rent. A part of her hoped her life would turn around completely in four weeks, but she doubted it.

A few moments later, she was hauling a suitcase with everything she owned inside of it up the front steps. Before unpacking, she fiddled with the air conditioner until it came to life. Relieved, she unpacked her clothes and counted out change for laundry, stacking the coins on top of the desk in the bedroom. It smelled musty and old within, but she thought better of opening the barred windows for air as twilight bruised the skyline.

She plopped in front of the window unit until her lips grew cold. Her stomach gurgled. So she fished out the macaroni and cheese packs she'd saved from her last grocery trip, cooked one, and relished each savory bite.

Looking out from the bars of her kitchen window, she saw two figures dance across the too-close windows of the apartment complex next door. Another individual did dishes above them. A family came and went through the window on the right. She wondered when she'd hear the thrusts of lovemaking in the unit next door, the shouts from the couple when their space or finances or expectations of each other overwhelmed them, or the laughter of the family during holidays, while she sat alone, nursing a bowl of mac and cheese and scrolling through social media by herself.

So this was loneliness.

She remembered being the life of the party once. Paying for rounds at the bar without batting a fake eyelash. Turning social media views into cold, hard cash. She was good at it, too. Internet famous for over a year, which was as famous as a nobody could hope for these days. But one small post about privilege—as ignorant as "let them eat cake" she now realized—and her celebrity status was canceled as fast as her maxed-out credit cards.

Turns out 140 characters was all it took to completely undo a person's life. Cora blamed her Gemini roots for being drawn to the superficial and opening her mouth without considering the repercussions.

Her online persona, her ideal version of herself, escaped with little consequence. She just disappeared. But not the real Cora. Not the pimple-faced girl in sweatpants who was handed an eviction notice and cried into the same silk pillowcase she'd hock on eBay the next day. That girl was collateral damage.

Since then, she'd turned in her fancy cellular for a prepaid phone with a cracked screen. She dyed her hair back to a mousy brown, her natural color, and let it grow because she couldn't afford to cut it. Her nails were thin and peeling from her picked-off acrylics. It would take months for them to mend.

Still, she was lucky it hadn't been worse than this duplex on the frayed edges of suburbia, where a handful of eyes could stare between bars into her kitchen. She could be couch-surfing or living out of her car. The debt monster was slowly receding back into the closet. But sometimes she still felt it might kill her.

Cora watched a cockroach scurry across the countertop and disappear into the sink drain. "Stupid house," she muttered through a mouthful of cheese. It dribbled down her chin and onto her shirt.

She didn't want to go to the laundromat in the dark. Walking after dark here was too dangerous. So she walked down the hall to the bathroom and doused the stain with cold water and cheap bar soap.

A thud sounded along the wall that split the duplex apartments. It was so light, Cora wondered if it was a knock on the door, if the landlord had forgotten something. But it rang again, louder, right beside her head, behind the propped-up dressing mirror.

She grasped the bath towel that shielded the dressing mirror and pulled it to the floor. The stain on her shirt was a neon yellow, thanks to the dyes in the mac and cheese. She'd have to wait until tomorrow to figure out if she'd completely ruined it.

Cora turned her gaze to the dressing mirror. The white-stained wooden frame was solid, but the paint along the edges and bottom was distressed, like it was an antique. Tendrils of woodwork arched over the top in a flowery vine design. It looked like a prop for a wedding dress pictorial in a fashion magazine. The video reels she could have made if the mirror had been hers before… Cora sighed and brushed aside the thought. This was the nicest thing in the entire duplex. Maybe the entire neighborhood. Her mind knotted itself around the puzzle of why anyone would leave it behind.

She stared at her reflection. The mirror made Cora look slimmer and taller. But she was gaunter than she remembered, a shadow of herself now that the ring lights and contouring palettes were gone. This was what months of convenience store snacks and powdered milk products looked like. Just sallow skin underneath florescent lights, malnutrition and dark circles. Cora lifted a hand and felt the rugged texture of her jawline, where acne had sprouted from neglect. She didn't remember the last time she'd looked at herself in a mirror this closely. Now that she had, all she wanted to do was look away.

In the mirror, her mouth pulled into a smirk. Cora's eyes widened. Her fingers climbed to her lips, still flat and expressionless. She froze as her reflection lifted its hand toward the mirror. The hand pressed against the glass and, with an iridescent wave, pushed through it. Fingertips stretched toward her face.

Cora screamed and grabbed her curling iron, batting the hand away. Her reflection winced and pulled the hand back through the glass.
Cora snatched the towel off the floor and threw it over the mirror. She backed into the hallway, ready to run. But her heavy, rapid breath was all she heard for the next minute. Nothing stirred below the bath towel or the empty bathroom.

She approached again slowly, wondering if she'd gone mad. "What kind of *Alice Through the Looking Glass* shit was that?" she whispered.

There was only one solution. She had to get rid of the mirror. Cora grabbed it by the frame and pulled, but it was too heavy. Even the rush of adrenaline couldn't help her push or lift it. Why had the landlord said she could just prop it on the porch? That was impossible. She struggled to grasp the corners of the mirror without bringing down the bath towel, and when the towel threatened to fall anyway, she scrambled to pin it in place, begging "No, no, no."

She finally gave up and leaned against the wall. "Okay," she heaved. "Cora, get it together. You're tired. It's late. You just need some rest."

A social media alert flickered across her phone screen. Someone she followed was starting a live stream. She turned it off, but then an idea came to her.

She navigated to her own profile with a mere 52 followers. The number both stung and pleased her. She was surprised 52 people still cared. Maybe they would be enough.

Cora typed out a title: *Help! My Mirror's Possessed*, and pressed the LIVE icon. In a matter of seconds, she could see her scared, pale face reflected back at her in the dimly lit apartment.

"You're going to think I'm crazy," she said to the camera, "until you see it happen, too."

She tip-toed down the hallway toward the mirror.

"I just moved into a new place, and the old tenant left behind a dressing mirror. I thought nothing of it, really, until my reflection—" she inhaled sharply "started having a mind of its own."

By the time she reached the end of the hall, her live stream was getting engagement.

Is this a prank?
Wait. I thought this account was dead.
10 people had tuned in.

Cora stopped at the bathroom door and repositioned the phone so viewers could see both her and the covered mirror side by side. "Behind here," she whispered. Her live stream hand trembled a little as she tugged at the towel and it fell.

The mirror glass was empty. Void of Cora's reflection. Only the shadows of the hallway and bathroom wall beside her shone through.

The viewer count crept up slowly.

Cora turned the phone so they could see the rest of the bathroom and the mirror from various angles. In every shot, her reflection was absent.

Exclamation points and vampire emojis floated across her screen.

Cora kept her voice low. "I'm not even joking, guys. Just minutes ago I was standing in front of this mirror, perfectly still, and my reflection moved on its own."

Gotta be a trick mirror, one viewer commented. *Funny but lame.*

"No," Cora insisted. "My reflection reached out a hand toward me, and the hand went through the glass." She said the last three words slowly for emphasis.

The emojis flooded her screen then. Faces of laughter, raised eyebrows, wide eyes and wide-open mouths.

This B* is crazy, one comment said.
Girl, get outta there!
The numbers ticked higher.

Then Cora saw movement in the mirror. "Guys!" Her breath caught. She turned the camera toward it. A shadow at the end of the hall. It sprinted toward her until her own face came into view, haggard and scowling. A hand pushed through the glass and snatched her phone. Then the mirror went black.

"Shit!" Cora stared at her empty hands. She couldn't believe how stupid she'd been. Not only had her counterpart stolen her phone, she also blocked her from the other side by covering the glass.

She waited for what felt like days before the mirror restored a reflection. Whatever her counterpart had put up to block the view must have fallen down, she guessed, just like the bath towel on her side.

Hesitating at first, she wondered if the reopened mirror portal was a trap. But as no one appeared on the other side, Cora placed her hand against the glass and felt its cool, smooth surface. It consumed her hand, then arm up to the elbow, then half her body.

She held her breath and closed her eyes as her head slipped into the glass.

When Cora opened her eyes again, her heart raced. The bathroom where she stood was a replica of the one on her side of the duplex. But this version was raw and dimly lit. Broken tiles scattered across the floor underneath a flickering light. Holes punctured the drywall to expose the tender, pink insulation. A bloody knife lay on the sink counter, handprint stains along the porcelain. The smell of diluted bleach hit her nostrils, barely masking the sweat and rot that filtered through it.

"Gross," Cora whispered. She covered her mouth.

Then a buzz came from down the hall, and Cora jumped. She pressed her back against the greasy hallway wall as she inched toward the bedroom. A putrid smell, like cat piss, grew with each step. Inside the bedroom, she found a mattress, soiled in browns and yellows, on the floor. The wall behind it had two long chains attached to it. They refashioned the desk from her duplex into a makeshift interrogation chair here, with straps to trap the arms, legs, and chest. An assortment of instruments, from hammers to knives and an electric shock device with rusty clips, were arranged on the desktop, glistening among the grime. Beside them on the wall were others. Chainsaw, swords, a baseball bat.

Cora shuddered. She remembered getting clobbered with a baseball bat while she was in high school softball. A loser from the other team took it out on her face because she hit a home run in the final inning and cleared the plates. Teenage girls could be so cruel. One swing and she was out cold for the next hour. The bruise took forever to fade. Reflecting on it now, that's what initially led her to delve into makeup and become an influencer. She obsessed, practicing everything she learned on video tutorials until she mastered disguising that bruise. It felt empowering to have that much control over how others saw her.

The buzz sounded again. Beside the instruments she saw it: two identical phones, side-by-side. One of their screens lit with activity.

Cora slunk into the bedroom and picked up the buzzing phone. It was hers. Her face automatically unlocked it, and a flutter of messages scrolled along the screen.

OMGeeee that thing got her!
Gotta be a hoax, man.
Is this account a place for horror movie previews now?

The live stream views reached over a thousand before the other Cora shut it down. Then it looked like hours passed and the comments and reactions trickled to nothing.

Her history showed another live stream, one she hadn't started. She pressed play. It was the other Cora, the lower half of her face covered by a mask. She recognized the eyes and eyebrows as her own. The other Cora breathed menacingly as she stared at the viewers, then giggled. The screen went black. Viewers heard a scream and a bludgeoning sound, firm at first. Then the sound became thick and sloshy. Cut to an image of blood dripping from dangling fingertips.

Then it stopped again. The comments went wild.

WTF is wrong wit u?!

She just trying to get attention. #desperate #loser

We don't wanna see anymore of this drunk-ass shit.

I admired you once, but didn't sign up for this. Delete!

Cora's followers disappeared one-by-one until only a dozen remained. She wondered if those accounts were even real.

The buzz she'd heard was an alert from the platform saying they were disabling her account because of inappropriate activity.

Cora picked up the other phone, and it unlocked effortlessly with one scan of her face. A social media app was also open on the other Cora's phone. The handle was BeautyIsPain. The profile picture matched the half-masked, sinister version of Cora. But her eyes—Cora's eyes—were made up with voluminous lashes and cat eyeliner, as sharp as a dagger. She'd picked a sparkling red hue that rimmed the entire eye with a deep purple fading to black at the corners.

Cora had to admit it was pretty.

As Cora scrolled through BeautyIsPain's content, she found photos and streaming snippets reminiscent of the post that brought down her own account. The bedroom mattress with a prisoner chained to the wall, and a bloodied bag over his head. A red handprint on the desk with soaked tools beside it. Rolled back eyes, disfigured jaws, and body parts. When she looked closer, she realized most of the victims were marred by botched aesthetic procedures before they met their end. Lips so full of filler, they burst open. Faces that had been subjected to chemical peels without a neutralizer. Layer upon layer of flaked skin peeled back to the bone.

She suppressed a vomit then realized her counterpart must have mixed up the phones. Since they looked exactly alike, BeautyIsPain accidentally posted to Cora's account, thinking it was her own.

But Cora's jaw dropped at the fanbase here, just shy of half a million. And they were adoring fans.

Sick. Ur content's wicked!

I own that same knife! Best tendon slicer on the market.

I gush for you. Black heart emoji.

The platform not only provided entertainment but also had a currency system in place, allowing fans to send gifts. In some of the reels, dollar signs danced across the screen as frequently as the adoration-filled emojis. Thousands of dollars had poured in for BeautyIsPain, thanks to the disturbing content.

Cora clicked through the list of people BeautyIsPain followed back. The entire platform was filled with gore and viewers relishing it, like some kind of darknet social media.

Cora wondered why she hadn't heard or seen BeautyIsPain in the duplex yet. She crept to the front of the apartment, and when she saw that was empty, too, she opened the front door. She expected to see a car or a windowless van sitting outside of the duplex. Because what else would a kidnapper and murderer drive? But she was alone. Instead of a decrepit neighborhood, she saw a narrow dirt road leading through a thick forest.

She pulled on the doorknob to the other half of the duplex, but it wouldn't budge. She peered inside the window, her eyes adjusting to the dimly lit room beyond the slightly pulled back blinds. Mirrors adorned the side wall, while leather lounge chairs were placed at the front. In the center, there was a vanity with black clothing, masks, and gloves neatly displayed on racks.

Cora imagined her counterpart came here to freshen up before she played with her victims. It was everything Cora could have hoped for herself, minus the murder theme.

Her gut signaled it was time to go, before BeautyIsPain got back and made her into a murder reel.

She grabbed her phone as she shuffled back toward the bathroom. But when she reached the mirror, she paused. She looked so tired—and scared. Not so much about staying, though. She dreaded going back.

Her counterpart had ruined every shred of hope. Famous to infamous. Not only would she never recover from the embarrassing and horrific post, but big trouble could also wait for her on the other side of that mirror. The social media team would identify her IP address and notify police. It was only a matter of time before they'd find and question her. And the answers she had would only make her sound crazy.

An investigation might produce nothing of substance. But it could take months, maybe years, to clear her already tainted name. Things would be off limits for her even more than they were now. Future jobs, her social accounts, even her ability to rent the shabby duplex—everything was threatened.

Cora felt the tears begin to well, then her tears turned to rage. She made a fist around her phone and threw it at the mirror, surprised at how easily it split. Shards fell at her feet, and she kept slamming her phone against it, until the white frame was all that remained.

Her battered phone fell to the floor, and she picked up one of the long glass shards. It reflected her bare and reddened eyes, her mouth hidden from sight. It gave her an idea.

She marched to the bedroom, double checked the straps on the chair and dug into each of BeautyIsPain's videos, studying how she used each weapon of torture. When everything was ready, she examined the assortment of instruments and selected the baseball bat. It seemed fitting for this occasion.

She couldn't use one of the pretty masks BeautyIsPain stored in the other half of the duplex. Not yet. So she made do with a torn piece of fabric she found on the floor. Probably from another victim. It didn't matter.

A faint crackling sound echoed in her ears, then grew louder. Cora peered out the front window as a van made its way down the dirt road toward the duplex. In the driver's seat was the other Cora.

Cora grabbed BeautyIsPain's phone and pressed the LIVE icon.

"Hello, devils," she said. The screen immediately burst to life.

BiP!!!

The goddess of death returns. Can't wait for this one!

Cora smiled beneath the mask. "I have a special treat for you today, not that you beasts deserve it."

Laughing emoji. Black heart emoji.

"Two kills in one. Mmhmm, that's right. But let me torture you with a little wait first, yes? Keep watching."

She propped the phone onto a chair, facing the doorway, so the viewers could see her positioned just behind it. She raised the bat to her shoulder and blew them a kiss. Then she pressed a finger to the mask as if to hush them.

Dollar signs flashed across the screen. First one, then another, then dozens more.

You finally did it, Cora, she thought. Back on your feet.

She took a deep breath.

BeautyIsPain parked the van, popped out of the driver's seat, and walked around to the side door. She whistled as she removed a gurney and clumsily hoisted another woman onto it. The other woman was passed out and tied up in ropes. A gag was in her mouth.

The door opened, and Cora hid just long enough for BeautyIsPain and her victim to slip inside. Then, with a joy she hadn't felt in a long time, Cora swung for the bleachers.

HOLE OF DARKNESS
-Alyssa Stadnyk-

As the tires of the truck crunched on the gravel, I looked in disgust out the window at the wilderness that now surrounded us. I growled in annoyance at the bumping of the trailer that was being pulled by what my friends called a camper's dream truck. In case anyone was wondering, I am NOT a camper. I hate nature of any kind, but because I'm a pathological people pleaser that can never say no, I agreed to go on an end-of-summer camping trip with three of my friends before we were all supposed to go off to separate colleges next week.

"Joys," I murmured with a grimace.

"It's just trees, Amber." My best friend Jenny Leong laughed.

"But they're all over the place," I grumbled. I was a city girl through and through, and I didn't find any sort of thrill in gallivanting through a forest like a wild animal.

"That's kind of the point of camping," Josh McKenna said, turning around in his seat to peer at me through his wire-rimmed glasses he thought made him look sophisticated, when really, they just made him look like a douche. Especially since he didn't actually need them. He liked their uniqueness. "You really *are* a girly-girl, aren't you? Maybe you should have just stayed home and gone shopping, or something."

"Fuck you, Josh!" Jenny snapped. "We can see Tiffany's hand in the front of your shorts, so don't act all high and mighty!" Josh's girlfriend, Tiffany Radcliffe, snapped her hand back quickly and, to her credit, started blushing so hard that her cheeks soon matched her red hair. I couldn't help but let out a small snicker at her obvious mortification.

I know it must sound like these people aren't actually my friends. Or like I could barely stand them. Except for Jenny. But the four of us have been a team since we were in diapers, and we like to give each other a hard time. And when Josh and Tiffany decided they liked each other as more than friends, our group became stronger. As hard as that might be to believe. Josh flipped Jenny off and turned around before shutting off the ignition.

"Okay. Let's get out and start setting up," he said.

"Set up? I thought we were sleeping in the trailer," I replied in confusion.

"We are, but we need to prepare the campfire, make sure that the food is secure in case of bears, etc. You know, normal camping stuff," Josh answered as he opened his car door.

"Bears?" I whispered in horror as I got out of the car.

"Don't worry, Amber," Tiffany said reassuringly, coming up beside me and putting a hand on my arm. "Bears are very rare and they tend to keep their distance. This is just a precaution."

"So people say, but then BOOM, bear attack," Josh shot back

"Ignore him," Tiffany said, rolling her eyes at her boyfriend. "That's what I do. Especially when he's being obnoxious."

"Isn't that all the time?" Jenny asked, raising an eyebrow.

"Yeah, but he's so cute when he does it," Tiffany answered, her eyes filled with adoration for Josh, causing a sickening sensation to rise in my throat.

"Josh, never let her go," I said as I swallowed my nausea and looked at the expanse of green and brown in front of me. "Let's get this torture over with."

"That's the spirit, Amber!" Josh said as he handed me a huge, bulky object. "Here, take these chairs and start setting them around the fire pit. Jenny, take the cooler out of the truck. Babe, can you get the bungee ropes from the trailer so I can secure the food?"

Wasting no time, we quickly got to work on our designated tasks, and in just twenty minutes, we were fully set up. I hadn't even noticed when it got dark, as we were so busy chatting by the campfire. Or, rather, Jenny and I were chatting while Tiffany and Josh were dry-humping in one of the chairs. I tried my best to ignore them, but their moans were a little disturbing. I turned to look at Jenny, and her expression mirrored my own disgust.

"Do you think if we threw a marshmallow at Josh's head, they'd stop?" I asked.

"Hmm, I don't know," Jenny replied. "Let me try something. Oy, rabbits, Amber's naked!"

"Jenny!" I hissed.

"Naked? What?" Josh said as he tore his lips away from Tiffany to stare at me.

"Pig," I muttered and laughed when Jenny threw a pinecone at Josh's head.

"Hey! You say my best friend since we were two is naked and expect me NOT to look?" Josh grumbled as he massaged the spot where the pinecone hit. "Do you not know me at all?"

"We do know you, Josh," Jenny replied, her chair creaking slightly as she leaned back. "We also expect you to not be a pervert and to pay attention to your girlfriend, who looks like she wants to rip your head off right now."

Josh turned his head to look at Tiffany, who was still comfortably seated on his lap, and flashed her a sheepish grin. Tiffany looked rightfully pissed. Although I loved Josh, a part of me couldn't help but be curious if she would actually throw a punch at him. The egotistical ass would have it coming. Much to my disappointment, Tiffany's cold expression softened and she shook her head.

"You're lucky you're cute," she said as she played with his messy brown hair.

"People say that all the time," Josh answered, smiling up at her.

"Maybe if you weren't such a dick all the time, people wouldn't put the "lucky" part in front of the "cute" part," I said as I leaned back in my chair as well.

"But where's the fun in that?" Josh said with a shrug. Undeniably, Josh's best quality was his ability to handle criticism gracefully. "But, to avoid further injury by pinecone, Tiffany and I will stop making out, even though my raging hormones need to be released."

"Thank the Lord," Jenny muttered. "Now, can we please talk about something that could distract us from the image of Josh's raging hormones?"

"Fine." Josh sighed. "Hey, did you guys hear about the fifteen-year-old girl who was killed in these woods three years ago?"

"Josh," Jenny admonished. "That's just a rumour."

"How can you be so sure?" Josh said, crossing his arms stubbornly. "The newspapers were filled with headlines about her disappearance, and this was the exact location where she was last spotted."

"But they didn't find a body," Jenny argued. "She probably just ran off and the press blew it out of proportion."

"And, now you sound like the police," Josh said in disgust. "The people who are supposed to help but won't fucking—"

"Wait," I interrupted. "A girl disappeared and was possibly murdered in these woods? And we're here because…?"

"She wasn't killed and nothing's going to happen to you," Jenny said soothingly. "Josh, stop freaking everyone out and let's move on."

"Fine," Josh agreed. It was nice to know he wasn't a complete dick. "But rumour has it that the killer is still here, awaiting his next prey." Never mind, he was a COMPLETE dick!

With a nervous gulp, I turned to Jenny, seeking guidance. She met my uncertain gaze and wordlessly advised me to pay no attention to Josh. I nodded in agreement to let her know. Josh's story seemed far-fetched, but my obsession with true crime podcasts made me consider the possibility. One thing was for sure, I would not leave the sides of my friends until we were safely back home.

***

I was able to keep that promise until later that evening. Josh and Tiffany had started grinding on each other again. Jenny was actively choosing to ignore them as she read. And what was I doing? The discomfort was unbearable as I squirmed around, urgently needing to relieve myself, only to realize there was no toilet in the trailer. And after the story Josh told, there was no way in hell I was going in the dark depths of the woods alone.

"Jenny," I murmured and blushed when she looked up at me. "Do you think you could maybe—"

"Amber," she replied. "I love you. You're like a sister to me. There are actually times when I love you more than my actual sister. But there is no way in hell I'm going with you to watch you pee. Suck it up and go. Bring a flashlight with you."

"But, Jenny…" I whined.

"No," she said. "Go. You don't have to go far and we're not going anywhere. Don't listen to Josh."

"Fine," I grumbled, standing up. "You can be a real bitch, you know that?"

"It is one of my best qualities," she answered as she returned her attention back to her book.

"If I'm not back in twenty minutes, send a search party," I said, feeling the weight of the flashlight in my hand and securing my dyed purple hair into a tight ponytail.

"Mmhm," Jenny answered, turning a page in her book.

"Here I go," I said as I walked to the end of the clearing. "About to go in the depths of the jungle."

"It's a forest, Amber," Jenny said. "Not a jungle."

"Same difference," I muttered.

"Except for the fact that the most dangerous animal you'll encounter in there is Bambi," Jenny replied from behind me.

"What about the bears?"

"They're not nocturnal," Jenny answered. "Now go before you pee yourself."

"I might do that anyway at the first snapping branch," I muttered as I took a deep breath and walked into the dark unknown.

***

While navigating the vast, shadowy forest, I focused my flashlight on the narrow trail branching out from the open area. I faintly heard that Tiffany and Josh stopped making out and were now engaged in conversation and laughter with Jenny. As I walked further, the surrounding sounds dissipated into silence, prompting me to find a suitable spot to quickly take care of my business and rejoin my friends. While searching for a suitable place to squat, reminiscent of a scene from a horror film, my flashlight suddenly died!

"Fuck," I whispered as I hit the side of it, desperately hoping that the light would come back on. "Come on. Not now."

There was a brief moment when the light came back on, but it immediately flickered out again. Despite my frustration, I resisted the temptation to throw it aside, knowing that doing so would worsen my already dire situation. As I took a few deep breaths, the crisp air filled my lungs, mingling with the anticipation of finding my way back to the campground. However, my search yielded no luck. Everywhere I turned, all I could see was darkness. When I looked up, a sense of calm washed over me as I saw the Gemini twins gracefully dancing across the night sky. My friends find it strange that I feel a strong connection to the zodiac, especially Gemini, even though I don't possess any of their characteristics. However, the fact that people have put so much importance in the stars for thousands of years strangely brings me comfort. Shaking my head, I strained my ears to see if I could hear my friends, but no luck on that front.

"Guys!" I called out. "Jenny! Josh! Tiffany! Can you guys hear me?" I just heard silence. "Fuck. I'm going to have to find my own way."

When I started to hear some chanting in the distance, a wave of relief washed over me. I had no idea what my friends were up to, but I didn't care. They meant salvation; them and their weird chanting. I took a few cautious steps towards the sound, relying on my sense of touch to guide me through the darkness. Luckily, I didn't trip over any tree roots, but I still didn't know where the hell I was, or where I was going. Despite walking for about ten minutes, I realized I should have reached the clearing by now or at least spotted some light indicating that I was going the right way, but all I could see was darkness. The chanting had ceased, leaving me without my sense of hearing to rely on. I sighed deeply and took a step in the direction I had just come from…and suddenly I was falling.

The next minute was kind of a blur. I can only recall my stomach in my throat, the rushing wind in my ears, and the certainty of impending death. As I collided with a hard surface, a sickening crunch reverberated through my body, momentarily eclipsing the pain. But above all, I was grateful to be alive. I was lying on my back, gazing at the sky above me, and realized that I must have fallen into a deep hole. Once again, Gemini provided me comfort, but I doubted their ability to rescue me from this situation. I couldn't even fathom what a humongous hole was doing in the woods. Maybe the hunter set up a trap to catch larger animals, but they should have put up some sort of barrier to prevent an unsuspecting person from falling into it. I sat up cautiously, grimacing in pain, and gradually rose to my feet. *At least I don't have to go pee anymore*, I thought to myself as I dusted off my jeans.

"Jenny!" I called, cupping my mouth with my hands. "Josh! Tiffany! Can you guys hear me? Can anyone hear me? I need help!"

I was met with the eerie echo of my own voice and the chilling sound of bats squeaking overhead. I thought I heard the haunting chanting start up again, but when I strained my ears, there was only silence. *Just my imagination*, I thought. I believed that if I waited patiently, my friends would eventually start to wonder why I was taking so long and come searching for me, but who knew how long that would take? Josh and Tiffany were likely engaged in sexual activities, and Jenny could easily lose herself when engrossed in a book. When she's engrossed in a book, what might take everyone else two hours could feel like just twenty minutes to her. All I knew was that I wanted to get the fuck out of this hole and that it was up to me to get myself out.

Slowly, I made my way to the wall of the hole and discovered what seemed to be tiny mouse holes that could be used as grips to pull myself up. I cautiously placed my feet in two holes, hoping that curious mice wouldn't nibble on my toes. Or worse, my fingers. I carefully put my hands in two more holes a little above my head. I knew I was going to have to be extremely cautious while climbing. If I made one wrong step, I could fall again and hurt myself more. I desperately clung to the earth wall, my muscles straining as I tried to hoist myself up with the little strength I had. Closing my eyes, I reached for another hole just above my current position while I moved my leg up to where my hand had just been. I was moving at a slow pace, but at least I was making progress.

"Please, God. Buddha. Allah. Artemis. Come on, my Gemini twins! Whoever the fuck is listening," I muttered as I moved my hand again. "If you can get me out of here, I promise I'll start lifting weights and doing pull-ups in my spare time."

Cautiously, I glanced upwards and felt relieved when I discovered I was halfway up the hole. I just had to hold on a few more minutes, and I'd hopefully be able to find my way back to my friends. It honestly hurt my feelings that they hadn't bothered to search for me yet. As my left hand reached for another hole above my head, I felt something smooth and slender, resembling a twig. I cursed when it came loose and hoped I wasn't about to lose my grip. My legs ached with soreness, and I could barely lift my arms. I couldn't risk falling now because then I'd never be able to get myself out again. I firmly planted my feet in the holes and clenched my hands tightly. Removing the twig would help me improve my grip. I removed the twig from the mouse hole and inspected it before discarding it.

Much to my horror, upon further examination, I realized it wasn't a twig, as I initially believed. It was a fucking bone! I let out a loud scream and accidentally let go of the bone. As I did, my grip slipped and my legs couldn't support me, causing me to fall back into the hole. I remembered to tuck my body into the fetal position, protecting my head from any potential injury. I had a rough landing on my side, causing me to lose my breath, but thankfully I wasn't seriously injured. Just tired, hungry, and fucking terrified. I checked out the tiny bone that made me trip and figured it was just some animal bone.

"Of course it is," I whimpered. "It has to be."

I let a stupid animal bone derail me so much that I ended up falling once more. My initial attempt left me too exhausted. Unexpectedly, there was a loud popping sound that came from above me, and a distinct crack immediately followed it. It sounded like someone was walking around about a foot above my head.

"Josh!?" I called. "Is that you?"

I didn't receive any response to my call. Only silence and a faint sound of cracking. That's when I began to panic, recalling Josh's tale of the girl who disappeared. I chanced another look at the bone and wondered if I was wrong for thinking it was an animal bone. Maybe it was human. Maybe it had belonged to that girl and whoever I'd heard walking around wasn't one of my friends, but the killer. Then I heard it again, the damn chanting! I looked at the wall of mouse holes warily and started shaking when skeletal hands started digging out of the dirt walls and the fingers started reaching for me. As I moved backward, I could feel my foot sinking. As I looked down, a chilling sight greeted me - the ground began to bubble and transform into a deep crimson hue, resembling blood. The chanting was almost deafening by this point. I squeezed my eyes shut, bracing for the sensation of being pulled into the ground or grasped by the bony fingers. However, when nothing occurred, I cautiously opened my eyes and observed that the ground had returned to its usual state. There were no hands emerging from the wall, and the chanting had ceased. And I was still in the fucking hole!

I breathed a sigh of relief that my mind had only been playing tricks on me and now I could concentrate on getting out of here. My heart raced as the cracking sounds filled the air once more, making me jump in fright. I hastily pressed myself into the darkness of the hole, desperate to shield myself from any danger. I hoped to remain unseen and not draw any attention to myself. The sounds grew nearer, causing me to tightly shut my eyes, desperately hoping it was just my imagination and not a murderer approaching to make me vanish forever.

"Amber?!" I heard a familiar voice call out. "Amber! Where are you?" My eyes popped open when I heard Josh's voice and the concern in his tone. "Come on, Amber, this isn't funny. If you can hear me, call out!"

"Josh!" I screamed, and I heard his footsteps stop. "Josh! I'm down here! Please, get me out."

I don't think I've ever been more thankful to see Josh's wire-rimmed glasses than when I saw his face peering over the edge of the hole. I couldn't help but smile to myself when I saw the naked relief on his face when he saw me, unharmed.

"Shit," he whispered. "Are you okay?"

"A little bruised," I replied with a shrug.

"Okay," Josh said. "I'm going to get some help. You stay there."

"Where the fuck would I go?" I whispered to myself when I heard him run off shouting in the distance for Jenny and Tiffany.

I sat down on the ground and rested my head against the wall, feeling better now that I knew I was about to be rescued. As soon as I relaxed, exhaustion washed over me and my eyes began to droop. I let out a frustrated sigh as I faintly heard my name being called and the sound of rope scraping against the ground.

"Amber," I heard Josh whisper as he put a hand on my arm. "I know you're tired, but you have to wake up so we could get you out of here."

"Josh?" I murmured as I peered at him with heavily lidded eyes. "How did you get down here?"

"I used the bungee ropes I brought to secure the food in order to rappel down here," Josh explained. "Jenny and Tiffany are holding the rope steady. Come on, let's get you up and out of here. Can you stand?"

"I think so," I replied as I stood up slowly with Josh's help. His arm was loosely wrapped around my waist, providing stability as we made our way towards the dangling red rope near the hole. He secured the rope tightly around my waist, ensuring our safety as he connected it to his own.

"Are you ready for this?" he asked as he smoothed a piece of hair from my face and I hated how I felt a little jump in my heart. *Stop it. It's just hero worship. You don't like Josh*, I thought to myself. *He's cute, but he's a pain in the ass. Not to mention dating your best friend.* I just nodded in answer to his question. "Okay. Hang on. Jenny! Tiffany! I've got her. Pull us up!"

As Josh slowly started climbing up the side of the hole, I felt my legs leave the ground and a wave of relief washed over me. I buried my face into his strong chest so that I could forget my ordeal for one second. Shortly thereafter, I noticed a second set of hands reaching out towards me. Even though they were smaller, I equally appreciated them. I chanced a look and saw both Tiffany and Jenny shining their flashlights on me and looking like they had been crying.

"Amber. Oh, my God," Jenny said as she untied the rope around my waist and pulled me into a hug. "Are you okay?"

"I'm fine," I murmured as I hugged her tightly. Tiffany's worried gaze met mine, and I extended my spare arm towards her. Her hug enveloped both me and Jenny, and I could barely hold back my tears.

"Fuck," I heard Josh mutter, and I saw him looking down into the hole. "It's gotta be, like, eight feet deep. It's amazing you didn't break anything. Is that a bone down there?"

"Yeah, but I think it's an animal bone," I replied as I let go of the girls and tried not to let it bother me when Tiffany curled into his side. "Thanks, Josh. For getting me out of there."

"Well, I couldn't exactly let you rot down there," he answered with a smirk. "Your mom would have my hide if anything happened to you."

I laughed because it was true. My mom was the definition of the mother bear. Speaking of bears, I wanted to get the fuck out of these woods before a bear decided we'd make a good breakfast.

"Let's go back to camp," I said as I leaned on Jenny for support, and noticed I was way off in my sense of direction when the group started walking in the completely opposite direction I had walked in before I fell.

"Josh," Jenny panted out. "Do you mind leading her back to camp? She's too heavy for me to drag all the way there."

"Sure," Josh answered, letting go of Tiffany's hand and coming over to put his arm around my waist. Over his shoulder, I could see Jenny winking at me before she went to walk with Tiffany. I blushed when I stumbled on a tree root. I was not this girl. And I was most definitely not the girl to lust over her friend's boyfriend. "Are you hurt anywhere?"

"Not really," I answered honestly. "I landed on my back when I fell, but I can still move so that's a good sign."

"For sure," Josh replied and I breathed a sigh of relief when I saw the clearing up ahead. "I'm going to deny I ever said this, but I was really worried about you, Amber."

"Really?" I said. "You weren't too busy making out with Tiffany to notice I was gone?"

"What?" Josh said in confusion. I shook my head, feeling ashamed about my bitter tone. It wasn't his fault that I'd found myself in that situation and I was fooling myself for thinking I actually had feelings for him.

"Nothing," I said. "Sorry. I'm just tired."

"Don't worry," he said, squeezing my waist in response. "Once we get back to camp, you can rest while we pack up. I think we're all a little too excited to spend the night here."

"Thank God," I murmured, feeling sleepy again. I felt him helping me into the waiting truck and I heard scraping and screeching as the girls folded the chairs. Although it was corny, I felt like it was my Gemini twins who led Josh to find me and subsequently led to my rescue.

I rested my head against the top of the backseat and closed my eyes. I winced when I heard the various car doors slam shut and the ignition start. As the truck finally drove away, I let out a sigh and was greeted by the soft murmur of Josh and Tiffany chatting in the front seats. When I turned my head to the side, I caught sight of Jenny giving me a concerned look.

"I'm really okay," I said. "I promise I'll get checked out at the hospital when we get home, just be sure."

"Good," she replied with a nod.

"I'm never going camping again," I groaned as I covered my face with my hands.

"It wasn't that bad, was it?" she whispered to me, keeping a close eye on our friends. "I mean, you finally realized the reason why you like giving Josh a hard time. You have a lady boner for him and I think he likes you too."

"Okay," I said, as I looked at her in disbelief. "Even if I could move past that little moment of insanity, which I will not admit to, I still have to go back to the fact that I fell down a fucking hole. I think that takes priority over whether I have feelings for Josh."

"That's true. We can focus on that if you wish," she said in consideration. She glanced back at me with curiosity, and I could honestly admit that I didn't like what I saw in her gaze. "By the way, how did you like my little hole of darkness? Kind of comfy, huh? Probably shouldn't have walked that far. What did you think of the chants? Were you frightened by my friends? They're particularly attracted to believers."

"What?" I spoke softly, doing my best to keep my voice steady.

"Shh," she answered, putting her finger to her lips. "Don't worry. They won't hurt you. We're going to have so much fun, you and I." Then she winked at me before turning her attention to the book laying open in her lap.

When I turned my attention back to the front of the car, I saw Josh's concerned expression mirrored in the rearview mirror. I shook my head to let him know I was fine when really I was reeling. Was Jenny joking? Could it be that she was a psychopath, and I was completely unaware? I realized neither answer would provide me with any relief. I couldn't stop thinking about the bone I came across. Was it human? Was it an animal? And if it was human, did Jenny have anything to do with it? And who was she talking about? Was everything I saw real or was it really just my mind? These were the questions I knew would haunt me all the way home and when I went off to college. Lucky for me, I had four years to figure it out.

Joys.

CANCER

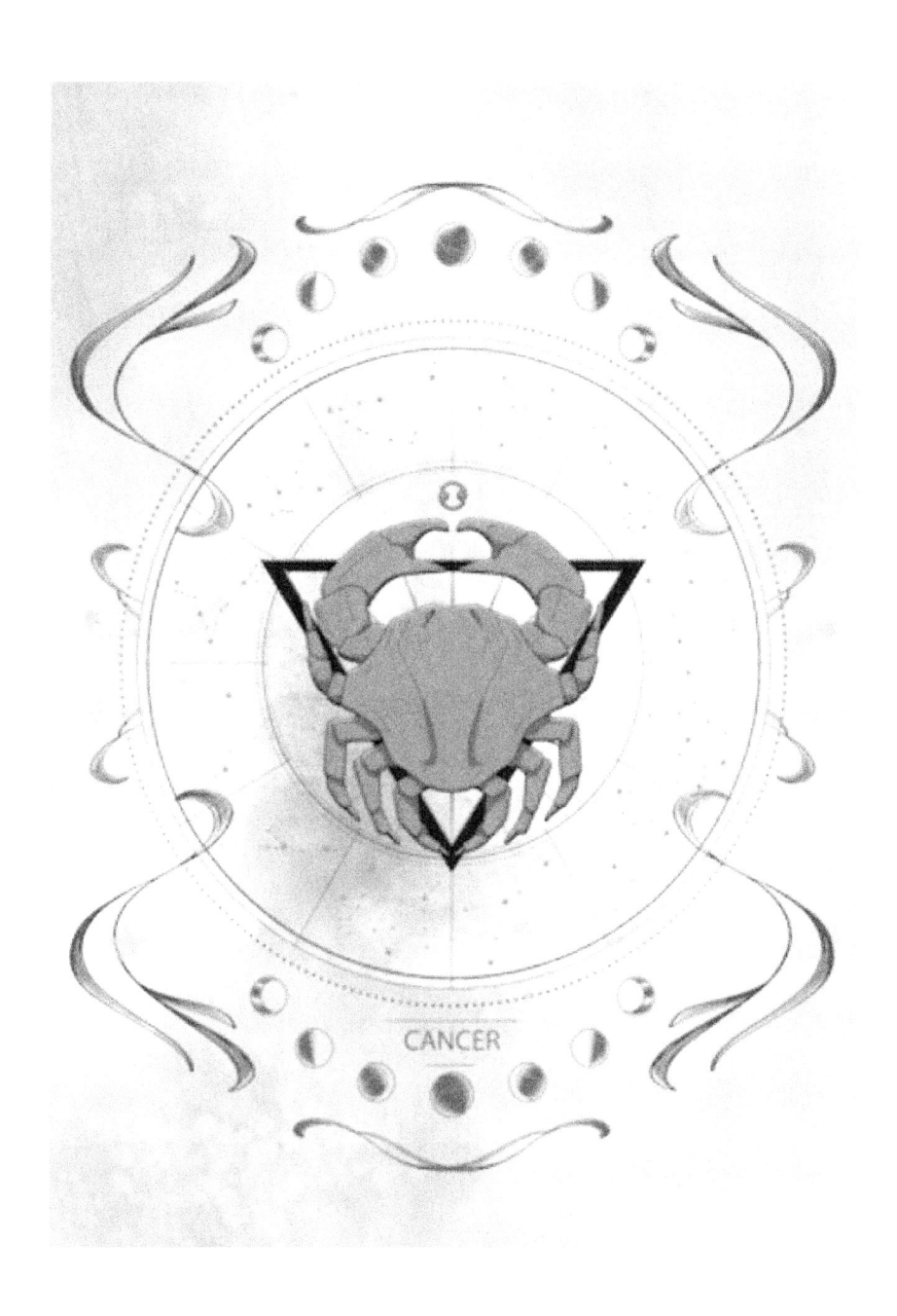

LOVE ON THE SHORE
-Alexander Michael-

The island sat in their sights, visible from the mainland.

Mudjimba Island—more commonly referred to as Old Woman Island by the locals and tourism rags—occupied the horizon, its body resembling a whale breaching the sea's surface. The hill rose to the sky. The island's single pine tree sat atop its modest heights like a beacon to the curious.

These curious; this young man and woman who had known each other a mere three weeks.

After navigating their way into the 'keyhole'—the natural pool lined by rocks—and pulling the kayak ashore, the love-struck pair stood at the edge of the sea and gazed back toward home, her arm around him.

If only she'd shown this warmth on the trip over, Cody thought, instead of criticising his rowing method.

It was a shame she was fast becoming a political light-weight in his eyes, her lack of interest in anything to do with politics so maddening.

"What a sight," he said, the sea bleeding sparks. "What a sight."

***

Again… Naomi thought. He said it again. How often can the same thing be announced? Just let the day be, you political bigot!

She sighed, trying to push away the realisation she had only known Cody for a week before they decided to start dating, and that only two more weeks had passed before the idea of spending a weekend on the island had struck them. "Are you ready?" he had said, his arms outstretched, proffering his adventurous idea. She thought she had been ready, but if he admired the day one more time, she might just leave him to it.

She had two and a half days stretching ahead of her to figure out what she saw in him.

But time enough for scrutiny later. How could she be upset when there was a turtle not twenty metres away, floating along without a care in the world? She smiled, shading her eyes from the sun. His were alight with hope and excitement. She kissed him nonetheless, there on the shore. His body smelt of sweat and salt.

"Wanna do some fishing?" Cody asked.

How was it she hadn't yet informed him of her vegetarianism, and how was it he hadn't noticed her eating only tofu when they had gone out to dinner? Her insides somersaulted.

***

Cody hoped he didn't have to listen to much of this flower child's tosh about 'an event of grand scale coming to shake the earth from its evil complacency', 'an arrival from the stars', numerous astrological predictions, and the fact that she is a Cancer. She sure was turning into a bit of a crab.

On the way over here, Naomi had even claimed that animals had rights. He had laughed out loud.

"Did you know," she had asked, "that once people pass away, their souls are transferred into animal bodies? I wish people knew that. They might treat animals kinder."

"Mmhmm. What animal would you want to be?"

"A crab, of course! Like my star sign!"

Oh Lord...

"Well," he said, "Let's hope someone grants you that wish. Maybe I can come too? So we can be together."

"If you're lucky..."

Rife with sweat, his shirt discarded, he made his way over to the pine tree. It stood solitary, an eternal vigil over this tiny island. The sparse canopy allowed a view of the sky. The clouds above were racing as fast as his blood. "What a sight..."

They went down to the shore together, a silence reigning between them. Having chosen their vantage point, they first decided to explore the island. As it turned out, the place they erected their tent was one of the few spots free of a plague-like cactus which had spread almost entirely over the island.

Among the pandanus trees were the ruins of the first and only house built on the island. They wandered among the destroyed walls, no sign of a roof above. Towers of grey and black stones still stood, moored in stubborn concrete from decades long past. They made their way through the 'rooms', alighting upon the remains of a bath or spa, the tiles still cream where they resisted time's decaying hand.

Cody examined the ruins. "Shame it's a bit of a shithole."

Naomi huffed. "I like it here."

The first day passed with the capture of three snappers, and how Cody wished to freeze time at this moment. He was already shirtless. His body glistened in the sun's last hurrah. She followed suit, untied her bikini top, and tossed it onto the sandy beach. The stars peeked their heads out from behind the celestial curtain.

Naomi stayed with him on the shore until the light completely left the world. Their bodies were warmed by beer and close proximity. When the sky was littered with worlds in their trillions, they made their way via torchlight up from the rocks and sand through the maze of prickly pear cactus. The sea was a constant rumbling din. The tent enclosed them.

The thin walls pent up his yearnings. All he could smell was her sweat. This was too much. Naomi saw his gaze. It was returned, and with a smile of her own to boot.

They undressed hurriedly, so intent on consuming and being consumed; to become something *other than*. In the dim light, her bare breasts gleamed like precious jewels, accentuating her flawless figure. The tent's skylight allowed the moonlight to gently illuminate the space, as if inviting the voyeuristic stars to join in. His mouth moved to hers.

Stars bled arousal. The lovers waxed the same. When her trailing tongue coaxed the brink ever closer, Naomi left off her labours and lay on her back. Now it was his turn. She was squealing in minutes. Skin pale as statuary, her body curled into a question mark in the gloom. She *was* a mystery, this girl he had known less than a month.

***

He awoke.

The tent was open. Night, deep.

It was empty. "Naomi?"

Nothing. He racked his brain. They had been together, hadn't they? She'd been on her back. Then he remembered her climbing on top and planting herself there like a vine taken root.

Then nothing. Blackness. Awakening.

The sight of the hill just as empty sent the first threat of fear into his spine. The starlight was shocking, its blaze so superior to anything mankind could conjure up. He stood back, his hands on his hips. It was easy to admire the whites, emeralds, and mauves of the Milky Way. The distant seaside towns all along the shore were entirely ignorant.

He was so alone. Only now did he realise.

A *squish* beneath his foot.

One of the day's catch stared up at him. Its dead eyes tried to guilt him. To his right was the second fish, a metre or two from the other. Sure enough, the third soon reared its head, the three corpses spread out in a trail. He entertained a lunatic thought for one second only: that they had opened the esky and leapt from their cold coffins onto the grass, intent on escape.

"Hi."

He leapt, turning for the source. The pine tree.

There she was, at its base, one hand on the trunk. Naomi wasn't talking to him. She was facing away.

He crept over to the pine tree. In one direction, the shores lit by electricity, dwarfed by the galaxy. In the other, dark out to sea, bilious clouds forming a more complete darkness. But the hill seemed to be empty of souls save theirs, so who the hell was she speaking to? Did she even know he was there?

"Hey..." he murmured, lightly touching her arm.

She jumped but did not break her stare, which was directed right up towards the stars. He threw a quick glance upwards, but could only see a mass of distant light. Her attention lingered on that firmament. In a moment of pointless realisation, he saw she was now clothed. So was he.

"What are you doing?" he asked gently.

She continued to stare into the canopy of the pine tree, where the stars sat close and so far. She opened her mouth to bestow a horror. "Don't you see her up there?"

He threw his glance skyward. Nothing to see but the expanse of space. Even in the moonlight, all absence of stars were merely the tenacious branches of the pine tree. He looked back at her face, her eyes so intent on their quarry.

"Honey..." he realised then with lunatic clarity this was the first time he had ever called her by a pet name. "There's no one up there."

"There. There she is."

She pointed. Ignoring common sense, he followed her finger.

An alien melding of starlight and night-blindness made him see someone crouching in the branches. He shook his head before looking again.

"She smiles at us…"

"All right. That's enough," he said. He grasped her shoulders, turning her from the sight of the tree. "Do you hear me? You're freaking me out. Snap out of it."

Words failed her. Her head turned itself upwards once again. "No!"

He tightened his grip, only for her to scream and thrash. The sudden destruction of the island's blissful silence was shocking. Her scream sent him leaping from his skin. It instilled rage in him instead. "Stop it! What the hell is wrong with you?"

At last her fugue broke, and his rage was proved miniscule compared to hers. She reached out and struck him in the groin. The air leapt from his chest. The ground rushed up to meet him. His curled form was a spoof of her body's earlier position in the tent.

"Don't you *ever* lay your hands on me again!" she cried, her body bent over under Anger's ugly burden. Was she waking from a nightmare? Did she know he was here?

He moaned her name.

"No more whining," she groaned. "No more *ignorance*. Did you know I was a vegetarian? Oh yes, killing fish seemed like a fantastic pastime for me! Why did I get into a relationship with a man *I don't even know*?"

She stormed down the hill, disappearing from view.

He was alone. Again. His balls sang a hymn to painlessness. Should he call out to her and receive nothing but another injury? She could have *told* him she was a vegetarian.

No, he shouldn't call out to her; whatever was wrong, the lunatic could work it out by herself. Who was Naomi, anyway? Why had he thought it a great idea—oh, the best!—to spend a weekend with this stranger in such a barren place? Struggling to his feet, he peered up at the night sky one last time.

Eyes.

Bright amid the black.

The crouching form shifted. Long hair trailed a face that was all leer. Two eyes—burning; eager—folded into the nothingness, simply closing their lids.

A tenacious gull screamed its distant delight.

Cody tripped backwards down the slope. Every collision coated his body in the spears of the prickly pear cactus.

***

The woman beckoned.

Her shape was a jagged scrawl on midnight's canvas. Fecund shadows bred trails as the woman walked on, a litter of nightmares at her feet.

Naomi followed.

The ruins reared up. Two towers of black stone and concrete. Naomi wasn't afraid. There was no fear here, only a blessed numbness. What could pain do? Pain was so fleeting. The shape ahead beckoned.

All she knew was that she had been sleepwalking. That *must* have been the reason for her little excursion, staring up into the night sky and into the gaze of the 'woman' that was leering at her from above. But why had the esky been destroyed? Why were the beers gone? She had found them at the base of the hill, shattered among the stones. She strangely felt no need for caution.

But still the woman called. Still, Naomi followed.

She always prided herself on her ability to *feel*, to read situations, and to discern the truth beneath normality's veneer. Whether this was true or not, she was fast doubting these abilities. Why did her life consist of these hasty decisions? Why couldn't she find value in herself until a man was buried in her? Was she so needy for affection she needed a living mirror to tell her what she already knew? She was somebody. She was worth something. But no, she was as shallow as the rest of the multitudes, seeking that 'partner' only as an extension of her vanity.

As soon as she shrugged off this simpleton that brought her here, she would 'fall' once more, a new living mirror delivering his affections upon her lovesick temple.

From out of the ruinous shadows came the remains of the house's shower. It creaked and moaned and she sat in it, huddling her knees to her chest. Why was she out here in the dark, sitting in a dilapidated bath built who-knew-when?

She was following a woman, wasn't she?

Was she splitting in two? That might explain why she had seen a figure among the pandanus trees; and in the pine tree, staring down at her and whispering dark truths about the world: which constellation was screwing which constellation; which parent Bastard Earth could call 'daddy'; the rumours of a black hole and its scandals; the sacred mystery at the root of this island.

The mystery she now discovered, standing up from the bath and moving to its underside as if upon instruction.

Yes, she *was* splitting in two. But what a pleasant experience to give up control.

There on the side of the tub, a little crab stared out at the world. She caressed the design with her thumb to see the concrete it was ensconced in fall away. The clatter of stone on stone was muffled by the roar of the waves nearby. The birds had been all but silent since their arrival, most of the gulls abandoning this barren rock for specks of land less charged with the anomalous.

The hole vomited blackness. The scent from within was musty, but spattered here and there with the remains of old incense. Was this some remnant of the house's cellar? Would bookshelves greet her from tapestried walls?

She inched her way inside the hole just wide enough to fit her too-skinny frame.

***

Since when had the earth been so *hard?* Cody lay prone. Stars tittered. Bones accompanied his balls, a riotous symphony.

The sea was near. It mocked him. Cody removed spikes from his skin, trying to ignore the sight of blood on the stones. "Fuck fuck fuck…"

His dinner had been fouled, the esky's ice thrown here and there, and he now noticed that all their drinks had been smashed on the rocks.

He was trapped on this island with a lunatic until morning. "Flower child! Fairy fucker! Why do I *do* this?"

Why did he throw himself into every relationship that came along? He had things to offer, didn't he? Why couldn't he find value in himself until he was buried in a woman? What a weekend...

The shore erupted in spasms.

A boulder tripped him. His arse slammed into the earth, adding further bruising. The splashing continued, forcing him further and further back into the dark.

Something was coming.

***

Naomi gawked. The space inside the rock was no bigger than the inside of her wardrobe. The blackness was utter. It smothered her, but she could not turn around in a hurry without scraping her body to bloody pieces. Cursing, she instead took a deep breath and tried her best to calm down. Her heart was a damned drum in her chest, vibrating her ribs and throat to no end. She was sweating, her skin slick. Despite the voices in her head, she used her sodden skin to slip deeper into this crevasse.

Before the need for light overwhelmed her, a sickly iridescence forced its way between her eyelids. Something here was glowing.

It became more obvious with every passing moment until she finally had to admit it was brighter in here than it was out under the stars. The light bubbled up out of the earth itself, or from the walls. She was not sure which, but the amber illumination painted the series of petroglyphs in its oils.

These ancient markings occupied the walls and ceiling of the chamber. Just how long had they been here, beneath this frequently visited fishing and surfing spot? A touch of the ancient in hiding beneath the commonplace.

She began examining the markings, but the nearer she got to the wall, the more they proffered themselves to her eyes. What she originally took to be meaningless spirals now revealed themselves to be whirlpools—in the very sea that surrounded her now, no doubt eager to press itself into this rocky sepulchre to claim her life. That was the nature of the sea, wasn't it? It took what it would, eager for vengeance against all those who filled it with trash and pilfered its living families. Much like Fisherman Cody, somewhere above, surely gazing at the stars with that idiot expression plastered on his lips: what a *siiight*!

Amid the spirals that depicted the sea was a pattern, or several married together, in which the sea threw up various forms of life. This wall was akin to a bestiary.

Sharks beneath the veneer of the sea. Fishes of all shapes and sizes accompanied these larger beasts from under their fins. Rays equipped with stingers of barbaric size and severity. Crab-life and crustacean. The graceful turtle, its image multiplied tenfold, even in this crude depiction appearing as a prince among the rest of the animal life.

Over on the far side of the cave, its depths still illuminated, one animal took up pride in place. It stared out at the world from the eyes in its bulbous head, that gaze displaying its vast intelligence. It was an octopus dominating one entire wall.

These pages of stone were carved upon by hands unknown, in times unknowable. For whatever reason, this artist—or artists — thought it crucial to immortalise the beasts that were to be found in the sea close to the island. And there it was on the wall, not too far from the god-like octopus: the island, drawn in shocking particularity as compared to the rest of the creatures here.

Only now, being this close to the monstrous octopus, did she realise where the light was coming from. The source of illumination came from its eyes.

She gaped like a stuck fish and edged closer to the wall. Standing on tiptoe, she put her eye to that of the animal's and peered within. There was a room back there, and in it, an occupant. The wall began to shift.

The occupant turned, a mess of shadow, long hair disguising features already disguised. It waved.

The vibrating earth ceased as the door completed its rotation. The light source revealed itself. It was a den, existing here beneath and between walls of stone. Littered around the place, a collection of lamps, their shades ranging from cloth to glass to ceramic, their light pure white or red or tangerine or rainbow. Fairy lights were strung about over the ceiling, the globes not charged by electricity but trapped fireflies.

Bookshelves suffering from their freight lined the space, the fact they still stood testament to their great strength. There was no way to see from here what tomes and manuscripts occupied those shelves, for her eyes were too concerned with the room's centrepiece.

This was more a garden than a den.

A bushel of vines erupted out of the earth in the room's dead centre—not quite a tree; not quite boasting a canopy—and stretched up to the ceiling in emerald profusion. Odd blossoms littered the foliage, their scent a mix between orange peels and spilt passionfruit. Some were tangerine, matching the glow from a few of the lamps. Others mingled turquoise with scarlet. Others still were the deep black of midwinter pestilence. Finally, some of the buds erupting from this strange marriage of vinery and bloom were as pink as the lips she harboured at her centre.

This shrub had the echoes of humanity and womanhood in its midst.

It was true: in the dim light, the plant—the tree; the vine; whatever the hell it was—appeared to resemble a woman standing upright, her body voluptuous, her stance that of a yawning feline recumbent upon an upright daybed. She had twelve arms; twelve limbs of some ancient tree, spiralling up through the firefly-light. A lifelong follower of the Zodiac, Naomi thought of the corresponding animals, and set a sight for her own limb on this tree.

It was she, this flora-woman, whose golden ambience filtered through the underground chamber to shoot through the eyes of the giant painted octopus in the next room. Her leaves *sweated* this light, a bioluminescence that laughed at the sun, and this human visitor desired to sit among her roots and bathe her.

Somehow, Naomi was certain this room functioned as the heart of the island. This womanly show of vines was the spine of the pine tree. It shot upwards through earth to become that lone pine ruling the sky and the hill: its heart; its soul.

Her gaze was drawn to the black figure sitting at the little table, and a wave of fear washed over her, causing her skin to prickle and sweat to form. The figure was hooded and hunched. There was a subtle glimpse of long hair trying to escape from underneath the black fabric. In the darkness, it gleamed with an icy, white glow.

She backed away towards the door to the petroglyph. "Who are you?"

The figure in black rose from the earthen table, and sidling over to the plant life growing in the centre of the space, plucked something from one of the blooms. It brought its bounty back to the table.

Still, Naomi was numb. Still, she viewed all this as a memory of a film once seen as a child. She knew she had to eat that which the stranger brought. Once thought, so.

The person beneath the hood slid the seeds into her starved mouth and kept them there as she chewed. Only once the seedlings were all mush, releasing a pungent liquid, did they remove their hands.

She swilled the liquid in her mouth before swallowing. It was thick, complete with a strange consistency. But to her delight, it tasted like whisky, unadulterated by either ice nor mixer. It eased her body. She chanced a smile. Her rising lips vibrated the world inside and out, and pleasure reverberated back at her. The occupant did not wipe the bliss from her face, so she indulged deeper, sliding into the fix with ease. Her limbs were loose, her eyelids heavy.

The hood had been thrown back during her ecstasies, and sitting opposite her was a woman of advanced age.

Her hair hung in ice-white profusion from her central part, complete with artful braids from crown to waist. The woman's garments matched the colour of the snowfall erupting from her scalp, but the clothing itself was a tunic not seen in several centuries. But her face… While aged, there was nothing there but exceptional beauty, her skin wrinkled but pearly and cool. Her voice entered the intruder's mind. Lips and speech were redundant in this holy place, so the interloper followed suit.

The herbaceous plant quivered, creating an unsettling rustle.

She heard the woman speak so clearly: *The man. He is here to hurt you. He wants to take you away. You must stop him before it's too late.*

He wants to hurt me?

Yes. She nodded.

Why?

Do the unclean need a reason?

He is unclean, isn't he…

The woman smiled, and her lips glowed a pinkish hue that Naomi yearned to kiss. *There are many like him. Those ignorant fools who come and kill the animal life, all for mere trophies. They actually believe that to extinguish life is a fun pastime. Animals, here and among the stars, have suffered for far too long.*

Yes.

To harm the natural life is a great crime. So the punishment must also be great. It is deserved.

Yes! Naomi began hyperventilating, her entire being in agreeance. *Mankind must suffer for its crimes against the wild.*

Good, child. You must stay here. With me.
With you?
This island is the last safe place.
Yes.
Keep me near. Become one with the stars and all its Houses.
Of course, she said.

Naomi found herself plucking one of the flowers from the woman-shaped vine and swallowing it whole, impregnating herself.

***

She crept along the shore, hunched and cadaverous, having spent too much time around harridans. A small axe sat in the palm of her hand. It was eager.

She knew there was another identity riding her like a horse, but the relinquishing of the reins was a blessing after so many years of pain. Her limbs were loose, her body warm.

Once they eliminated the man who threatened an end to this bliss, then nirvana could last forever. This was what the woman promised, if she did this one small thing.

***

Cody did not have time to see what the ocean was disgorging onto the sand. All he knew was that it was large, salt water falling off its back and head in rivulets. There was the sound of shifting rocks and the squelch of wet limbs.

He was far more concerned with the sight of Naomi.

The shadows moved away, allowing her to emerge from the pandanus trees and step into the moonlit area. Cody failed to recognise her at first, so fast was his heartbeat and the racing of the blood in his veins. There were dangers on all sides.

She continued to approach; her eyes wide in a perpetual stare. She grasped something in her hand. It glinted. He threw a glance back to the shore and cursed.

The entity crept closer and closer in the dark. He felt its breath already, coming from a bloated body six feet long with a head four feet tall.

He fled from the sight instinctively, but only then remembered the other threat: the young woman, once named Naomi, approaching him from the other direction, her back hunched, her eyes locked on his, her mouth now in a constant grimace. How had he once doted on those lips? Now they quivered and gyrated, as though she very much wanted his blood. The axe in her hand reinforced this fear.

"Honey... What are you doing?"

The monstrous octopus slid closer.

Naomi failed to answer. Her face was frozen, but her limbs fluid. She lifted the axe.

"Stop!"

The moon found it again, adding its desire to the blade.

The beast let out a guttural dirge. Foul. Fetid. Whether it came from its maw or its belly, Cody never wanted to discover.

Naomi launched herself at him, screaming all the while. She swung the axe. It struck nothing but the air. Ducking, he shoved her chest, and she fell back to strike the hard earth. What hurt more than anything was the sight of her on the rocks, pain on her face.

The axe! It had fallen from her hand!

The moon hid its face now. Cody picked up the weapon and readied himself.

The giant octopus! Where was it?

The beast of Old Woman Island reached out with three of its tentacles. They were as wide as the trunk of the pine.

Naomi rose to her feet, the monster at her back. It concerned her none; did they—woman and beast—both belong to the same governance now?

She ran at him again. Her hands were claws. She raked her nails across his face before he could block her.

He screamed, but his cry was barely heard over her guttural wail. "Stop it, Naomi! Stop!"

He tried to fend her off with one hand, the other occupied by the slickening axe. Blow after blow she rained on him. She then put both her feet onto a boulder and launched. Her attempt failed to topple him, but she planted both hands around his throat. She squeezed. Her nails were sharp. They entered his throat.

Warmth drenched him there as she throttled. Horror, horror, *horror:* her fingers slowly entered his skin, seeking his windpipe bone to bone.

Against all his fears and his pleas, Cody swung the axe.

A dreadful silence.

***

The cephalopod king wrapped its tentacles around both itinerant explorers. It dashed their skulls together.

They fell to the sand, sacks of wide eyes and fresh wounds.

Old Woman Island was returned to silence just as the ignorant morning reared its head.

The octopus was not unfamiliar with irony: both man and woman had fallen in a way that looked to be an embrace. Here they were, joined at last. The cost of loving.

Beneath the island, in a grotto never known by the sun, the king lay on its throne of carcasses, human fodder dispatched over the years on instruction by its mistress. It admired the two new additions to its collection, running its tentacles over their staring eyes and gaping wounds.

As long as humanity existed, they would always fail to show kindness to those they deemed unworthy: as long as this paradisiacal shore had visitors, the beast could swell the number of its trophies. What a blissful life.

***

In the shallows just off the island, two crabs abruptly stirred, as though waking, and turned their stalked eyes upon one another.

Naomi and Cody bemoaned their misery.

You and Your Cancer
-Ashe Woodward-

Any peace offering
Release, relief
Wavers and sizzles
The heat too heavy
Thick air rising in an already blackened lung
The lightning bugs are impaled
on spikes of fragile bush branches

Too far to see details
Too hot to try to reach
The entrails of tepid spring
Or the tendrils of leafy autumn
Sand still lingers on the bottoms of my feet
A single grain rubbing a rash between my toes

Swatting, always swatting…
Fly away past where the weight stays holding
Past where I remember your birthday
      still.
every.
single.
year.

On the smell of a warm wool picnic blanket
We move on to where you left us
Where stones uncoil
Where the forest of bones cools my skin and
I dream
instead of simply sweat

CONTROL
-Anthony Taylor-

'A home isn't a *home* until a family resides within it, and you won't have one unless you find a man willing to love you.' At least, that's what Michaela Blaire's mother insisted upon while combing her hair. Her aged cornflower eyes interlocked with hers in the mirror, instilling a generational curse - as she called it - to be ingrained in her mind from age six. From that moment, and others that followed, Michaela spent most of her adult life searching for a man - *any* man - to love her unconditionally, to no avail.

However, tonight will be different.

Michaela stared at herself in the full-length mirror, admiring her beauty. Her light orange hair was rockabilly-style, pinned with a bow to complement. She looked immaculate in her black and white polka dot dress, the epitome of perfection. Though her nerves bested her, her legs trembled with anticipation. Closing her eyes, Michaela envisioned how the night would go, creating scenarios in her mind. She exhaled upon opening them, smiling at the thought of finding true love.

She straightened her dress and brushed away the fabric's wrinkles, revealing her fertility goddess-like curves. Michaela's golden brown eyes shot glances at the clock, curious as to where her date could be. She often spoke about the importance of punctuality, yet he disregarded her expectations of a partner. Her anxiety flared, overthinking and feeling unnerved as her heart palpitated. A subtle glimpse into the mirror evolved into a stare-down at her reflection, unraveling every aspect of herself.

Was there too much blush?

Do polka dots compliment her figure?

Was he deliberately ignoring her?

Was her eyeliner symmetrical?

Michaela scrutinized herself, pondering if her lipstick shade - a matte red called Ruby Woo by MAC - was too overwhelming.

Only a duplicitous man with an insatiable, lascivious appetite and lustful heart will want you, Michaela. No man of nobility would love a woman who presents herself as a harlot.

Closing her eyes, Michaela respired, ignoring her mother's vocal opposition as she had during her youth. An extroverted child, carefree and joyous, Michaela lived in her rose-tinted world, sheltered by innocence and her father's love. Miles Blaire, a respectable family man, lived a wondrous life, spoiling his only child to the dismay of his wife. She, however, coveted control and yearned to rule with an iron fist.

Whenever she and Michaela were alone, Margaret Blaire whispered 1950s female ideologies, hoping to instill a *proper* upbringing while young, and continued their private conversations through adolescence. Miles saw the once eccentric and lively child transform into a near-identical clone of her mother, yet he assumed she had simply matured. It wasn't until her 15th birthday that he overheard a conversation, interjected, and refused to allow Margaret to taint their child further. Arguments ran rampant in their home, bringing forth discussions about separation; however, it never came to fruition as Miles passed unexpectedly overnight. His death was labeled "inconclusive" as examiners couldn't determine the cause.

Margaret and Michaela grieved during his funeral, yet Margaret's hand rested steadily on her shoulder, strengthening its grip daily.

Once Michaela turned 18, she desired freedom - a new life - by attending social events and out-of-state college visits with friends despite her mother's disapproval. Margaret recognized her little bird attempting to fly and clipped her wings before flight. She leaned on her far more than a parent should, using her grief, "crippling" health, and guilt to control, a tactic that worked. Michaela no longer associated with friends - declining invitations, ignoring calls and texts - and withdrew applications to colleges outside her mother's permitted radius. Michaela compartmentalized her collegiate dreams and allowed her friendships to wither away, utilizing her time nursing her mother back to health. In order to appease her mother, Michaela made the difficult decision to drop out of community college, succumbing to her mother's expectations and being guided into womanhood accordingly.

When her mother passed ten years later, Michaela felt sad yet relieved. The harrowing weight lifted from her chest; the overbearing thick, gray fog dissipated, and though she felt alone and lost in her death, it allowed her to breathe. Her absence brought comfort in knowing Margaret Blaire could no longer burden her with guilt or grief nor coerce her into living the life Margaret expected. But even in death, Michaela remained haunted by her tyrannical mother, whispering doubts and fears into her ear as she had while living.

When Michaela opened her eyes, she gasped, expelling the breath from her lungs. A black apparition emerged behind her with two cornflower eyes peering over her left shoulder. Michaela trembled, her chest tightening and unable to move as those familiar eyes remained fixated on her. A withered, putrefied hand reached out of the black fog and grazed her soft skin with its decrepit, bony finger. Michaela flinched, releasing a guttural scream, and spun around.

Her eyes were brimming with wonder and fear as Michaela looked about her bedroom, searching for those familiar eyes. Silence flooded the room as a disconcerting stillness sucked the air out and left her questioning her sanity. Had she seen them? Those cold, haunting cornflower eyes.

Was it *her*?

"No," Michaela dismissed, shaking her head in disbelief. She sat on her chaise lounge; her hand pressed delicately against her chest. Michaela's heart raced as she tried to catch her breath. Her flooded brown eyes scanned the room again, praying those vengeful eyes weren't staring back at her.

The buzzing of her cell phone broke her almost hypnotic trance on the vanity. She grabbed it and noticed an alert, indicating her date had arrived at the Winstonian, her favorite restaurant. Since discovering the place three years prior with another failed suitor, Michaela has raved about it to anyone who'd listen, especially Jonathan, her current interest, hoping he'd take her there.

Nevertheless, she sighed and brushed off the frightening occurrence moments ago. Though ecstatic about a night at the Winstonian, Michaela's frustration overwhelmed her sense of happiness. Why didn't Jonathan tell her he'd meet her instead of picking her up?

It's what a gentleman would do, she thought.

With a strike against him over being late, Michaela added another for miscommunication. It wasn't how a date, or a man, should act, nor will it be tolerated. Michaela grabbed her purse and keys from the hook before leaving through the front door. Jonathan's negligence would be confronted and immediately corrected if they were to have a future together, and she planned on handling this problem once she arrived.

***

She trudged toward the Winstonian entrance with her arms wrapped tightly around her body, shivering over the crisp autumn air. The calm wind blew gently while a mist of rain caressed her soft alabaster skin. Fallen piled leaves painted the sidewalks and roads as they squashed beneath her heels. Michaela regretted not grabbing a coat before bolting out the door, but she pressed on; her rage kept her warm enough.

Michaela took a deep breath and opened the door, determined to confront Jonathan and hold him accountable for his transgressions. She pushed through the crowd, all expressing disgust and whispering amongst themselves about her abhorrent behavior. Michaela ignored their hushed whispers and passed the hostess station.

Overwhelmed with reservations, impatient guests, and the incessant phone ring, the hostess exhaled and glanced from her screen. She noticed Michaela's erratic behavior and called: "Miss, wait!"

However, Michaela ignored the woman and continued searching for him through the boisterous, well-dressed patrons, eyes bouncing between tables. They looked up from their meals and idle conversations, annoyed from being disturbed by the distraught woman. Michaela halted, both feet planted to the floor, and immediately spotted her prey at a further table. A request Jonathan implemented as he desired more privacy, a fact known since their first date.

Michaela respired, collecting herself and appearing much calmer. She ambled toward his table, catching him mid-conversation with a brunette woman, his date.

When the wine glass touched his lips, Jonathan noticed Michaela standing beside their table, furious as a woman scorned. He swallowed his wine, feeling the bitterness slide down his throat. His eyes widened in awe.

"M-Michaela," Jonathan spoke, seemingly bewildered yet afraid. He placed his glass back on the table, shooting glances between her and his date. "What, uh, what are you doing here?"

She pursed her lips, nodding her head listlessly. Michaela snickered, vexed yet amused by his question; her left hand hovered over her mouth as their eyes met. Is this the game he wanted to play?

He stared, utterly dumbfounded and confused.

Apparently, she thought.

"Seriously?"

Jonathan remained silent.

"We had a date tonight, or have you forgotten?"

"A date?"

"Yes, Jonathan, a date!"

"Um, Michaela, what are you–"

She interjected, holding a hand up. "That's enough! Any excuse you have won't do."

Jonathan shifted uncomfortably in his seat, offering a glance toward his date, who appeared just as uncomfortable. They exchanged unsettling expressions, hoping the other understood.

Crossing her arms, Michaela informed: "I have high expectations for the men in my life, Jonathan, and I had high hopes for you, too. It's one thing to lack punctuality, but to ignore me, leaving me to wonder what had happened, is insulting. I never would have known you expected me to drive here, much less be on a date with another woman, if it hadn't been for the alert on my phone telling me you arrived at the Winstonian! I truly cannot believe you, Jonathan. I thought you were different and *man* enough to tell me when you're no longer interested!"

Jonathan's expression drastically changed from confusion to horror, and asked, "What was that about an alert?"

"Huh?"

"You said, 'If it hadn't been for the alert on my phone telling me you arrived…,' What alert are you talking about, Michaela? Is that how you knew I was here?"

Michaela stood in silence, unsure of how to recover.

"Are you tracking me?" Jonathan questioned, retrieving his phone. He scanned the apps quickly and noticed one unfamiliar one. His eyes grew with realization. "Oh, my God. This explains everything! How you would always be wherever I went. When did you find the time to download this onto my phone? Was this when you were over at my apartment and left it to charge on the counter? Jesus, Michaela!"

She stared at Jonathan, falling into a trance.

Oh, my sweet child, an ominous but familiar voice whispered. She felt a cold, decrepit hand brush against the nape of her neck, wincing at its touch. Michaela knew the voice was real, not imaginary. It was her mother, and she had followed her there, anticipating this outcome. She shivered, her heart pounding as she tried to comprehend what was happening. Why was her mother haunting her? What did she want? *How will you ever get out of this one?*

"Quiet, Mother," Michaela whispered.

Mother knows best, dear. No man would dare love a woman such as yourself: an insecure woman who overcompensates by dressing as a harlot.

Jonathan watched intently as she twitched and mumbled to herself. He debated whether to interrupt but asked, "Michaela, are you alright?"

Perhaps you were too overbearing.

"Michaela?"

Or perhaps he, too, realized the type of woman you've become.

The brunette woman mouthed 'what the fuck' and carefully sipped her wine, considering whether to run out the front door.

Maybe you're a failure as a lover as you are as a daughter.

Jonathan mentioned her name again, unable to break her trance.

Her mother's condescending and callous voice whispered, 'I told you so' in Michaela's ear, drowning out the world around her. Sweat slid down her temple; her eyes forced themselves closed as she shrugged her mother away, audibly shouting: "Shut up, mother!"

The other guests fell silent, gazing at Michaela in fascination. A few whispered amongst themselves and commented on her mental well-being.

A concerned Jonathan stood from the table slowly, disregarding his date's caution not to interact with the deranged woman. He reached toward her, delicately placing his hand on her upper arm. Jonathan peered into her tearful eyes and asked, "Are you okay?"

Embarrassed, Michaela wiped the tear sliding down her cheek and smudged the makeup alongside it.

The Winstonian's owner walked toward them with trepidation. He looked at the three of them, reading their expressions, before repeating the same question to Michaela. He hoped she'd remain calm; otherwise, he'd be forced to get the police involved. The man smiled, extended his arm, and suggested: "Perhaps we should move this conversation toward the front and away from my customers. We don't want to disturb them and their meals."

"Don't bother," Michaela stated, pulling from Jonathan's hold. "I was just leaving."

Turning on a heel, Michaela walked through the crowd of whispers and sympathetic stares without speaking another word. She noticed all eyes were on her as she approached the front door, but the only pair not looking at her were Jonathan's; he couldn't bear it. She turned away in shame, eyes flooded, wishing for a different outcome. Michaela pushed through the door and ran home, not looking back.

***

Michaela entered her moonlit apartment, makeup trailing down her face, and flicked on a nearby light. She flung her purse onto the floor beside her nightstand and collapsed onto the bed, burying her face in a pillow. She wept silently, pulling another pillow closer. Michaela felt the emptiness of her bedroom that night, the weight of her loneliness overwhelming her as she tried to process what had happened. She flipped onto her back, staring at the ceiling with the conversation repeating in her mind. How could she allow herself to reveal the truth? How could she let Jonathan know she had been tracking him? It's not like it's that big of a deal! A lot of people track their partners! Doesn't he understand that she did it out of love? For them? She did it so he would realize that *she* was the only woman for him, not that brunette! She would *never* love him like she does!

"That brown-headed harlot would *never* go to these lengths to show her love and devotion!" Michaela yelled. She stood from her bed, tossed the pillow aside, and paced around her studio apartment. "How could he choose her over me? I have gone above and beyond to show him how much I love him and how devoted I would be as a wife, and this is the thanks I get! How could he be so heartless? How could he be so naïve? At least I remembered our date! He acted clueless, like I just made it up!"

Michaela sat down on her chaise lounge, releasing a deep sigh. Her tears slowly dried as she stared at her reflection in the mirror. Michaela had to accept that Jonathan may never understand, but a part of her hoped that one day he would.

Oh, my sweet child, a piteous voice spoke. *Let Mother help.*

Michaela stood apace and knocked over her chaise lounge with the back of her legs, the audible thud echoing off the floor. She scanned her apartment, expecting to see her mother's decomposing hand reaching from the black fog, but she was alone. Michaela felt her heart slamming against her chest, anticipating that hand.

"Please, Mother, leave me alone!" She pleaded.

Behind her, the fog appeared as a hand reached for her shoulder. A bony, fleshless finger grazed her skin, causing Michaela to shriek and turn around. She stared at the black fog with astonishment as it grew in length. Out from the dark abyss stood a full-bodied apparition: her mother.

Michaela, startled and afraid, fell onto her bed with eyes filled with terror as her mother silently crept toward her. She felt her body grow heavy, unable to move. Her mother inched closer with arms outstretched. Before Michaela could dare speak, her mother's hands wrapped around her neck and forced her mouth open.

Her mother opened her mouth to release a guttural sound as her raspy voice stated: "It's… my turn… now."

Michaela watched her decayed mother transform into the black fog again, swirling above her body, before it dived into Michaela's mouth. The putrid stench of decomposed flesh burned her nose and throat as it made its way through her body. Her blood boiled; her flesh burned. Bones cracked as Michaela convulsed erratically.

Moments passed before she stopped twitching over the agonizing pain and stood to her feet as if nothing ever happened. She straightened her dress, wiped her eyes clean, and went to her mirror. Michaela stared at her reflection, noticing her cornflower eyes staring back. A smirk grew across her face, saying, "Now, my dear, let's go get our man back."

LEO

LEONA
Hayden Robinson

  Entering your apartment, dark as that cave
cold and black as death in those days of old when we,
the creatures long forgotten, roamed free.
  Heat blasts my skin like your belly's fire;
the familiar sense of fear crawls within me as I
remember the winter's night when I hid from you
  Behind stone walls and in the golden lake
itself; I beheld you as the fearsome monster,
your sharp toothed grin, your armour-like skin.
  Now, in your kitchen, you hide in this form,
a human woman, standing tall and strong,
by the table, your pour wine into two gold chalices
  Which surprises me; you speak with a grin,
"I was expecting you, Leona, the lion elf,
the one who defied me in those days of old."
  Removing my hood, my human ears grow tips,
my flesh glows pearl white in its natural hue,
and with glowing yellow eyes, I gaze up to you.
  "Zehava," I say, "it's been too long since we
agreed to live among humans in peace,
only to be like humans ourselves." To this, you laugh.
  I add, "Gone are our days of glory and might;
here are the days of new; rejoiced on Christmas Eve."
I peer to the window, watching snow fall.
  Your grin, with sharper teeth than ever, widens
and you ask, "Why do you come now, little elf?"
I reply, "To bring you back what is yours."
  The heinous grin falters, brow now lowered,
puzzled by my words. I almost chuckle at how
a dragon woman can look so confused.
  From my rucksack, I rummage and scoop out
a dark red gem, the size of a heart,
and, peering up to you, I hold it to your gaze.
  Taking it in both hands, you turn it over once,
then sniff it like a cinnamon bun; you smile
as if an old friend has returned home.
  "Painite," you whisper, then to me,
you say, "You stole this great treasure for your king."
with a tut, you add, "Why do you give this back?"
  "A truce," I reply. "In time, all us elves shall be

gone, along with giants and pixies and goblins.
And dragons too." I state this, neither glad nor sullen.
        Suddenly, I am raised by black scaly wings,
the longest and softest wings I ever felt; I stare
into your eyes turning pure red as you snarl in delight.
        Your curly hair twists into horns;
your breasts and stomach scorch red with heat;
you cackle, growing into the monster I know.
        "Dragons remain," you snarl in your true voice.
"And you shall not." Your jaw unclenches and I see
a fire burning from the back of your throat
        As you draw me near, intending my life to end
inside your fire, but no, dear dragon, it is not to be
for now I let out the bellowing of my mind.
        Unyield! obey! cool your flames! I roar;
this roar is not of dying elfs of old
but of my own taken from the lions before me.
        Your jaw snaps shut and you throw me away
but I land on my feet; glaring over at you,
your dragon form shrivels back to a frightened lady.
        After running fingers through my mane,
I smile with delight and state, "Now you have yours
and you, Zehava, cannot take what is mine."
        I take a gold chalice and gulp down the wine,
remembering Christmas eves in the forests,
drinking wine, eating bread, singing jovial songs.
        I also recall the trees falling with screams,
blood coating the grass; bodies scattered like stars;
these memories made my modern life hard.
        With that, I leave you to quiver, knowing
that all the years of masking my flames
have been released to you, my old enemy.
        Now I walk down the snow-filled street,
hearing carols sung from churches nearby;
I am Leona and it is I who shall remain.

SINS OF THE FLESH
~Emma Jamieson~

When we are born, we are blessed with the perfect canvas. I desired my creation to be adorned with captivating hues that leave people breathless and images that unravel tales, eagerly devoured by hungry gazes. I wanted to be a thing of beauty, a walking exhibition, a masterpiece amongst the mundane. It had been almost a year since I was first marked by the needle; a beautiful serpent, winding round my thigh. It was a sensation like no other as it slithered into my skin. Alongside the pain, there was an overwhelming euphoria coursing through my veins, as if the adrenaline had ignited a powerful high within me. Esme could feel it every time she worked on me, the ecstasy pulsing through me, matching the vibrations of her gun. Even with my eyes closed, I could sense when she glanced up, watching as a state of heavenly bliss would float serenely across my face.

  I'd found her by chance. Tattoos hadn't even been on my mind that particular night as I'd made my way home from another gruelling and painful shift at the restaurant. It was dark, and I'd always stuck to the well lit main streets, yet I was also in a hurry to get home, to wash the screaming children, the snooty, middle-aged alcoholic women and the greasy, slimy old jerks with wandering hands from my body. Against my better judgement, something told me to cut through an alleyway. It would easily shave 10 minutes from my journey and I was driven by the prospect of a hot shower, the warm water spilling deliciously over my cold, bare skin. I pulled my coat tightly around me as if it would make me invisible to any potential threat and scurried down the gloomy backstreet. There she was, standing outside the doorway of a small shop. Her face, cloaked by the darkness, lit up from time to time as a neon sign that simply stated 'Creator' flashed erratically. I smiled briefly as we made eye contact, my brow furrowing slightly at the unusual sign. What exactly are you creating down here?

  'Do you like art?' She called out as if she had been privy to my thoughts.

  'That depends on the artist, I guess.' I replied, looking back over my shoulder, shrugging, and allowing my pace to slow. She stepped out from the shadow of the doorway and approached me, swishing her long black hair behind her. I came to a halt and turned; my head cocked in intrigue.

  'Ever thought about tattoos?' I couldn't help but notice the vibrant blue of her eyes as she came closer and stared into mine before taking my hand, moving her gaze to inspect it and rubbing her soft fingers gently across the back, sending goosebumps rippling up my arms. 'You have the most perfect skin.'

  My hand flopped limply at my side as she dropped it, reaching out to stroke my cheek as our eyes met again. Hers were hypnotic and I could feel myself getting lost in them, bewitched by this stranger.

  'I've always wanted them.' I whispered, leaning into her touch.

'Then come with me. I have something especially for you.' She smiled, taking my hand again, and led me to the doorway. Swept up in her spell, I was unable to resist and together we retreated silently into her sanctum.

The room was a visual masterpiece, with beautiful artwork adorning every surface. Salacious demons danced while victorious creatures emerged from the flames, as alluring women with naked curves seduced you, their knowing expressions fixed on the walls. I explored the colours and the shapes while she cleansed and prepared. The smell was overpowering, causing me to feel even more lightheaded than I already did. I drifted between each picture, feeling as if the flames were licking out at me, as though I could reach in and grasp each demon by its rough, crooked horns, as if these were more than just something created from an artistic mind. Esme instructed me to remove my trousers, then ushered me to the bed and settled me on it. She sprayed something onto a paper towel then wiped it over my exposed thigh, caressing and massaging as she went, greedily admiring the emptiness she was about to take from me. I could hear her muttering to herself. What was she saying? The words blended together, and I closed my eyes, feeling a drowsiness wash over me. Her foot tapped the pedal attached to the tattoo gun and the heavy whirr of the mechanisms woke me from my haze.
'What are you going to do?' I slurred.
'Your spirit will guide my hand. Are you ready?'
I nodded. At no point in time had I seen amongst the paintings any official licence or permits. But that didn't matter to me. When Esme penetrated me with her ink, she took me to places I had never been.
Over the months, we had created many beautiful things together. I was slowly working on becoming a showcase of her talent, her creations. Along with my snake, I had a caterpillar creature that crawled creepily up my arm, each segment an all-seeing eyeball; a skeletal siren luring you in with her sweet song graced my calf and my favourite piece to date was a ferocious lion emblazoned on my chest, its full, wild mane cascading across my ribs. So many tattoos in such a short time should have taken a toll on my body, but with each one, I grew stronger, more confident. I walked with confidence and pride, feeling as majestic as the lion. I wanted to be seen. I wanted to be watched. I slogged Monday to Friday at the restaurant, serving uncultured swines who were beneath me, but it was on Saturday nights that I came alive, performing at a high-end evening establishment. As all eyes were on me, I savoured every single moment, basking in the attention. I loved the control, enticing people in with promises of my beautiful body, slowly peeling each item of clothing sensually to reveal what an exquisite piece of art I was. And the crowd went crazy for me. They feasted hungrily on my flesh. On Pandora, the painted lady.

***

'What's wrong?' I asked as I sat in the chair, Esme poised next to me, eyes closed, with her gun hovering over my arm. The air was infused with a scent I had become familiar with every time I visited the shop.

'Nothing speaks to me. I cannot see anything. There is nothing here for you today.' Her eyes flicker open and her blue eyes burrow intensely into my core. 'I think you are done.'

My eyes wander over every plain and unmarked inch of my body. I am not done. I have barely begun. I am a work in progress.

'What do you mean? That's not true. There is plenty of space for more. You must have some idea, some design you can do?' I pleaded insolently, although I knew in my soul something was amiss. The atmosphere was different. Everything felt cold, sterile and my usual trance like state evaded me. The women on the walls glowered at me sullenly, the raging fires from before were merely smouldering embers and no creatures danced gleefully, instead they were brooding in murky, overcast scenes. The colours were dull. All that had been flowing with life was now stagnant.

'You are done.' She echoed, a sterner tone in her voice this time as she stood up from her stool, placing her tools down. 'There is nothing more I can do for you.'

'Fine!' I snapped, clambering angrily out of the seat. 'I'll find someone else who will do more for me. And better!' I snatched up my jacket and stormed out of the shop. As the door swung closed behind me, I heard her call out.

'Keep your vanity at bay, Pandora!'

The fury consumed me completely, leaving no room for any other emotion. How dare she refuse to work on me! I was her muse. I had allowed her free rein on my skin and this is how she repaid me? Had I not shown the world her skill? Displayed her creativity? If anything, she should be thankful for me.

My performance that night was fuelled by rage. I thrust, I kicked, I writhed as the anger spewed forth from every pore. I was beautiful but bitter that it was she who had made me that way. Alone in the dressing room, I sat in front of the mirror, feeling the sweat bead on my skin, and my eyes couldn't help but fixate on the bare patches. They ruined me. I grabbed my water bottle and took a sip to cool down and as the cool water ran down my throat, I felt something move inside me. More than the liquid I had just ingested. Desperate for relief, I took another quick drink, but instead of soothing the discomfort, a sharp, throbbing pain pierced through my chest. I doubled over, caught off guard. Was I having a heart attack? I'm far too young for that. Sure, I was mad, but not THAT mad. I stood up from my chair, stumbling slightly as I clutched at my torso. I needed to find help. I wobbled my way out of the room, my legs feeling like rubber bands as I neared the stage. There was a surge of agony throughout my entire body and I collapsed to the floor.

Weakly, I crawled up the steps to the stage, my hand outreached as I gasped for help. That is when I saw the skin on my arm move as though something was wriggling underneath it. I dragged myself up each step; the pain engulfing my entire being as though my skin was alight. The blazing lights overhead dimmed to a spotlight on my body, curled now into a mass of excruciating wretchedness and, expecting this to be part of a performance, I could feel eyes on me as I lay in a tormented heap.

No - I could feel eyes IN me. The skin where the wriggling had been was now bubbling red and angry. A scream released from me that made me sound as if I was no longer human as the bubbles of stretched skin exploded, spraying blood and pulp across the stage. Something emerged from within the torn remnants of flesh hanging onto my limb. A black, spindly pincer waved disjointedly before finding the ground and tugging the rest of itself out of the hole in my arm. I watched in horror as an eyeball, covered in a slick crimson substance squirmed, looking around before more followed, each with their own set of disgusting appendages thick with blood and tissue. It crept across the stage, trailing my ooze with it. I could hear muffled voices and chairs scrape from the auditorium as I lay on my back, my breath rasping. There would be no reprieve for me though as I felt a burning in my thigh. The pain ripped through my leg as one again. My body throbbed, skin stretching as something internally pounded, twisting through my muscles to escape from my body. I could feel as the skin, pulled tight, tearing open like a weakened seam but I could not move to fight it. I understood my fate. I heard the hiss and felt as a forked tongue gently tickled my leg before something warm and scaly slipped down the rest of my thighs and calf. Or perhaps that was the blood as it flowed from my wounds.

As I stared into it, the spotlight diminished into a tiny pinprick of light and just before I died, there was a rippling in my chest followed by a deafening CRACK as my sternum splintered into a thousand pieces...

***

The audience, frozen in a new level of fear, watched as Pandora's torso erupted. Her flayed rib cage jutting out at unnatural angles. A large paw loomed, sharp claws glinting in the spotlight that illuminated the decimated carcass that had once been their favourite dancer. An ear protruding from a thick, golden mane followed the paw, streaked with scarlet and marrow and with that came a muzzle baring thick, white, deadly teeth in a frothy jaw. As the lion clambered free from her body, the crowd could see it swell and grow, forming regally on the stage above them. It shook itself out, spattering the audience with wet meat before turning to what remained of Pandora. Letting free an almighty roar, it reached its enormous mouth forward and sunk teeth into her calf, twisting and pulling, devouring the flesh from her lower leg that had once been home to a siren tattoo. A fishtail dangled out, flapping erratically before being swallowed whole as the lion returned to sink its teeth into the mangled corpse. Trampling across broken glasses, overturned tables and chairs strewn haphazardly, the crowd scrambled towards the exit as a hysteria unleashed. But there was no way out. A guest who had watched this ghastly spectacle from the shadows had known to leave early, swishing her long black hair behind her and barricading the doors as she left. The horrifying screams and cries of the dying club patrons echoed through the building as they were bitten and stung repeatedly, filled with agonising venom then savagely mauled, ripped apart as the dreadful fangs of the glorious beast stripped every ounce of flesh from their bones. Each one consumed right down to their very soul by her creations.

The Burning Night
-Lucy Grainger-

Within the depths of darkness, she does dwell,
A deadly fire goddess, unleashed from Hell.
Her mane ablaze, a lion by her side,
Together they bring terror far and wide.

      Her eyes, like embers burning bright with rage,
      Igniting flames that dance upon life's stage
      With every step she takes, destruction reigns,
      Leaving behind a trail of charred remains.

She roams through forests, engulfing all in fire,
Consuming souls and hopes with wild desire.
Her presence leaves a mark of death and pain,
A haunting reminder of her fiery reign.

      The lion follows, fierce and strong in stride,
      A guardian protecting his queen with pride.
      His golden mane reflects the flames' cruel light,
      A symbol of their power in the darkest night.

Together they embody doom and despair,
A lethal combination beyond compare.
They hunt their prey with ruthless, savage glee,
In this gothic tale bound by destiny.

      The lion's roar reverberates through haunted lands,
      As darkness spreads like tendrils from their hands.
      The world quakes in fear of their relentless might,
      As they unleash the horrors that dwell in the night.

Beware of this deadly duo made of fire,
For once they strike, there's naught you can acquire.
Inferno's rage will leave no soul unburned,
For no stone will be left unturned.

VIRGO

IMMACULATE
Harriet Everend-

"Did you know?"

"What is it, St. Mary?" A small child quips. I couldn't help but roll my eyes. A saint? This woman? There's a good chance that she's a con artist. As I casually walked by, scrolling through my phone to check the weather, I stumbled upon a cluster of individuals huddled around a destitute woman, her tattered garments begging for replacement. Her disheveled gray hair matched the dirt smudges on her face. It is clear that she is a member of the homeless population. However, I can't help but stop to hear what she has to say. Pausing for a moment, I quickly send my friend a text to inform them I'll be running a few minutes late for our lunch meeting. Afterwards, I redirect my attention to the scene ahead of me.

The old woman clears her throat. "We've all heard stories of the Virgin Mary, right? You know, she is the mother of our Savior, Jesus Christ. "The one and only..." Her words taper off, and a dreamy look appears on her face, as if she's transported back to a bygone memory. "Oh, Jesus, what a wonder you turned out to be..."

"Is it true," a taller girl of eleven or twelve chimed in, "that Mary nearly died after giving birth?"

From my secluded position, I could catch faint murmurs and whispers of people expressing their disapproval of the statement. Even though it's clear that she is insane, I can't resist the temptation to get closer to her. I go unnoticed by everyone as I get closer, and I can only make out the old woman. As I watched, Mary took a step forward and gently placed her hand on the girl's head, emanating a grandmotherly warmth.

"Yes, my darling..." Her face twitches ever so slightly. "But let us not get into the gory details. It's important to protect your innocence from the harsh truths of this cruel world."

"What happened? If you said she nearly died?" Another child asks. Was it God's doing? Or the angel Gabriel?"

A chuckle escapes from Mary's lips. "God? Oh, no, no. This was the working of a special angel," her voice more excited with each passing word. Are you familiar with the angel Parthenos?But without waiting for the crowd's response, Mary went on. "She goes by another name — Virgo. She is the angel and the protector of virginal maidens."

This catches my attention, and I can't help but stifle a laugh. *Really*, I thought. *We're getting astrology tied up into this? Surely, people don't actually believe this, do they?* Right as I have this notion, several people start making negative remarks, accusing her of being deceitful and arguing that astrology and religion should not be intertwined. "Thank goodness," I whisper under my breath, grateful to come across people who possess some intelligence.

"I promise you!" Mary exclaims above the roaring crowd. "It is indeed real!"

More scoffs and vulgar comments come her way. "How did she survive?" one man asks. "It's not as though there was a supply of blood stored in a cooler or a proper way to give a transfusion!"

"She would have died from the blood loss or given the wrong blood type!" shouts another.

All the while, these comments and questions were being hurled at her. Mary stood patiently and waited. I, too, am curious why she isn't doing anything but merely watching. There is something about her behavior that strikes me as unusual. With a statue-like stillness, she smiles patiently. Then I see her eyes flick slightly toward me. Or at least in the direction I'm in. Her gaze is piercing, as if it could sear through my very being. *She's not looking at you. Stop imagining things!*

"How do we not know it isn't real?"

I notice her eyes diverting from me to the ground, showing that a young girl made this statement. Whether it is directed to Mary or the crowd, I am unsure. But I see Mary wastes no time. "I'm shocked. This little one has more faith in me than most of you who should know better. But that is okay. We tend to underestimate the extent of knowledge held by young people, even though they often possess more than they reveal."

I cannot see Mary anymore as she has dropped to her knees, either to connect with the child at their eye level... or because she has finally been freed from the entity that had taken control of her. "Okay, that wasn't nice," I muttered as I made my way through the crowd; no one giving me a second glance.

"Virgo is real. Just as real as you and me," Mary spoke. "She's the one who saved the Virgin Mary."

Silence swept through the audience as they fixated their gaze on Mary. There was a peaceful look on her face, as if she had finally let go of a burden that had been weighing her down. Taking a long breath out, she questioned the crowd about how the angel Virgo came to the rescue of the Virgin Mary. One said it was her belief in the Lord; another said it was a healer who happened to be strolling by. As different responses were shared, Mary kept her silence, giving no indication of confirmation or denial. I can't help but watch her; to see what she says. While I don't believe in God, I respect others' right to have faith. Even though I think it's all nonsense, it's intriguing to see how passionate others are about it.

"Those are all good theories," Mary whispered, her voice barely audible, her eyes darting to her right side as if acknowledging an unseen presence. Rising slowly, she makes her way towards a young woman standing nearby. Without making eye contact, Mary reaches out and holds the woman's hands. "But what it really is." Her head turns to face the woman, a smile spreading on her wrinkled face. "I'd like to show you."

"Sh-show me how, St. Mary?" The woman timidly says as Mary turns her head back to the right, the smile still adorning her face. For some unknown reason, I experience a chilling sensation in my chest and instinctively move backward a few steps. All eyes in the crowd are fixed on Mary and her companion, who appears visibly uneasy. Mary chuckles.

"If you're afraid of pain..." Her eyes flick over. "It's only for a second."

Before anyone can ask what she means, a blur darts past them with such speed that they can only see a streak of movement, and the young woman is gone without a trace. Everyone around me gasps and starts panicking, wondering what had just happened. Startled by a piercing scream from above, we look up to see a woman, her gossamer gown billowing around her, and translucent black wings outstretched; her white hair flowing in the wind. In her arms, the young woman from before trembles with clear panic. My eyes focus on this winged being and the girl struggling in her arms. The angel's (or demon's?) face contorts briefly into a grotesque mask before sinking its teeth into the woman's throat, causing a rush of crimson blood to cascade down her body, saturating her garments and flesh. She attempts to scream, but the flow of her own blood stifles her voice, causing her to go lifeless in the angel's embrace.

As this grisly moment unfolds, the air is quickly filled with piercing screams of panic and chaos. Mothers snatching their children; the men trying to hurry the women and children. Shouts echoed through the air, forming a chorus that warned of the approaching danger posed by a formidable demon. I appear to be the only one who notices the angel's silent presence as it delicately carries the lifeless woman to Mary's side, who greedily consumes every drop of blood until the body becomes a pale, lifeless husk. I'm hypnotized; I can't take my eyes off of what's happening. I observe the transformation in Mary's appearance. Her gray hair darkens to a chestnut brown; the wrinkles disappear before the transformation stops. Letting out a vicious snarl, she lunges at another woman, effortlessly overpowering her and tearing open her chest. I struggle to hold back the urge to vomit on the spot. I can only observe as she consumes her prey, her nails transforming into sharp claws and her appearance growing younger.

As I turn my head, I catch sight of the demonic angel, its menacing gaze fixed upon me. Although I understand the need to escape, I find myself unable to budge. I try to maintain a calm facade as she draws nearer, despite the fear pulsing through my veins. I feel the sting of a sharp nail being dragged across my face as she observes me, her comrade feasting on the second corpse beside her. My eyes linger on her, mesmerized by her extraordinary beauty; her skin appears to be chiseled from pure marble. If it weren't for her black wings and red eyes, one could easily mistake her for a divine angel.

"What are you?" I breathe.

"I'm the fallen angel, Virgo. I am—was—the protector of all virginal maidens before I was disgraced for helping the Virgin Mary."

"What happened?"

She tilts her head to the side. "It was made clear to me I should not meddle in whatever unfolded for Mary following the birth of the Holy Son. But I felt that what was happening to that poor, innocent girl was not right. I disobeyed God and provided aid to her. I saved her life."

I swallowed hard, trying to calm my nerves. "So, how did you pull that off?"

A devilish smile played across her lips. "I ended the life of the first virgin I happened upon, extracting her untainted blood and presenting it to Mary for consumption. I knew the blood of a virgin would help save her, but…it came at a cost."

"But why the blood of virgin girls?"

"The purity of their blood surpasses all others. Its powers remain a mystery to most, except for those of us with divine yet malevolent abilities. The blood of man is too corrupted to be of any use, and I refuse to target innocent children."

I can't help but gasp. "So, you're a vampire? A selective vampire?"

She chuckles lowly at my comment. "I suppose you could say that, but I don't think of it that way."

"How can you not?" I point to Mary, who was done with her victim and lapping up any remaining blood before something dawns on me. "Is that… is that…?"

Virgo nods. "Yes, that is indeed the Virgin Mary. She's been around for over 2000 years now. Of course, I take great care to ensure that she isn't discovered or identified. Can't be having that." She chuckles again. "I may be a disgraced angel from the Holy Father, but I am not about to work for Lucifer."

"I need more!" Mary howls as she searches for anyone else nearby. Our eyes meet. It's true that she was beautiful, but the sight I witnessed was absolutely horrifying. Her face is adorned with blood, dripping from the corners of her mouth and eyes, perfectly matching. An enormous grin dons her face as she takes a step toward me; however, Virgo holds up her hand.

"So…she," I point to Mary, "has been around since the birth of Christ? No… Jesus and God are stories from myth written by men. It's not possible. It's not real."

"Not real? Oh my child," Virgo purrs as she grabs my arms tight. "It's all very much real." She turns to Mary once again, that wicked smile spreading on her face again before turning back to me. "But you won't be given the chance to see that."

Virgo beckons Mary over. I struggle against Virgo's grasp, knowing what's coming next. Despite my efforts to scream and fight, I am fully aware that it is pointless. The demonic angel has me in a vice grip as Mary descends on me. The last thing I feel is a searing pain in my neck as I gurgle on warm, thick blood.

Beneath The Archives
-Jack Finn-

Ya-Wei Technologies' DRAGONLink system is recognized as the most advanced high-speed, low-latency broadband internet service on the commercial market. The company's constellation of highly advanced satellites operating in low orbit around the planet eclipsed that of even their American competitor, StarLink.

Initially founded by scientists at the Chinese Academy of Sciences in Beijing, Elon Musk and members of the Western defense and technology sectors decried Ya-Wei as a tool of China's Ministry of State Security, the country's principal intelligence and security apparatus. A claim that Ya-Wei Senior Engineer Fang Chu had to admit was completely accurate.

Therefore, it was even more surprising that the Vatican, the West's most iconic and influential religious institution, chose Ya-Wei over more politically favorable, albeit technologically inferior, Western competitors to be the Catholic Church's global internet provider. According to the online investigation website BeijingCat, the enrichment of private Swiss bank accounts of several senior Vatican officials played a significant role in the contract award. A claim that both Ya-Wei and the Vatican emphatically deny.

As with all Ya-Wei DRAGONLink contracts, the company required the installation of all proprietary hardware and software to be conducted only by Ya-Wei employees. Due to this non-negotiable clause, Chu and his five-person team of engineers found themselves in the telecommunications power nerve center twenty-six levels below the Vatican Apostolic Archive.

Chu glanced over at their Vatican escort, the quietly snoring form of Father Joseph, as the man sat slumped in his chair with his meaty bald head resting on his chest. His dark, intense eyes lingered scornfully on the priest; their work here would be far more accessible than his superiors thought. The West produced nothing but lazy, complacent people. The two men monitoring the power control panels sat studying the readings across their screen, indifferent to the sleeping priest and the Chinese technician.

The senior engineer looked at the reflection of his white jumpsuit emblazoned with the curled red dragon emblem of Ya-Wei on the computer monitor. Since his eighteenth birthday, now over twenty years ago, he served the Communist Party and, for his loyalty, received an unbroken string of promotions. However, a move into the Party's upper echelons, where true power and privilege lay, continued to elude him.

Chu's selection to lead this effort would change all of that. Hidden deep within the equipment his team installed in the Vatican telecommunication systems was software that would read and re-transmit even the most highly encrypted messages. His work would give the Ministry of State Security insight into the Vatican intelligence service's efforts to hamper the Party's work worldwide.

His Bluetooth headset buzzed as one of his men keyed the transmission button in four quick successions, the code they established for essential communications. Chu keyed his transmission button once, the signal for acknowledgment.

"I am going across the hall to the generator room," Chu had never learned Italian, so he spoke to the men in perfect English.

The two men in their dark blue Vatican overalls just looked at him with disinterested eyes and then over to the slumbering priest and shrugged, returning their gaze to the computer screens.

The twenty-sixth level, the bottom-most subterranean floor of the Vatican Apostolic Archives, consisted of the control room and the large room across the hall that housed the four Rolls-Royce MT30 gas turbine generators, each feeding 36 megawatts or 50,000 horsepower into the Vatican's telecommunication network. The building generated enough energy to power two conventional aircraft carriers.

Above them lay the central repository for the Holy See, containing fifty-three miles of shelving with over thirty-five thousand volumes of knowledge. The thought of Chinese scholars one day pouring over such ancient knowledge made Chu smile.

He stepped out of the control room into the dimly lit corridor. One end of the long corridor contained the elevator, which took them to the surface; the other end held an emergency stairwell. Both were electronically locked and required one of the Vatican personnel to enter a code.

Inside the generator room, a dozen blue-clad Vatican technicians milled about the four massive generators. Three of Chu's technicians were working alongside them, connecting the power cables that ran the DRAGONLink system, all young men fresh from their graduate work at the Chinese Academy of Sciences. The two other men on his team drew Chu's attention. The shorter man, Xiuying, sat with his squat, round face intensely staring at the computer tablet in his hand; beside him, the large, heavyset technician, Cheng, stood nodding his head thoughtfully.

"Sir, we have an anomaly," Xiuying spoke in Chinese. The Vatican technicians could not understand them.

"What is it?"

"I was looking at the power readings with technician Cheng. The generators are only putting out a total of seventy-two megawatts of power." He handed the tablet to Chu and pointed at the data filtering across the screen. "Seventy-two megawatts are unaccounted for.

"They are not running at full power?"

"That's what we thought at first," Cheng's slow, deep voice held the accent from one of China's rural Western provinces.

"I checked all four generators and found they are indeed running at full capacity," Xiuying pushed his thick glasses up to the bridge of his nose, a nervous habit that irritated Chu to no end.

"Then we made a discovery," Cheng's voice lowered conspiratorially. "If you look over my left shoulder, you will see a cable from generators two and three meets and goes down into the floor."

Chu looked and saw that amongst the cables running upwards from the generators, one lone cable thick as a man's arm extended from each generator met in a 'y' shape that continued into the floor.

"According to my readings, there is no power running to the cables that go upwards," Xiuying was failing to keep the excitement from showing in his voice.

"They are dummy cables," Cheng looked at his supervisor with dire seriousness. "We think they installed them to mislead us intentionally. Generators two and three are powering something below the twenty-sixth floor."

"Below the twenty-sixth floor?" Chu could not mask the surprise on his face. "There are only twenty-six sublevels below the archive. Our intelligence services confirmed this."

"Sir, the data is unmistakable," Xiuying tried to hand the tablet back to Chu, who waved it away dismissively. "The Vatican is diverting enormous amounts of power to a lower level."

"A secret level." Cheng raised an eyebrow. "One that even the Ministry of State Security is unaware existed."

"It must be a separate system from the main Vatican telecommunications network. But why keep it secret? It must support the Vatican intelligence service." Chu was nearly breathless with the scope of their discovery; this would propel him to a senior position within the Party.

"It must be." Even the customarily subdued Cheng could not suppress his smile.

"Can you attach DRAGONLink to it without being detected?"

"It's possible, but this configuration is highly unusual," Xiuying eyed the y-shaped cabling suspiciously. "An error might lead to detection, possibly even jeopardize all of our work here on DRAGONLink."

"Then we will not make an error. Is that understood?" Chu was not about to let this small-minded technician ruin his chances for wealth and power.

"I can do it." Cheng squared his shoulders and jutted out his jaw. Chu smiled at the big man; ambitious men like this could be useful to him.

"Cheng," Xiuying's worried look filled Chu with disgust at his weakness. "We would have to run tests to see if DRAGONLink could handle the current. The power and telecommunication lines intertwine within those cable sleeves; without further tests, we would be working blind and could as easily cut into a power line as we could a telecommunication line."

"We do not have time to run tests," Chu let his annoyance punctuate every word. "We are required to finish our work in the generator room today."

"Sir, it will be done!" Cheng gave a confident nod.

"Good, I will provide a distraction, so their technicians do not question your work."

"Gentleman, gentleman, please, a moment of your time," Chu stood at the front of the generator room and beckoned the men to join him. "Please, come here."

The three Ya-Wei technicians quickly stopped what they were doing and stood in front of their supervisor. Chu watched the Vatican technicians exchanging looks as he continued to wave them over. A silent discussion of rolled eyes and annoyed expressions seemed to pass between the technicians until their supervisor finally gestured for them to all walk over to Chu.

Chu smiled warmly as the men gathered around, but his eyes kept sliding toward Cheng as he knelt by the y-shaped cable and began his work. For an unrehearsed speech, Chu had to admit he sounded outstanding. He exuded the very model of Chinese friendship, giving the technicians platitudes for the hard work and cooperation they have provided.

A sharp crack and flash of light stopped his speech mid-sentence as a ripple of electricity coursed through the room. The assembled technicians uttered a startled cry as Cheng was propelled backward and landed in a crumpled heap, dark wisps of smoke rising off his lifeless body. A blackened sunburst scarred the wall above the sparking y-cable he was working on.

One level below, the woman sat quietly in her room when the power went out. The single light in her room went dark, and the white noise device that filled her head with an endless amount of disorienting static ceased broadcasting. It was only for a moment, and then the lights and static returned.

"That has never happened before," she thought as she walked the small square chamber, running her hands along the wall. "Something feels…different."

She ran her hand over the cold steel door; the ever-present electrical thrum that indicated the magnetic seal on the door was absent. Curious. She grasped the metal door handle without experiencing any painful jolt. Curiouser still. She pulled, and the door swung open effortlessly. The cool air of the corridor blew into her face, and she smiled. In the cell across from her, she could see the old, one-eyed man staring balefully at her through the viewing slit in the door. She gave him a wicked smile and blew him a kiss.

She could hear the guard in the corridor working his way toward her cell by cell.

"Thirty-two alpha secure, thirty-three alpha secure, thirty-four al…" the black-clad Swiss Guard gaped open-mouthed at the woman standing in the open doorway. Her eyes were jet black and hawk-like on her long pale face. The woman's long hair was the color of the darkest night, and she was clothed all in a thin black robe that followed the contours of her lean body. The guard's hand reached for his gun, but her arm shot up and turned into a line of thick black smoke as she pointed at him. The line of smoke ran through him like a spear and materialized back into her hand as it withdrew from his chest, his throbbing heart in her hand. She laughed wickedly as the guard collapsed dead and crushed his heart in her hand like a sponge.

"Goodbye, my Nordic neighbor." She waved her hand at the one-eyed man as he pounded on his cell door and roared furiously at her for his release.

Two black-clad guards rushed down the corridor towards her, their assault rifles raised and ready to fire as they ordered her back into her cell. She stopped walking towards them and raised her hands, palms outwards. A wicked smile crossed her face, and she slowly closed her hands; as she did so, the two guards screamed as their bones splintered and they curled into balls like crumpled paper.

The woman turned and looked through the viewing slit in the door to her right at the small dark-haired woman with blue swirling triskele tattoos on her face that glared disdainfully at her.

"My dear, I would say age before beauty, but as you see, I have them both," she laughed as she walked down the corridor lined with cells.

When she reached the doors at the end of the corridor, there was a muffled thudding noise as the elevator reached the twenty-seventh level from above. She raised an eyebrow in curiosity as the elevator doors opened, and nearly a dozen guards stood in the crowded space. The woman exhaled a deep breath onto the guards in the elevator, and they began to scream as the men in their twenties and thirties aged into their eighties and nineties within seconds; their hair turned gray, their skin wrinkled, and their strong bodies became frail and stooped with age. One by one, they collapsed like dried, empty husks.

The woman stepped amongst the bodies and studied the control panel for a moment before depressing the button for the first floor. The elevator started its slow ascent to the surface and then stopped suddenly. She glanced above the doors and saw the number twenty-six illuminated as the elevator doors slid open.

She smiled at the two control room technicians as their eyes opened in surprise and terror at the sight of her amidst the desiccated husks of the guards.

"Hello, boys," she smiled as her hands shot out and grabbed the men by their throats before they could utter a cry.

Their vertebrae cracking and bodies slamming to the floor were the only sound in the corridor as she glided out of the elevator onto level twenty-six.

"Sir, he's dead," Xiuying knelt by the body of Cheng and searched for a pulse.

"What have you done?" the senior Vatican technician gestured animatedly to the sunburst shape scorch mark on the wall. "Generators two and three were not on the work authorization for DRAGONLink."

"Your faulty equipment has killed my man," Chu confronted the man with false indignation in an attempt to deflect the direction of the conversation. "My superiors will demand a full account of your negligence."

"My negligence?" The technician roared with outrage at the Chinese engineer, and several of his men closed ranks around him, ready for the confrontation to become physical.

"Alfredo," one of the Vatican technicians tapped his supervisor on the shoulder.

"What?" the supervisor snapped, irritated at the technician, who only pointed towards the door.

The attention of the senior technician and the others in the room quickly turned to the pale woman who had just entered the room. The length of her silky robe made her appear to glide across the floor as she walked into the room and looked about, her long black hair sliding across her shoulders as she turned to look at them. The senior technician watched her dark piercing eyes move down his uniform to stare at the Vatican crest on his overalls pocket. A sereness filled her face, and she closed her eyes as if listening to music.

"Death is like a symphony," she raised her hands like an orchestra conductor.

Her hand swooshed through the air as if she were directing an orchestra's strings and woodwind sections. However, as her hands gracefully cut through the air, those in her path appeared cleaved by an invisible sword. Horrific wounds opened in the technicians' bodies, splitting some men in half at the mid-section while others were sliced open from neck to groin. The floor became slick with gore as she walked through the room, conducting her symphony of death.

None escaped her death song as the terrified men tried to flee or hide. After a wave of the mysterious woman's hand decapitated his three technicians, Chu shattered the glass window containing the emergency fire axe and grabbed it from its bracket, indifferent to the jagged glass that cut into the backs of his hands.

Chu hefted the axe and turned to face the woman; of all the technicians who filled the room moments earlier, only Xiuying remained alive. Xiuying stood rooted beside Cheng's body, immobilized by sheer terror. The woman looked at Xiuying and cocked her head in mild curiosity.

Her body transformed into a line of pure black smoke that shot through the air, and Xiuying's body was like the bolt of some ethereal ballista. Xiuying's mouth gaped open, and his eyes rolled in his head as he fell to his knees, a sizeable scorched hole through his torso. The woman formed back into her physical form as Xiuying fell face forward onto the ground.

She stood with her back to Chu, studying the scorched sunburst on the wall and the sparking y-cable. Chu released a primal scream and raised the fire axe over his head in a two-handed grip as he charged at the mysterious woman. Without turning from her study of the wall, the woman raised a pale, slender hand, and Chu froze in place, axe raised high in the air.

The Chinese technician's eyes turned coal-black, spreading out from his pupils and swallowing the white of his eyes.

"Is this what caused the power to fail?" the woman's voice sounded in his mind.

"Yes," his voice sounded distant in his ears.

"Very interesting," her voice echoed in her head like a wisp of wind.

She turned to face him and seemed amused by the axe frozen in his hands high above his head.

"With your axe like that, you remind me of a cuckoo clock I used to enjoy watching in Vienna. Little wooden men would come out the little doors on the clock and swing their hammers onto a bell every hour. It was a marvel of artisanship. Tick tock, tick tock, then the cuckoo would coo, and the wooden men would swing their hammers."

Her thin lips curled into a smile of pure pleasure.

Father Joseph groggily awoke from his nap to find himself alone in the control room. He stretched his protesting limbs as he stood and walked into the corridor. A dark-robed woman walked out of the generator room into the passage at the exact moment. Behind her, he could glimpse a scene of utter carnage as the door closed behind her. He turned to run towards the elevator and then saw the crumpled body of the two technicians, their heads laying at an impossible angle.

She smiled maliciously at him, and he felt frozen in place. He tried to run and scream, but his body refused to respond. The woman moved to look directly into his face; her breath was ice cold on his face as beads of sweat ran in rivulets down his bald head.

"The one true god, what an interesting phrase your kind have created," her dark eyes were cold and filled with malice. "Pity one true goddess would not have been acceptable."

"What is it you priests say," She brought a long pale finger to her lip and raised her eyes as if in thought. "Oh, yes, god created man in his image. Interesting. Or is it that you created him in yours? Well, priest, I have a message for your pope. Tell him that today I will turn 'the one true god' from a statement into a question."

As the priest stared wide-eyed with terror, the woman's body unwound into a long tendril of impenetrable black smoke that snaked down the corridor and disappeared underneath the steel door of the emergency staircase.

The main tactical operations center of the Pontifical Swiss Guard was a scene of utter chaos as Bishop Karis, head of Vatican Security, glowered angrily at the guard captain. Behind them, a wall of thirty-six screens transmitted cameras scanning the Vatican grounds. Black-clad guards shouted orders into phones or reviewed streams of data scrolling across their computer screens.

"We have had a breach in the containment level," the flustered guard captain ran a nervous hand through his dark hair. "There…there have been deaths."

"Captain Grech, I need to know who has escaped and, more importantly, where they are now."

"A woman, the prisoner in cell thirty-two alpha." Grech felt his cheek twitch as he looked into the red-bearded Bishop's stormy face.

"Captain, I need you to tell me who the prisoner in thirty-two alpha is." Bishop Karis tugged agitatedly at his beard as the Captain conferred with a guard seated at the nearest computer terminal.

"Your Excellency, it was Lilith," even as he spoke, Grech winced at the Bishop's expression.

"Captain Grech, are you telling me that I must inform the Pontifex that one of the most ancient beings on earth has just escaped our impenetrable prison?"

"There was a power failure," Grech explained, but the Bishop cut him off with an agitated hand wave.

"Just tell me where she is now."

"She's right there." The guard at the computer terminal stood and pointed at one of the monitors on the wall.

The Bishop felt a cold chill of fear run down his back as each monitor came to bear the image of the pale, dark-robed woman one by one. Conversations in the room ceased as all eyes turned toward the woman on the monitor. She stood amidst a crowd of milling people and stared directly into the camera.

"She's in Saint Peter's Square," one of the guards in the room called out.

"All units to Saint Peter's Square," Captain Grech ordered into a walkie-talkie. "All units proceed to Saint Peter's Square."

"What is she saying?" Bishop Karis squinted to see the screen better, but thought he saw the woman's lips moving.

One of the guards zoomed the camera in close, and the woman's pale face filled the screen. Her mouth moved as she smiled maliciously.

"Your Excellency," the guard at the computer turned to face the Bishop, a confused look of uncertainty on his young face. "I believe she is saying the word 'cuckoo' repeatedly."

"What?" the Bishop looked from the guard to the woman on the screen. Her lips did indeed seem to be forming the word.

Twenty-six levels below the Vatican archives, his eyes as coal black as night, Senior Engineer Fang Chu raised and swung the axe like the wooden men in the cuckoo clock. The blade sliced through the y-shaped cable in an explosion of sparks and electric tendrils that struck the engineer and cooked his skin black to the bone.

The lights went out on the containment level, and the electric seal on the level's hundreds of cell doors failed. As the red glow of the emergency lights activated, cell doors swung open, and long-contained prisoners stepped out.

A tall, muscular man with the antlers of a great buck sprouted from his head, reached down and tore the door to the emergency stairway off the hinges. On the other end of the corridor, the one-eyed man pulled open the elevator doors and stepped among the withered bodies of the guards inside. He reached up, tore down the metal ceiling of the elevator as if he was peeling open a banana, and climbed up into the shaft.

"We have a complete power failure on the containment level," the guard's eyes were riveted to the monitor as he watched the images of prisoners streaming up the stairway and elevator shaft.

"My God," Bishop Karis staggered backward in disbelief. "Lilith has freed all the old gods. She's let them loose upon the world again."

IMMORTAL VIRGO
-Allison Hillier-

"Damn. Damn. Damn," I curse at myself for running late, again. I take a few seconds to run my fingers through my unruly brown hair, but it refuses to be tamed. I grab a rubber elastic band and rope my curls into a ponytail, knowing it will hurt like hell when I take it out later. A faint horn honks outside the park, and I know it's Jules waiting for me. I quickly grab my boxing gloves and stuff them into my gym bag before quickly scanning the trailer home and forcefully closing the door. I sprint behind the trailers, hoping to avoid Duke, my landlord, since the rent was due three days ago, and I'm still behind. Since nightfall, the temperature has dropped considerably now that it's October, causing a noticeable change in the air. The sun sets ridiculously early now, but I don't mind; I prefer the cold and long nights, anyway. The sight of Jules patiently waiting for me never fails to bring a smile to my lips. She's not only my ride, but my best friend as well.

"Sorry, Jules, running late again," I say quickly as I open her Jeep door and slide inside the passenger side.

"Did you forget anything?" She smiles at me. She's always in a good mood. "I don't think so," but then I realize I forgot my tape. Before I can sprint back, she finishes for me. "I have extra tape in my bag if you need some."

"You're a lifesaver, Jules. I don't know what I'd do without you," I smile back at her. As she pulls out of the park, I can hear the smile in her voice when she says, "Let's hope you never have to find out, Quinn."

***

I've known Jules since grade school. Throughout the years, our friendship has thrived despite us being complete opposites. She used to help me in my classes, and I used to beat up anyone that would bully her. I learned how to fight from an early age and got better with every fight. Now, boxing has become my side gig to support me through college, and having Jules as my manager feels like the perfect fit. "So I've been reading up on the zodiac. What's your sign again?" Jules asks, interrupting my thoughts.

"I'm not sure... I think I'm a Virgo," I reply.

She snorts. "You are such a Virgo."

"Is that a good or a bad thing?" I reply, already bored with this topic.

"I used to dismiss the zodiac as nonsense until I delved into it. It makes perfect sense that you're a Virgo. Virgos are usually loners, stubborn, mysterious, but also incredibly determined to achieve their goals. That's you in a nutshell."

Before I can reply, she says, "Think about it... you don't have any family, I'm your only friend, and yet you're paying your way through college by kicking the crap out of other women three times a week in a boxing ring. You're also really difficult to get close to. You are a total Virgo."

"So if I'm a Virgo... what does that make you?" I ask as we stop at a red light.

"A Libra," she says softly. "Isn't it obvious?" She tucks a strand of her blonde hair behind her ear before she lists the traits on her fingers. "Sociable, charming, loyal friend, but I also get distracted easily." She then grips the wheel and continues to drive.

"I thought that last part was your ADD," I reply, as she pulls into the packed parking lot. "Or maybe it's both, Quinn."

After she parks, I say, "Don't you think a person's trauma, family history and life experiences influence someone more than say… what month they're born in?"

"Your psych major is showing again, Quinn."

"Of course, it's relevant, but don't you ever think about how lucky you are to be alive? Out of all the times your parents had sex…"

"Woah, Jules, not a visual I need right now," I interrupt.

"You're here, born in September. And you're a total Virgo. Fight it all you want, but it's all here," she continues, ignoring my sarcasm.

She does have a point. However, I can no longer concentrate on astrology and change the subject. "Tell me about this new opponent. What do I have to know about her?"

***

The moments before a fight are always a blur. As I enter the ring, the rush of adrenaline takes hold of me, making my body shake with anticipation. Jules always helps me prep before a fight. My curls were straightened and my hair was expertly braided into a single, thick braid that cascaded down my back. Jules already filled me in on my opponent, but conveniently omitted the detail of her immense size. These fights aren't monitored in any real capacity compared to an official boxing match, but going up against this woman will be a challenge. She is huge; her biceps look larger than my head. I look back at Jules with wide eyes, and I see her mouth, 'Don't let her see your fear.' That's always her mantra: stand strong, move fast, and never let your opponent smell your fear.

***

"Quinn, you did it, you actually did it! You won!" Jules exclaims.

"I did?" I ask her, my ears ringing.

"Yes, yes, yes!" Jules shouts over the music. "I thought this fight would be a waste of time, but you actually beat her. Everyone was betting against you. I can't believe you did it!"

I can barely register what Jules is saying. The entire fight is a blur, just as it always is. I don't remember any of it. I ask her to slow down a bit. The world around me appears hazy, as if covered by a thin veil, while my legs seem to have turned into quivering, gelatinous masses. I feel my face and realize my nose is broken. It isn't the first time I've broken it.

Jules has brought me into a quiet back room and pulls out her first aid kit. "I'll set your nose after I can get this cut to stop bleeding."

"Thank you… how much did I win?" I ask slowly.

"Probably over 500 dollars, after everything," she responds, finally calming down and treating my wounds.

I sag back in the chair in relief. That will pay my back rent.

***

"Come on! You can't be ready to head home yet. It's Friday night, and it's only 10 o'clock!" Jules insists.

"Jules, I'm telling you, I'm tired. One drink, and then we're out of here," I speak slowly but firmly, making sure she understands that I'm serious.

"Okay!" she says cheerfully. "I'll grab us some drinks. Stay put." She sashays over to the bar and speaks with the bartender. The crowded bar buzzed with energy that remained electric after the fight. A few people come over and congratulate me on my win, even though I cost them some cash by winning. Just as I'm waiting for Jules to bring my beer, I feel a tap on my shoulder. I turn and see a young man I've never met before.

"Can I buy you a drink?"

Before I can explain that I'm waiting for my friend to return with my drink, I spot Jules, and she's chatting with a guy at the bar. He already has an extra beer in his hand, so I graciously accept. "Thank you."

"That was some fight," he says smoothly. "I've never seen a woman dance around a ring like that before." He looks sweet, with kind blue eyes, round glasses and jet-black hair.

"Thanks, I've always been scrappy."

"You're very impressive, Quinn. I knew when I saw you this evening that I should bet on you." he smiles, showing all his teeth, and I notice the points of his canines. "I appreciate your support," I say quickly. Before I can say anything else, he adds, "Maybe we could get out of here, go somewhere a little quieter?"

"I really shouldn't. I'm going home with my friend, but I can give you my number." I never give my number out, but there's something charming about this man. I write my name and digits on a cocktail napkin and hand it to him.

"Thank you. I'll be in touch. I'm Henry, by the way." We shake hands. "Good evening, Quinn. It was lovely meeting you."

What a strange man, I think, before wandering over to Jules. I interrupt her conversation and say, "Time to go, Jules. I'm beat."

She squints at me and says, "I can't leave yet, Quinn. I've just met Kyle here, and we've been chatting about what it's like to be your manager."

"That's great, but I need to get home, and you're my ride."

Instead of leaving, she rummages around in her purse, pulls out a $20 bill, and pushes it into my hand. "Here, call a cab. I want to stay. The night is still young."

I know there is no way I can convince Jules to leave when she doesn't want to, so I ask her to drop off my winnings in the morning. "Will do, hun. Goodnight!" And then she's immediately sucked back into her conversation with Kyle.

***

I'm waiting outside for the cab, but twenty minutes later, there are no cabs in sight, so I stop at a local coffee shop and spend $8 of the $20 Jules gave me on an overpriced cup of coffee. As I sip the warm liquid, I feel a comforting sensation spreading through my body, soothing my frayed nerves. Stepping out of the coffee shop, I am greeted by the empty street, devoid of any other people. I only have about a mile to walk before I reach the trailer park, but I can't shake the feeling that I'm not alone. I consistently check behind me, but I see no one there. Trusting my instincts, I opted for the faster route home and ventured through the dimly lit alley. I'm almost through it when I'm suddenly being pulled backwards by strong hands and everything goes dark.

***

I wake up to a loud banging. "Quinn! Wake up!" I hear Jules shouting outside. I'm sprawled on my couch and unsure what happened. The only memory I have is of going through an alley, but I can't recall anything that happened afterwards. How did I get home? I get up, unlock the door, and squint as the daylight pours in.

"Hi, Jules… you're here awfully early. Please say you brought breakfast."

"What are you talking about?" Jules asks as she steps inside. "It's after lunch. But I brought you coffee." She hands me a large cup.

"You are a saviour. Thank you." The coffee burns my mouth as I drink it, but I don't care. I need something in me to wake up. "How did it go with…" I ask, forgetting his name.

"Oh, Kyle? Definitely passing on him - He's a Capricorn."

"Wait… now you're choosing your partners based on their signs? That's crazy."

"No, it's not! Our signs just aren't compatible. Capricorns are too focused on succeeding. I want to have fun. Why waste both our times when I know it won't last in the long run?"

"Whatever you say, Jules. It just seems like a shame to not even give him a chance."

"That's okay. There's always more fish in the sea, or whatever they say." She hands me an envelope. "Here are your winnings from yesterday. It was a great fight." She stands and kisses my cheek. "But I've got to run." She wrinkles her nose before she continues. "And you could use a shower."

***

The mirror is completely fogged up when I get out of the shower. I wrap myself up in my towel and wipe the mirror clear with my hand. I'm expecting my reflection to look terrible - it always does after a fight, especially with a broken nose. Much to my astonishment, I see myself and realize that I appear perfectly fine. In fact, I look better than fine. I look great, and my nose has completely healed. How can that be in just one night? I slowly take off the bandage and gently wiggle my nose, but no pain comes. The cut on my cheek is also completely healed. How could this have happened in one night?

Before I can investigate further, my stomach rumbles. I haven't eaten in a while. I had planned to spend the day studying at the college library, but will definitely need fuel before I can get any work done. I quickly grab a pair of leggings and an oversized sweater. I manage to wrangle my curls into a bun. While checking the bus schedule, I make myself a slice of toast. As I continue to scroll, I receive a notification from Jules. She just texted me my daily horoscope. "Thanks, Jules," I mumble under my breath, but I open the notification anyway. It reads, "Prepare for a big change. You might be tempted to act swiftly, but consider all possible decisions before taking action." I can't help but roll my eyes when I see it; it seems so incredibly vague that most people will find this resonates with them. I'm about to respond to Jules while taking a bite of my toast. But… it doesn't taste like toast. It tastes like sawdust in my mouth. It's disgusting, and I can't help but spit it out. What is happening?

Before I start to panic, I realize that my bread has simply gone bad. I can't help but laugh a little. Of course, it's gone bad. I've been so busy studying for midterms that I haven't gotten any new groceries in a few weeks. I throw out the stale bread, grab my schoolbag, and leave the trailer.

Before I get on the bus, I make sure to drop off my rent money at Duke's. There are few clouds interrupting the sunny autumn day, allowing the vibrant colours of the leaves to shine. My feet crunch when I walk through the leaves to Duke's trailer, and it always reminds me of being a kid again. My mom used to rake all the leaves in the park and make a giant pile for me to jump in. I make sure to apologize to him again for being late, but we both know it won't be the last time I'm behind on rent. I think he has a soft spot in his heart for me, as he was close friends with my mom before she died. After she passed, I stayed in the trailer park, and he's tried to help out whenever he can.

The bus ride to school is short. However, I have noticed a pounding sensation behind my eyes that continues to worsen since I left the trailer. Is this what a migraine feels like? I've never had one before, but I can't ignore the deep desire to be indoors. Arriving at the library is a relief. The short walk from the bus to the building was a painful one. My headache has intensified, and now everything appears hazy and distorted. I bumped into someone accidentally and made him drop his books. I normally would have helped him pick them up, but I was too dizzy to do anything but stumble away awkwardly. Once I'm in the library, I take a few moments to collect myself. My vision clears, and my headache dims to a gentle pulse. I collapse into a lounge chair at the entrance, taking a few deep breaths. I feel my heart rate is slowing. I make a mental note to check in with the school nurse on Monday when campus opens up again. Maybe I got a concussion from the fight yesterday and need to monitor any symptoms.

I decide to splurge and order a small coffee from the library's cafe before finding a quiet spot to work. I sip it gently and feel the relief wash over me, knowing that no matter what's wrong with me, I can still enjoy a hot coffee. There are only a few other students working at the library on a Saturday afternoon. I'm thankful for the quiet where I can spread my textbooks and papers out on the table. I begin to read my textbook on child psychology, but my attention is constantly being pulled away by a persistent scratching sound. I look up and see a man write with a pencil in a notebook. The scratching sound persists while he is writing. Is it possible I can hear the lead move across his paper? How is this possible? Once I realize that I'm hearing his pencil, I hear everything. I can even hear him swallow his saliva. I can hear the tap, tap, tap of a woman across the room typing on her laptop. I can hear the security guard speak into his phone, but also hear whatever is being said on the line. All the noises suddenly become very overwhelming. I grip the arms of the wooden chair to steady myself until I hear a crunch. I somehow have crumbled the arms like I would a piece of paper. How could I be this strong? I stare at my hands in disbelief and notice that I'm trembling.

I don't know what to do, and in my panic, I grab my phone from my bag. As I'm about to text Jules, or anyone for help, I get a text from an unknown number. The message makes everything still as I read it. 'Notice any changes yet?'

I text back quickly, 'What is happening to me?' I stare at my phone, willing for a reply until my phone dings. 'Meet me behind the library after the sun sets. I will explain everything to you then. In the meantime, stay away from other people and don't go outside.'

How do I know I can trust this stranger? They seem to know what's going on with me, but I don't know if they're telling the truth. I don't know what to reply, so I write quickly, 'Who are you?'

I don't have to wait long for the reply, and it's a simple answer. 'Henry.' Who the fuck is Henry? My hands are shaking as I hold my phone, and I realize that I'm very close to crushing it as easily as I crushed the chair. I went from being scared to being furious. Who is this mysterious stranger writing me cryptic messages instead of showing his face? It just dawned on me I've actually met someone named Henry before. I met him after the fight yesterday. Before I can write a reply, I get another message from him. 'I will answer all your questions after the sun sets... just stay away from people until then.' I decide to listen to Henry and gather my books. I have another hour before dark. I can't leave the library even if I wanted to; the idea of that migraine returning is enough to convince me to stay inside. I can go to another floor and hope to be alone and get some work done.

I end up falling asleep on my books. The stress from the last 24 hours has finally taken a toll on me, and as I have nothing in my system, it makes sense that my body crashed. It's dark outside now. I gather my supplies and sprint to the elevator. I enter and see the same man I bumped into earlier. Before I can apologize for acting erratically earlier, I realize all I can hear is the thumping in his chest. I can hear the rhythmic flow of blood coursing through his veins, and it triggers a thirst within me. It smells delicious. He smells delicious. My mouth waters at the thought of sinking my teeth into his throat and draining him dry. I can feel my canines lengthening at the thought. Before I can move, he asks, "Are you alright? What floor do you want?" I'm snapped out of the daze I was in, and mumble "ground floor". The entire elevator ride is torture as I fight with the part of myself that wants to open a vein and drain him dry.

As soon as the elevator opens, I sprint out of the library and don't stop until I see a figure leaning up against the library, smoking a cigarette.

"Are you Henry?" I ask, as it's too dark to clearly see his face.

He looks up at me and nods. He looks completely different from yesterday. Yesterday, he looked like a kind college student, but now I can see the real him. He's probably in his mid-forties, with graying hair and he's no longer wearing glasses. Before I can ask him what the hell is going on, he cuts to the chase. "I know this is upsetting, but if you had come home with me last night, I could have explained the truth. You have been chosen from my coven."

"Your coven? Like witches?"

"No, of vampires. Zodiac vampires. We pursue people who are perfect depictions of their zodiac sign. We turn them into children of the night, give them strength and speed."

"I never asked for any of this." I say simply.

"I know you didn't," he states. "I know this might be difficult to adjust, but when I saw you fight yesterday, I knew you would be the perfect Virgo."

He lets go of his cigarette and extinguishes it under his foot. "We do, however, give you a choice. Join us with power and immortality, or let the rest of my venom infect you and you will die in a few hours."

"That's it? Those are my choices? Live as a blood-sucking vampire or die?!" I am furious now, and I can feel the rage throughout my body. My fists are clenched, and I'm ready to beat this man to a pulp.

"I know it's not much of a choice, Quinn. I apologize for that. But I couldn't resist biting you last night in the alley."

"THAT WAS YOU?!" I scream.

"Yes, it was, and I brought you home safe. I would have stayed, but I can't be out in the sunlight, as I'm sure you know why. My venom also healed your wounds," he whispers.

Before I can stop myself, I ask, "What zodiac sign are you?"

"Gemini," he replies with a grin. He can see I'm considering his choice. "Being a Gemini vampire gives me the chance to change my appearance as I need to."

"Like as a charming college student at the bar?"

"Precisely," he smiles. "We've never had a Virgo vampire before. I'm so curious to see what you are capable of." He extends his hand to me. "Join us, Quinn, and I'll help you reach your ultimate potential."

Before I can stop myself, I whisper, "I don't have much of a choice, do I?"

LIBRA

By The Scales
-Elliot Ason-

The tearoom on the Isle of Shifters is one of my favorite places. The serenity, the calmness—it all makes me feel right in the world. And it's my job to stock shelves, fill carafes, sort and store leaves, and replenish the tableware drawers.

But there are certain characters who frequent it I'm told to stay away from, to never bother, even if they visit too often, linger too long.

Faysal is one of them.

He lives his life by the will of the scales, saying the goddess herself blessed him with the knowledge of the Libra.

I see him walking around, weighing fates as if he has a say. And maybe he does. None are truly certain.

His long black cloak brushes the dark burgundy tablecloths of the tearoom as he saunters around, surveying ones he deems less. I'm not going to lie and say he's not terrifying—he is—but when his black eyes are trained on you, there's no helping the shiver their intensity lets loose.

But I don't have time for that nonsense right now. My hands are full of dirty cups and saucers and I'm trying to rush to clean up a spill before it stains the off-white accent pillows.

Weaving through the small round tables, my foot catches on a woman's long dress, tripping me and pivoting my body right into Faysal's back.

He whips around, painfully pulling my arm up, markedly not to stop me from falling but to ensure I don't touch him further. The glassware in my hands crash to the floor.

"Fool! Back away!" he all but yells.

My blood freezes as our eyes meet, black connecting to blue. But he doesn't let go of my arm. In fact, his grip tightens.

I whimper, saying, "Please, I meant no offense. It was an accident."

His eyes narrow. "Accidents do not happen. All is determined by the scales."

"I assure you, it was not on purpose."

With one final, disgusted look, he wrinkles his nose and thrusts my arm away.

I don't look at him again as I scramble to the back, grabbing a broom and cleaning supplies.

When I return to clean the mess, Faysal is nowhere to be found.

***

The rest of the day goes much smoother with no more sightings of the black cloak. Though there are several times I would have sworn I felt eyes boring into my back, but every time I'd turn around no one was looking, let alone staring, at me.

Exhausted from another long shift—and weary of the feeling of being watched—I stop by one of the many cafes on the Isle's property for a quick bite to eat before heading home.

Walking down a side alley, the wind pricks my neck—sending the same shivers I felt earlier when looking into Faysal's eyes—down my spine.

"You're next." A menacing whisper brushes against my ear.

Spinning around, faltering on my feet, I look for who could have whispered in my ear but see no one. Nothing.

My human ears and eyes aren't sharp like the shifters and monsters that populate this Isle. The only reason I'm even here is because my distant cousin is a concierge and got me the job.

Not wanting to fuck around with whatever's out here, I run full speed to the employee housing just outside the main campuses.

My one bedroom bungalow's front step light is on, just like it always is. Having home in sight, my body relaxes a small fraction, though that doesn't slow my pace wanting to get into the safety of my home.

Closing and bolting the door behind me, I move to turn on all the lights, can't be too cautious after all, while turning the TV on.

Seeping a cup of magnolia tea, I settle in to watch a few episodes of *Parks and Recreation* while doing some word search puzzles.

An hour or so later, I get up to take a shower and settle in for the night. After putting my teacup in the dishwasher, turning the corner from the kitchen to the hall, I see the living room lights flickering. Rushing over, I check the plugs but everything seems fine. The flickering stops, all lights remaining solid, so I just turn everything off, not planning to come back out here tonight.

That was strange.

I dart to my bedroom, turning on both the ceiling fan and nightstand lights.

After whipping open my closet door, I go back out to the hallway and check the coat closet too for good measure. I feel silly, not sure what I was expecting, but at least I know there's definitely no boogie man hiding out in one of the closets now.

I just can't shake the feeling that someone's looking at me.

Turning on the TV in my room to drown out the silence, I do one more look over before heading to the bathroom.

Taking a few moments to decompress, I lay my head against the cool shower wall, letting the warm water cascade down my body.

A loud crash sounds from the living room. Quickly shutting the water off, I wrap a towel around me, grab my razor, and slowly creep to the front of the house.

Reaching the living room—with my razor clad hand extended in front of me—I don't hear or see anything out of place.

What the heck made that noise?

Tentatively, I peek through the blinds but see nothing strange outside either.

My phone dings from the bathroom so I go check it, shooting a text to my cousin while I'm at it, letting him know that I'm kinda freaked out.

Waiting for his reply, I do my nightly bathroom routine, then head down the hall toward my room so I can get some pajamas.

But before I can make it, a hand grabs at my shoulder, pushing me up against the wall and knocking the breath out of me. I try to scream, but another hand is slammed over my mouth before I can even part my lips.

I then notice the long black cloak resting against my thigh. Horror-stricken, I meet the black eyes of Faysal again.

He grazes a long fingernail down my cheek, bringing a sob out of me. The pressure on my shoulder is painful. I struggle but can't move an inch.

His face gets close to mine, almost touching, as he says, "I weighed you and you've been found singular, remarkable even."

Shaking my head, I try to talk but he hushes me by pushing harder on my mouth before saying, "I'm going to devour you."

JUST *~*LIBRA*~* THINGS
-Kassidy Van Gundy-

It began with just one outfit.

Feeling especially anxious that day, Lindsey decided to sew one of her favorite Squishmallow micromallows, a small gray sea cow with a monotone spotted belly, to the front collar of her oversized sweater, giving it the appearance of a soft pendant against her neck. She loved the fact that she could grab onto it whenever she felt nervous or shy, especially as she met all the other new students during her college freshman orientation. To her surprise, plenty of other students came running up to her of their own accord just to gush over her fashion choices, wishing they had the guts to do the same.

She smiled to herself as she reminisced on all the compliments she received that day as she worked late into the hours, hand stitching even more tiny plushies onto her sweaters. Her pendant became a full on strand of pearls, with sea cows swimming about peacefully along her neckline.

This time, she made sure to film her process and posted the results online.

Lindsey twirled about in her new outfit as hundreds of likes and comments came pouring in, encouraging her to make even more. She began stitching even more micromallows onto her clothes, creating intricate argyle patterns on her pullovers until she was practically drowning in plushies. With every new look, Lindsey would film part of her process, but it became clear that most of her audience was only there to see her model the clothes, so Lindsey adjusted her content again and again. Anything to chase this newfound feeling.

They even gave her a name for her own aesthetic: Lindseycore.

She absolutely loved being able to share all of her stuffed animal creations online with thousands and thousands of strangers. However, in the back of Lindsey's mind, she knew that her Squishmallows weren't the only reason people were falling in love with her.

As much as she didn't want to admit it, Lindsey was beautiful. Absolutely beautiful. She checked every box when it comes to conventional beauty standards: thin ✓ ☐, white ✓, blonde ✓, and young enough to still date Leonardo DiCaprio ✓ ☐. On top of all that, she'd never had a pimple a day in her life, so didn't need a lot of makeup, if she decided to wear any at all. She quickly became the envy of anyone who glanced upon her.

In all honesty, it didn't really matter what she wore. Anything Lindsey put on her body would drape off of her like fine silk. She could pull anything off, and as a result, she had far more creative liberties with her style than most people. At first, Lindsey had a hard time wrestling with her pretty privilege and the opportunities that were manifesting for her online directly because of it, but eventually she came to terms with her budding influence, even if it came about through superficial means.

It's not like she can control how people react to her, anyway. Why shouldn't she take advantage of it while she still can?

After her first couple of sewing videos went viral, Lindsey became obsessed with the positive feedback she was getting. She would lie awake at night, just staring at the dark ceiling as the hundreds and hundreds of comments would play back in her head, illuminating her thoughts for the rest of the night. Their siren song pulled her back into the stream of unregulated chaos, a sea full of other content creators fishing for an ounce of the magic that she already possessed. She needed a niche, and now that she's found hers, she's never letting it go.

Inadvertently, her TikTok handle was perfect: @Just*~*Libra*~*Things. It's a name that embodies everything about her profile, while also capitalizing off of the current astrology trend on the app. Lindsey really was a Libra, but she didn't know enough about astrology to really tap into the market fully. She knew Libra was ruled by Venus, the planet of love, beauty, and aesthetics, which seemed to fit her nicely, but her people pleasing tendencies only seemed to stretch so far.

Truthfully, Lindsey did give in to quite a lot of her follower's demands. She would post room tours, vlogs, and sewing tutorials whenever they would ask. However, this was never enough. They soon began asking her to open up her own Etsy store so that they could buy her creations and wear them themselves, but Lindsey didn't want this. She couldn't conceptualize making the one thing that made her stand out, the one thing that made her unique and special available for anyone to purchase online. If everyone wore her sweaters, then they wouldn't be as impactful on her. She would be doomed to be solely another microtrend, fading out in a surprisingly short amount of time.

Lindsey had to protect herself.

When she refused, some smaller accounts decided to take matters into their own hands. They made knock off versions of her sweaters and sold them online as if they were the originals. Naturally, Lindsey reported these accounts, hoping that someone would punish them for their blatant plagiarism, and more often than not, her wishes were granted. Many of these people got their stores taken down and their accounts banned, which was just a sheer testament to the strength Lindsey's influence over the company of TikTok itself, but not all of the other creators thought this was very fair.

Because she was deemed too big to fail, even more accounts took to the challenge of knocking her down. Several profiles began re-uploading her content without her consent. Even though every time Lindsey put in the work to copy strike them and get their accounts banned, two or three more would appear in their place. They multiplied just as quickly as the newly emerging gray hairs on her head. They must be bots or something, she always told herself. There's no way they could keep this up forever, especially since so many platforms are trying to reduce fake accounts these days. It'll stop eventually.

But it never did.

Every time she opened the app, Lindsey would be bombarded by her own videos being posted under various handles, some even being so bold as to appropriate parts of her own username: Libra*Tings, Libra~Thingies, JustLibraThings, etc. The list became endless. Just a shameless stream of people copying her for clout. Lindsey couldn't wrap her mind around it. She felt herself getting more and more worked up by the second, alternating rapidly between shock, disappointment, and anger every couple of seconds as more and more content trickled down her feed. It pulled her heart down with them, leaving her mind adrift in this madness with nothing to ground it.

It was exactly in this state where she saw it, a new video of herself.

One that she never recorded.

There was no mistaking it. That was her face. Her long blonde hair tucked behind a strawberry beret. Her slender body modeling a gross frilly pink cardigan with plenty of little Brina the Bigfoot Squishmallows sewn over where the buttons should have been. There was just one problem. Lindsey didn't own a strawberry beret, and she most certainly did not have any Bigfoot Squishmallows in her collection.

"Is this AI Generated?" she thought. "Can it even do something like that yet?"

To her dismay, a familiar voice responded to her internal questions.

"Sure, why not?"

Lindsey covered an audible gasp with her free hand as she watched the video reply directly to her.

"After all, with enough technical knowhow, anyone can be anything these days."

The girl in the video let out a condescending giggle, soaking up all of Lindsey's delectable panic. Sweat dripped down the side of her face as she double checked the bottom of her screen. This wasn't a live. This was a prerecorded video, and to make matters worse, it came from her very own account.

"W-who are you? H-how are you doing this?" Lindsey stammered in a hushed whisper, careful so that no one else outside her dorm room could hear her talking to herself.

"Well, that's easy," the girl said as she flipped her hair over her shoulder. "I'm you, silly."

Lindsey shook her head back and forth.

"N-no that's not possible-"

"Isn't it?"

The girl in the video raised her left hand above her head, causing Lindsey to immediately do the same. Lindsey's eyes widened in response, but the true dread didn't set in until she realized that she was unable to lower it.

She'd lost all control.

"S-stop it!!"

The girl mocked her and her pathetic protests.

"You've been letting us pull the strings for a while now. What's up with the sudden change, babe?"

Lindsey tried to pull against the girl's influence, but it's no use.

"You don't like being our little toy anymore?"

Lindsey found herself lowering her hand in time with the girl in the video. Both of their index fingers headed towards the phone, aiming right towards the bright red record button on the bottom of the screen.

"No worries. Soon we won't even need you -"

Lindsey's survival instincts overcame her sense of shyness. She let out a horrible scream, but no one seemed to hear her. No one pounded on her door to check on her. No one came running to her aid. Although at this point, it's doubtful that anyone could have actually helped her at all.

As soon as Lindsey's finger made contact with the screen, every cell in her fingertip gradually fell apart and reformed into a single strip of matter, building upon itself until it finally turned into visible strands of thread. This supernatural transformation continued through her hand and traveled up her arm, slowly making its way up to her head.

"You can't do this! You won't get away with it! People will miss me once I'm gone -"

The girl scoffed at her.

"Oh please! Individuality is dead. Everything is made up. Nobody's going to be able to tell the difference, anyway."

Lindsey muttered some inaudible sounds before the rest of her body was consumed by her own thread. As a result, she could no longer maintain her grip on her phone. It fell through her loosened fingertips and drug through the air until it finally hit the floor with a loud crash. Her screen cracked as the girl kept staring at what was left of Lindsey with her fractured smile.

"We're all just copies of each other at the end of the day, aren't we?"

The girl's voice drifted away, back behind the screen as Lindsey was finally laid to rest. She was nothing but a pile of string on the floor, indistinguishable from the countless other fibers discarded from finished and unfinished projects alike. Lindsey became interwoven back into the scraps of her early beginnings, back to that brief moment where she made art for fun rather than for content. What once was a source of comfort became corroded by consumerism and clout, choking her from the inside out. Of course, like every single other influencer, she didn't recognize this until it was far too late.

LORD OF DEATH
-Sabrina Voerman-

The earth trembled as she screamed her despair into the soil. Screams that shook and shuddered the entire world; every last drop of her pouring out through tears and what was left of her scratched-up vocal cords. It gushed from her body until there was nothing left inside of her to cry out. When she was naught more than a husk, she began to feel nothing, which was better than everything.

How long she lay there could not be determined by time, could not be dictated by such human concepts. Hours, days, millennia, she endured, until her bones formed with the roots of the trees that grew around her. Until grass, weeds, flowers, and fungi sprouted from her living carcass. The perfect host for she contained an abundance of life-giving qualities.

Yet she would not give life in the way she was supposed to.

All this time and yet not a second went by before he heard her cries. No, not just heard, but felt them as they broke through the levels of soil and earth, deep into the core of the realm. Through hers and into his. Echoes shattered the walls of his dark palace, cracking the empty throne that sat beside him. Never had the Lord of Death heard such sorrow. It snaked underneath his bones and stung him right where his heart should have been. That empty void within him, for the first moment since the universe burst into existence, felt something.

Pain.

He ran his finger down his throat and over the clavicle, veering slightly to the left where his heart would exist if he were more than a concept—only in existence because people believed in him. A gasp tumbled from his pale pink lips; he ached for someone he did not know existed.

She summoned him with her bellows of agony.

His tether to his throne, having been unmoving for centuries, was shattered. With forced movements and stiff bones, the rocks that held him there broke free from his force. His ethereal grace allowed this to appear effortless, but the pain weighed him down in ways he was struggling to fathom. The souls that lingered in his hellish kingdom hushed as he took slow, steady steps. Ascending thousands upon thousands of steps, he made his way to the surface he had not seen since time began. In his world, time meant nothing, for what was time to the Lord of Death?

The surface, oh what a place of beauty, burned him. His flesh tightened, his eyes narrowed. Even though the sun was gone, the moon still shone with the brilliance of life that he had not ever seen. Drawn still to the tether of pain that guided him, he walked for years and milliseconds at once, until he arrived.

A grove of trees that shuddered in the late-night winds sheltered her body. Long tendrils of willow branches touched her marble frame. She was curled in on herself, knees tucked under her naked body, head to the ground, hands above her head and fingers digging into the soil as if in prayer.

Is this why he had heard her?

As he neared, the pain scorched him; fire did not harm him, and yet he felt the burning through his flesh, into his nerves, sparking neurons to tell his mind that he needed to get away. But this, *feeling* itself, was more than he could bear and everything he ought to bear.

"Who did this to you?" he found himself asking, the words scarcely more than a whisper in the winds.

Her marble body cracked as she turned her head. Eyes grey like the throne he spent eternity within, looked through him. She turned back, slowly, as if each movement was a century. She did not breathe; she did not cry; she did not speak. Her nothing intrigued him.

He crouched down and touched her cold flesh. "You have suffered greatly."

"I wish only for death."

"Then that is why I am here," he said, both to her and himself.

This caught her attention. The marble woman turned her head again, eyes trailing from his hand where it was gently touching her in what could be considered a gesture of solace, to his arms, veined and tinged grey. She assessed his torso, sturdy and strongly built, then his face. Sharp features, as though he was carved from rock, with a gaze so black they could only be the night sky captured and encapsulated within his eyes.

"You are—"

"The Lord of Death," he told her. Looking where his fingers were on her back, he saw the brand of Libra. "You have fallen from the realm of Zodiacs."

"Yes," she replied.

"Even stars must die." They could have turned to stone in the silence that passed. "I can offer you what it is you desire."

"Please," she whimpered.

The Lord of Death removed his cloak and draped her under its ethereal blackness. Her body cracked as loud as tectonic plates breaking apart, and she accepted his gesture of assistance when he picked her up. Once she was in his arms, she leaned her head into his chest and closed her eyes. She trusted he would deliver her to the world of decay. Under the warmth of his offered clothing, she slept deep enough in his descent into the underworld to forget all that she had lost.

While she was able to separate from her agony for a flicker of time, the Lord of Death felt his knees threaten to buckle under the weight of her pain.

He sat beside her as she slept, waiting for her to wake but not daring to rouse her, should she take any of that pain back. He could bear it, for he had not felt this, anything, before. How agonizing, how foreign, how tantalizing. He wanted it. To take her pain, to be able to feel something, and to offer her reprieve.

It felt like purpose.

It might have been years when she woke with the Lord of Death still at her side. She wore a veil of neutrality when she came to.

"Where are we?"

"The world below, or after."

"Have I died?"

"Part of you, yes." He knew this was true as he spoke it, though he had not known it seconds before.

"Not all of me?"

"Like a flower in winter, you have died in some form, and yet, you exist still, alive in some capacity. And until you are ready, you can stay underneath," he told her. "You need not surface until you wish it."

"And if I never wish to surface?"

"You may remain here." He stood up and began to take his leave.

She looked around; a four-poster bed supported her body. The rock walls were jagged and uneven, with no windows to reveal light or sun. It smelled like fresh rain upon hot rocks, and this association almost put a smile on her face. Until she remembered; then the pain was sucked out of the air and slammed into her. A crack spread along her chest, beginning at her heart.

The Lord of Death looked to her. "Stop."

She looked up at him, holding her chest. "I—"

"As long as you are here, I will take your pain." He walked over to her and sat beside her now, holding his hand with palm facing up. She looked at his hand. Hers moved towards it, hovering over it now, but not daring to touch him.

"If I don't feel it, then it wasn't real," she whispered, the terror shaking her words.

It was his turn to crack, the perfect flesh he bore starting to form jagged lines, black in colour. "Let me feel it for you. This way it still exists, it was still real, but I…I will bear it."

She took half a dozen breaths, then placed her hand in his. Her cracks closed as her body healed, while his tore wide open, spreading over his chest. Black cracks like ribbons. She looked over his body, then her own. Her free hand that was upon her chest moved with a will of its own and touched his. She could feel a different texture there. It was smoother than the rest of his body, like obsidian glass.

"When you're ready to feel again, just say the word," he said quietly, breaking the silence in the room with dulcet tones.

"And if that time never comes?"

"Then this is your kingdom as much as mine." Something shifted on his features, a smile. "I can show you your throne."

She never spoke of her pain nor what caused it. She channeled it into The Lord of Death, who grew to desire not only her, but to absorb her suffering. As souls slipped through the earth and into this realm of his, she remained unaffected by their sorrow. She assisted greatly in his task to house the dead, for she did not feel. Having a Zodiac of justice in his realm brought a balance.

Meanwhile, the pain that she caused him grew over the years. It turned into something more than sadness and despair; it was a loss that she felt when he discovered her, when he rose to the surface to find what was shattering him. First, he ached for what she gave to him, that suffering. But now he ached for what she could not give him.

Love.

This absolute absence of feeling, since he bore it all in black marble, did not permit her to love. The Lord of Death entered the throne room, where she sat with profound beauty of unmeasurable proportions, and felt his body tremble at the sight of her. Arriving at her feet, he knelt down. Not to one knee, no, but committed to both knees on the rock floor below. He placed his hands around her waist and rested his head upon her lap. The obsidian of his eyes was now almost all of him.

"Please," he whispered into her.

"Please what?" she asked, her voice lacking the curiosity that it should have held.

"Please love me," he begged.

She placed a hand on his back as he had done a thousand years ago. When his fingers traced the branded symbol of what she was, a Zodiac removed from the heavens, from the realm where her kind reigned until they no longer existed. Because of her.

"But to love, I must feel pain," she replied. "That is something I am not ready to bear again."

He nodded, tears brimming in his eyes.

"If I were to choose to feel, it would not be you I loved," she told him. "The absence of love is better than the kind of love I can offer you. If I am to feel again, I would love another, and the pain that would seep into my cracks would be the death of me."

"I thought you wished for death," he said, regretting speaking the words the moment they left his lips.

"I have," she said as she ran her fingers through his chestnut hair. "You have given me death in this realm, so that I may live whilst simultaneously being dead. For I feel nothing, as though I were not alive. That is the greatest gift you could give me."

"Just a drop," he said. "Take back one crack and let me in."

She made a soft, contemplative sound with her closed lips. "You will not want a damaged version of me."

"I want every version of you." He looked up now. "Now that I have learned what it is to feel, I wish only for you to have it, too. How beautiful the world is when you can feel pain."

She remained so still that had she not blinked, he might have thought her a statue.

"I need to know if you can love me." His tears spilled. They were black, landing on her sheer gown.

Her lips parted, and a gasp emerged. Black tendrils like veins spread over her thigh. They bloomed like flowers. Warmth burst through her body, and it was not the coldness of pain she felt, but the hotness of desire and love that filled her. Her shaking hands touched his chin and lifted him to look at her. Tears continued to flow, burning her with their affection, until she was filled with the love he had for her.

His cracks slimmed, no longer consuming his entire broad frame, but outlining him with breathtaking streaks. Marks like watercolour spread over her body; the sharing of love and pain, the equilibrium of these feelings, shared between two people.

She hadn't thought wholeness could exist within her, and perhaps it still didn't. But between the two of them, wholeness could be moulded and shaped into what they determined wholeness was.

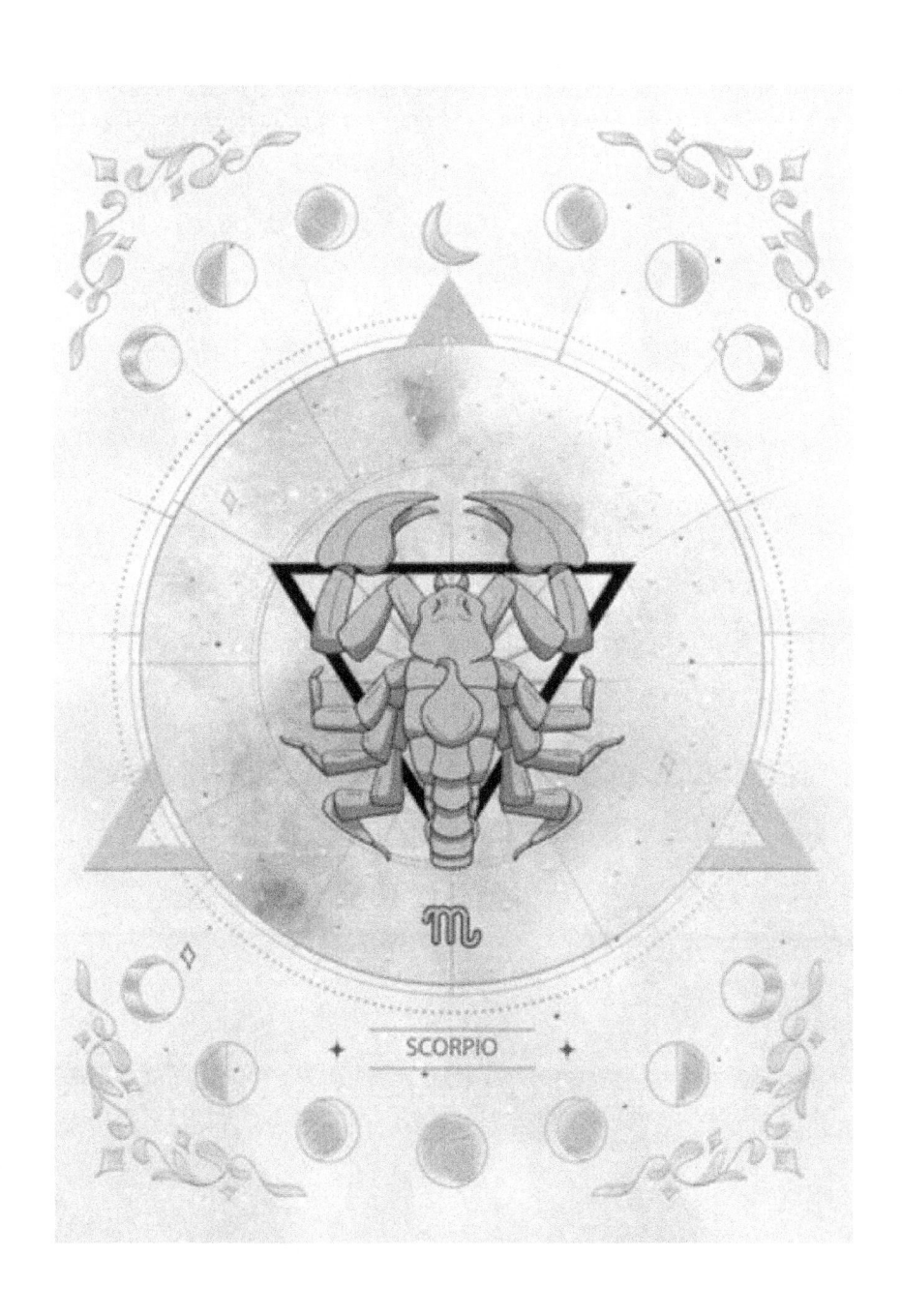

SCORPIO

Scorpio in Dreams
-Morgan Chalfant-

She's a Scorpio in dreams
Every night
is fight or flight
she's not the one that screams
in the melancholy moonlight.

She is a Scorpio insane
Every lie
is do or die
her own tail punctures her
in her trauma-poisoned brain.

She's a Scorpio that stings
Every time
dime and chime
when her phone rings
at two o'clock in the morning.

A Cold Winter's Call
-Alex Tilley-

Like a port pub in a Herman Melville novel, depraved seafaring folk occupied The Frigid Crone. Those with scarred hands and thick beards. Those with salt burned cheeks and eyes like deep grey storms. Sasha was told he would find work here, as times were tough selling cockles for a penny. He would've bet his life that church pews collected more at a Sunday service than he did haggling his burdens.

The pub was filled with noise. Clunks, chinks, and chatter. There was a cold dustiness, but Sasha caught the eye of the man he sought. A man no less coarse than sandpaper. The man sat with a mate. A small lass with red hair that reached to her thighs. They talked like a pair of marionettes with mugs in their hands, taking synchronised sips.

"Pardon your ass, lassy," a tall and skinny man croaked as he slid behind Sasha.

"I'm no lass," Sasha snapped back.

The tall man stopped between the backs of two chairs and turned back. A grin split his face like cracked ice. "You hear that, lads? This here ainny a lass!"

The pub laughed in unison and cheered the fine joke, but went on about their business. The man Sasha sought did not.

The lass with flaming hair and the broad shoulder man eyed Sasha with their stormy eyes. Neither grinned, nor looked like they were open to offering jobs. Sasha held their gaze and walked over to them.

"You mind if I join you?" he asked, as he summoned the confidence of his youth.

"You payin'?" the red-haired girl returned, and Sasha pulled out his pockets to show lint. "This boy ain't worth beans, Sloan."

"I... I need work. I'll work the line. Maintain the deck," Sasha said, summoning his haggling charm. "I sailed a whaler under Captain Emerson for a season. He's gone south now. You can put me in chains and bait me to the rats if I don't satisfy you. You can pay me seventy-five percent the lowest seaman or seawoman." Sasha nodded to the red-haired girl. "Please, sir. I got your name from Mr. Rickman, down by Cherry's Mill."

"What does Mr. Rickman know of the brittle bone-teeth of a winter sea breeze? Yer baby skin would crinkle like a walrus' if ye'd sail with me, b'y." The worn captain grabbed Sasha's wrist. "Eh, look at yer hands. Like polished marble. My daughter has more calluses than these. Ye don't have the mind for netting lobster from here to St. Ant'ony, b'y. Ye once did sail a whaler, eh?" The old man sniffed and took a swig from his flagon. "Let me tell ye there, ye ain't here yet a sailor, until ye heard the cold limbed maiden's cry. The Black Dread. Her soulless eyes will be the last to see yer frozen tears as she pulls ye under."

"Aye," the red-haired table mate affirmed.

The captain's eyes sparkled like a reflection of lightning across a black ocean. He had the gaze of a monarch that weighed Sasha's resolve. The captain brought his foamy draft to his lips and drank then clunked it back to the table.

"There's not a thing ye could offer. Yer better off in a library, as the snake-limbed maiden would have ye dead. Bone-shaking nights, salt burn, rashes upon yer face. Ye'd dwindle, then she'd catch the scent of fear and curse us man and crew… The silent waves aren't a place for a lad like yerself."

A voice came from behind. A woman's voice. A voice like a minstrel singing a lullaby. I was drawn to it. I was *pulled* to it. "Are you a man who carries suffrage without courage, captain?" Sasha turned then and caught his breath. Her face was oval and thin. She put an icy hand onto Sasha's. Her whisper was like a breath of wind against his ear. "Are you afraid, sailor? Who are you to these salted dogs? These sopped mutts wouldn't make it a league from port before the wind turned them back. Let me help you find a crew that'll show you the true kiss of the sea."

"B'y, watch this slithering water snake's tongue, shedding naught but rotten things to the weary and the drunk. She's a wandering crow without a feather. She'll peck upon yer skull and yer decaying bones among heathen corpses."

The woman smiled at Sasha. Her eyes plummeted deep into his soul, delving as far as the depths of Marianna's Trench would've taken her. He felt her inside him. He felt nothing of beguile. Her voice was of the wind and the wind pushed him to sea.

"Please," Sasha released, pulling out of his stupor. "You won't regret me."

"Aye, but the sea ain't for carryin' regrets; it carries bones," the captain said.

The conversation turned to the captain and his ship, *Mary Anne's Hope*. The captain spoke of his crew of east coasters and a boatswain from the islands north of Australia. After a few pints and some general hullabaloo, the sun fell from the sky to the sea. All was left in blackness, for the moon had forgotten to show. Maybe it was his inebriation. Maybe the woman frightened the old captain. Whatever the case, Captain Sloan and his lead hand, Dayton Ploo, invited the mysterious woman, whose name remained unknown, and Sasha to join them at sea.

***

Beauty stayed with Sasha through the weeks that passed, Beauty being the name he had given the woman, for she gave no other, though he had a mind to call her Scorpion because of the black tattoo on her hand. She had asked him why he was driven to sea, and he had told her there was nothing for him to return to on land and he needed work. His only prayers now were that a crew took to him. He asked of her the same, and she said that she sought her mother. She spoke little but could always be found on deck watching the water sink into the horizon. The cold seemed not to touch her skin.

It was a quiet morning when Sasha had awoken to work the deck on the seventh day since they had taken to the water. Early rising calmed his nerves. Beauty was waiting for him as he stepped up from the crew's cabins. She smiled her white-toothed smile. Her winter nebula eyes held him like a planchette.

"Morning, lass," Sasha greeted her. "Are you not cold out here in that? There's warmth among the flesh and cots below."

"You think I am here for the comfort of flesh?" she whispered, somehow louder than the waves that slapped the stern. She had a penchant for asking him poison-tipped questions when he was least hoping for them. "Fear is for children, and I took you for a man. Would you have me be a maiden below deck pruning the crew? You think me depraved? Am I but a slave to the appetite of bottomless carnivores? Child."

"Why do you abuse me so, woman?" Sasha sighed, as began to work the line.

"Woman? I have seen beyond the furthest reaches of your ideations lack. Woman? Child! You dare scold me under the sun, and yet seek my bosom when all else sleeps. That is but a child. A child who hungers for its mother's milk. Woman? Pah, I am the master of myself. I am deeper than black. I am the daughter of the sea. I am-"

"Eh, stop yer hollering water snake," Captain Sloan interrupted. "'Til ye can haul line handsomely, ye best away as we get tackin'."

Beauty scolded the round captain. Her black cloak snapped in the wind, and although a sense of dread sent shivers to Sasha's bones and the sea frost burned his skin, Beauty's fury tempered his heart.

While they tacked, the sea winds rocked *Mary Anne's Hope* like a cradle. Barrages of white-tipped waves broke upon them in sprays of stinging foam. It was colder than Sasha could ever recall on the water, and the crew seemed to wear the same sense of suffrage. Blue lips, pale knuckles, high collars. They all seemed to bear the weather's punishing bite, like walking corpses.

On the fifteenth day from port, an angry lashing of waves swallowed the rowdy, red-haired Dayton Ploo as a storm turned noon to night. Beauty claimed Dayton was coming to clear the deck when she caught sight of Beauty clinging to a line. Dayton rushed to rescue Beauty, but the wave swallowed her as she made a grasp Beauty's hand. Nail marks were left like seared brands across the scorpion tattoo on Beauty's hand. The loss left a sombre mood on the crew, and Beauty grew more resilient in her determination to find her mother.

On the twenty-first day of November, which marked the seventeenth day from port, what was left of the Autumn sun began to kiss the horizon beyond the azure sea. Sasha had lost the feeling in his fingertips and his eyebrows and nose hairs had become uncomfortably crisp. There was himself, twelve mates, the now languid Captain Sloan, and Beauty. Catch had been wholesome, but disgruntlement grew in the misunderstanding of the purpose of the trip. The crew became almost mutinous in their discouragement and distrust in the captain after losing Dayton. The weather seemed to match their fury, as the abusive winds and the frigid water burned eyes and skin. Beauty alone watched from the forestay, the cold seeming not to mar her skin, despite her hair a tempest of flowing black fire.

As the water calmed at midday, Sasha turned up from his bitter duties to spy on the woman. He couldn't help but notice that the world seemed to grow silent in her presence as she stood like a siren guiding from the bow. Sasha looked around to see if others had noted the sudden silence, but Rick Slither and Bastion Crye worked away in the misery of their own duties, their eyes reflecting the automaticity of their errands. Sasha returned his gaze to Beauty and found that she was looking at him with wide, spooked eyes. Her notoriously untouched skin appeared pallid. She suddenly jumped over to Sasha and gripped him with fingers like catfish teeth.

From the quarterdeck he heard Captain Sloan call, "Ahoy! There she is, lads: Black Dread! Ho! Shift the boom with me!" Suddenly, like a geyser bursting forth, a black snake-limb fled the sea. "Heave the line. B'y! Heave!"

Water exploded, turning the sailors who were left on deck to jetsam. Mates, untied barrels, and chunks of wood rained as debris. Panic blinded Sasha, as he and Beauty were tossed down the deck. Icy burns were forgotten as black arms twisted among the forestays, up the hull, and up the masts.

Sasha heard Beauty laugh as she caught the prow. "I am here, Mother, with an offering of freshly caught prey!"

Sasha gave her no chance to exalt further as he wrapped his arms around her midriff and pulled her away from the railing. "Don't go near the water!"

His words were swallowed by the deafening noise of smashing waters, screaming, and cracking wood, creating a chilling scene of wintry horror. Water burned upon exposed skin like rampant flames. Sasha tried to pull Beauty to the quarter's hatch, but her resistance made the effort futile.

Beauty broke from Sasha's grip and tripped up the stairs of the quarterdeck to face the great black head of an ancient beast of the sea.

Sasha dashed up the steps and grabbed Beauty's waist again as she reached up to the monster with a smile of carved admiration.

"Mother of the depths, take this offering I bring forth to thee!" she wailed. Sasha lifted her, her arms became like flailing clubs, but he persisted and pulled her to the edge of the prow. The great beast shadowed them in deathly silence outside of the maelstrom that consumed the rig. "Child, I am a daughter of the sea. A water death will not come for me."

Whatever the truth of her words, Sasha made no hesitation as he lifted her with the final dregs of his strength and threw her overboard. He had no moment to reconcile or justify his actions before the tentacles of the deep, black monstrosity crashed around him.

He followed the woman's screams into the cold winter blackness below. He could see her tattooed hand reaching up toward him until the darkness consumed her.

It was an eternity of frigid suffering until the darkness, an ever hungry beast, consumed Sasha too.

Venom of God
~Byron Griffin~

I tell thee my dear, not all that thou wouldst consider to be malignancy be wholly evil, for blessed is God's left hand as much as his right. Let me tell to thee the tale of the scorpion. It was during the season of moribund trees and stygian skies that I came upon the scorpion. 'Twas the twenty-ninth of October, whilst I was busied with mending the arms of the vicar's cassock and my mistress and he sat in the drawing room, for this did happen during calling hours, when that fateful knock came upon the door, which I answered; upon the doorstep stood a woman of much advanced years, whose eyes were as cloudy as the sky, come to sell divers things. The woman entreated entry, for she wished
that I should lead her to my mistress, for she hoped to entreat kindness; I bade the woman remain at the door whilst I went to Mrs. Dacre, that I might ask her if she wished to purchase from the woman. Mrs. Dacre did indeed wish to go to the woman yet, Mr. Dacre admonished her for this and thus I was sent back to drive the woman from the house however, ere I returned to the doorstep she had already departed, no sign of her left save for a statuette. The scorpion, a small figure wrought of darkest ebony. I brought it to Mrs. Dacre, she held it in her hands and inspected it; as she looked upon the statuette the Vicar returned and upon seeing the thing bade her cast it away, for he said it was a pagan fetish not fit for his home yet, as she did try to cast the statue into the fire her left arm was stabbed by the stinger. She entreated my aid in disposing of it, for upon being stung by the scorpion she became afeared to touch it again and thus, bade me throw it into the fire.

Mrs. Dacre was much ailed after the morning incident and became confined to bed thus, in the twilight of eventide whilst the vicar presided o'er evensong, we were left alone however, we could not take pleasure in it for dearest Victoria succumbed to sopor, for three days she remained thus. It was midnight on All Hallows, when she awoke from her stygian slumber, for indeed the visions she recounted to me upon waking seemed the stuff of the infernal realms, she spoke to me of being visited by a woman whose lower aspect was as that of an owl and from whose vulva did crawl a scorpion which did sting her left arm, whereupon she found herself cocooned in inky black waters, thick as blood. Upon her arm, where she had been stung, was a black mark that bore the form of a stinger.

In the days that followed Victoria's recovery a number of events which many would regard as being marks of a most evil fortune did befall those in my mistress's life; we received news that her father, with no male heirs, did contract and subsequently die from the King's evil and a legacy, consisting of twenty thousand pounds and the deed to his house in London, was bequeathed to the Vicar. However, he had become weak and wan in the days after Victoria's recovery and when the letter, which informed us of her father's death, did arrive he began to cough blood; Dr Carter was called and did confirm the Vicar had contracted consumption, which he soon after perished from. Thus, during that sombre season of death my dearest Victoria became a most wealthy widow, unburdened by the weight of accusations one might be subject to if the angel of death had manifest in other ways.

That which most wouldst have termed a cursed object, for indeed I am most sure that the scorpion brought Samael to the Vicar, was indeed a blessing.

SAGITTARIUS

Dark Arrow
Jelena Vuksanović

"Ancient object from afar,
It looks like a star
So bright, is that alright
Or is someone going to die tonight?"
That hauntingly yet melodious sound
No, no I cannot become spellbound

I run and run…
Keep going…
Soon the voice dies…

Before you, an archer in black
With an arrow blacker than midnight,
Yet glowed with an unnatural radiance
Eying it, something comes. A flashback.
You saw this arrow once before - a time most grand.
"I am in search of the light arrow!" I say.
"I will not rest until I seek it and be in my possession!"

'They are not everlasting.' Another voice.
'You will search forever and ever.'
This is the archer, cloak lifted. Eyes black.
As he extends a hand - the arrow! It speaks!

'No, it is the dark arrow you wish to possess.'
'How dare you think it will not enchant you!'
'Avenge your ancestors! You will have success!'
'For you know, little one, it is long past due!'

It is calling. To ME. As I grasp the obsidian weapon
The screams reach my ears. This feels right. So complete.
Poison and ill intentions fill my head - so enthralling!
I will commit. I will submit. I will commit. I will submit.

'Use it well,' says the voice. Under its spell I shall not stray.
Righting the wrong done to my ancestors I daresay….
Watch me wield it - I know Okan well and will obey
Pain and suffering is coming to my enemies - time to play.
Not the time to pray…it is time to slay.

Bog Hag
- Caleb James K. -

Misery be in the air tonight,
hiding within those crimson eyes,
for we cry crystal tears stained with dye,
red as her beating heart,
where the fire lies,
oh yes,
red as her beating heart,
where the fire lies.

Illuminated by the sun's hot rays, molten dewdrops dripped down an ancient yew's gnarled branches, hitting the soft soil below with a rhythmic tap tap tapping. Around the tree's girthy base, the drops cooled in a growing pool, darkening and darkening and darkening, until the drips stopped still and the red blood chilled.

Death had returned to the bog.

***

Two holy men from a nearby village stood aghast, gazing upon the gruesome scene.

"What devilment has befallen these wetlands?"

"You fret over the land, Tadg? What of the poor soul strung up before us like some beast after the hunt? Do say, what evil has defiled this man's corpse? Oh, the brutality. The sacrilege!"

A third man pushed through the surrounding foliage. "Perhaps his demise can be attributed to simple misadventure." He cleared plant debris from his forest green robe and then joined the others.

The man beside him—adorned in the same attire—shook his head. "Brother Cian, only the dimmest stars must shine upon you. How could any man fall prey to a misadventure such as this? Even a blind beggar could see that his entrails have been removed!"

Cian squinted and studied the figure swaying from one of the bigger branches. Sunbeams hugged the back end of the corpse and their marigold fingers reached around the man's front to illumine his gore-caked torso. Wind strummed the jagged rib bones protruding from his gaping chest cavity; a hollow whistle played among the windswept leaves.

"Golmac, I fear as always, you have seen the truth my failing eyes could not."

"Perhaps," Tadg interjected, "it would be best if blindness struck each of us at this moment and all memory of this misery be forgotten."

Golmac furrowed his brows. "You mean to say we go about our way and shant speak of this again?"

"Speak of what?" Tadg asked, turning from the yew tree and heading back the way they had entered. "And brothers, do not forget the herbs," he added, picking up his creel containing the efforts of his foraging. "A brighter day shall smile upon us on the morrow."

The other two men watched as Tadg maneuvered through the wood. Golmac leaned in close to Cian. "I fear no bright days lay ahead," he whispered, "for a shadow has fallen over this land." With that, he picked up his creel and followed Tadg's path.

Cian stood firm, staring at the body. His poor eyesight blurred the details, but in his mind, there was no denying what the men had stumbled upon. There had been a sacrifice. In the name of what God or demon, he could not say, but somewhere, deep in this bog on a foggy night, a man's heart was ripped free of his breast; his screams no doubt muffled by the dense vegetation.

"May your spirit now rest, brother," Cian said in a hushed voice.

With little vim in his stride, he worked his way back to the main road and walked along until he caught up with the other two. It was quick going as he had no creel to carry—for he had forgotten it near the mighty yew—but that mattered little after having tasted death's foul air. He vowed never to return to the bog again.

***

An afternoon drizzle dampened both the village of Aslen and the mood of its inhabitants. Inside the dim and dreary Dodder's Tavern, a group of laborers grumbled away the day as they filled their bellies with stale bread and tepid ale. The group sat huddled over a crude wooden table. Their disquiet, made evident by their surly temperament, tainted the Tavern's normally jovial atmosphere. No man so much as feigned a smile or allowed a peal of laughter to be had.

"Why should one dead man keep food from my family's mouths?" a laborer lamented. "There is no good reason to stifle a day's work on his account."

Another laborer gulped down a mouthful of bitter ale. "I agree, Sean," he said with a grimace. "Even if a madman lurks around the bog, I see no reason to cancel the day. No matter his cunning or brawn, he be no match for the likes of us. Seven strong men could put down even the most ruthless of assassins if united in the task." The laborer took a smaller swig of ale but the bitterness was just the same.

"Aye," Sean agreed.

"Be no madman that stirs the Court to action." Everyone turned their heads toward the grizzled blacksmith sitting alone at an adjacent table. He was partaking in a humble mid-day meal of meat and oat mash. "If a killer was on the loose, the Royal Guard would hunt him down. I suspect something far more wicked resides in that bog. Something no number of men could stop."

Sean rubbed his scruffy chin. "Far more wicked, you say? You speak of a beast?"

"Nay." For several moments, the blacksmith stared silently at his food. "Do you men know the tragic tale of Máire Ó Luain?" he finally asked.

"Know it?" one of the laborers at the far end of the table bellowed. "There is not a man, woman, or child in all of Aslen who has not shed a tear for that poor woman."

Sean tipped his mug toward the laborer. "Aye." He then looked back at the blacksmith. "He tells no lies, sir. You know as well as we, few have suffered as Máire Ó Luain. My own mother, when she was but a little girl, paid witness to Máire's final breaths of life. The memory haunted my dear mother until the day we purified her body with fire and spread her ashes over the sea."

A young man seated across from Sean cleared his throat. "As you men know," he said in a loud, clear voice, "My bloodline does not originate here as I had only arrived in Aslen but one year ago. So great in the knowledge that I am lacking, I would be honored, Sean, if you could educate me. I would like to learn of this poor Máire Ó Luain's fate."

"My apologies, Fionn. I did not think before I spoke. So much like a brother you have become this past year, I forgot you are not a native of this land and do not know of our histories."

"No need to apologize," Fionn said. "You have all welcomed me with such open arms that I want for nothing but to become learned as one born of Aslen."

"Fair enough." Sean looked to the blacksmith. "Would you care to grant the boy's wish and regale us with Máire Ó Luain's sad tale?"

The blacksmith responded with a single, slow nod.

***

A low rumble of thunder rattled the windows as fat raindrops began thumping the thatched roof. Flames flickered in the hearth, and all the while the sky darkened and the tavern darkened and the patrons' moods darkened, blacker and blacker and blacker until only the fire's orange glow gave muted music for the shadows to perform their grim dance to.

"All of you are too young to have seen Máire Ó Luain in the flesh," the blacksmith began. "Truth be told, I only laid eyes on her but once myself. When I was a very small boy at that. But she was not a woman one could forget.

"Even when I was a boy, rumor stalked Máire like a hungry wolf. You see," he paused and took a sip of ale, "it was said that at one time, she was the most beautiful and most coveted woman in all the land. So great was her beauty that noblemen from all over sought her hand in marriage, but she rebuffed them all, choosing a simple life on the bog.

"This caused little harm to her reputation. In fact, quite the opposite. With each man she turned down, her purity and loveliness grew in the minds of the villagers. Eventually, all common folk who gazed upon her were compelled to turn away. No one felt worthy of seeing such perfection. It was thought that to do so would be an affront to the Gods.

"Over time, more and more men demanded her attention. It got to where she could no longer trade goods in Aslen without some man of high standing pulling her aside and whispering sweet nothings in hopes of winning her favor. Through the village, every way she turned, a suitor was sure to follow. But the more hands that reached for her, the more reclusive she became.

"Her home, a crumbling round-house deep in the bog, became a sanctuary for poor Máire. It was the only place where she could go that the men would not follow. That was until the night one vile man, lost in the throes of lust or madness or both, found innocent Máire's home, and it was there that he stole her beauty and corrupted her purity."

"You mean to say this man took her chastity?" Fionn asked.

"By force," the blacksmith replied, his face hard as stone.

"And her beauty? How could one steal that away from a woman?"

The blacksmith swallowed hard. "With fire."

Outside, the blustering wind battered the tavern with terrible tenacity. If the laborers had not been so engrossed with the blacksmith's story, they might have rejoiced in having been freed of working in such dire conditions. Perhaps then, their collective mood would have elevated and merriment would have reigned until the setting sun signaled the day's end. Alas, the tale ensured no cheer would be had.

"The man," the blacksmith continued, "named Vulcan Volesus, was a Roman patrician who had stopped in Aslen on one of his many travels. Not much is known about him, but it has been said that he was tasked with spreading his culture throughout the land. It was a cruel, violent task, and Vulcan excelled at it by imposing his will upon the innocent. As you men may know, the Volesus name still carries weight in some parts, and that is due to Vulcan's efficiency at propagating his seed.

"He cared little about marriage, and so the rogue patrician was not interested in taking Máire's hand. No, the rotten louse, the villain," the blacksmith rained down a heavy fist upon the table, "all he cared about was destroying beauty! All he desired was to quench his lustful thirst, and Máire was the sweetest wine.

"I will not pretend to know all the details of the night in question. Nor shall I speculate about the events. What I can surmise is that Vulcan Volesus was not entirely successful in executing his dastardly plan.

"That part I know to be true because Máire spoke of it herself. You see, he forced his way into poor Máire's home and then fell upon her with great violence. But his brutality did not stop there.

"After deflowering her, Vulcan realized consequences would soon follow his actions, even to a man of his standing. To steal the purity of such a coveted woman could only end one way. In death. He accepted this, but being the lecherous dog he was, it was not his death he had in mind.

"This is still a history muddied with rumor, but Máire's account to the Court described Vulcan's scheme to dispose of any evidence linking him to his evil deed. That evidence being Máire herself."

***

With the afternoon creeping by, the heavy rain slowed, and the heavy slaps on the thatched roof slowed, but the heavy words flowing from the blacksmith's lips did not slow. It was as if each word was a raindrop, filling the empty basins in the laborer's minds until the images overflowed and ran down into their hearts.

In detail, he relayed what Máire had supposedly told the Royal Court. About how Vulcan had stalked her for many weeks. How even though she had refused all of his advances, he had persisted. This all culminated with the tragedy that had befallen her.

She told them that Vulcan had ravished her, and how after, he had stripped her naked, taken a switch to her back, and whipped her raw and bloody. And then once his arm had tired and she no longer had a voice to scream with, he had cut her throat with a dagger and removed a piece of flaming timber from the hearth. This he used to set her home ablaze while she lay inside, nude and dying in a pool of her own blood.

What Vulcan did not know, she had told the court, was that in his haste, or due to his lack of combat experience, he had missed cutting her jugular and instead sliced the area beneath her jaw, thus spilling much blood but not killing her. The fire, too, had failed in ending Máire's life. And though she had been badly burned, the dampness of the bog may have kept her body from mortal injury, even as her home burned to ash around her.

"Even a Roman patrician such as Vulcan Volesus could not escape the noose," the blacksmith continued. "Once Máire spoke her truth and the people of Aslen learned of Vulcan's evil acts, the Royal Court had to take action. And take action they did, chasing the fiend to the edge of the bog where they hanged, drawn, and quartered him."

Fionn raised his index finger in the air. "How was it that Máire made it to Aslen and got herself in front of the Court?"

"That ends the known history," the blacksmith said in a forlorn voice, "and so the story of how Máire managed to claw her way free of the rubble and speak her truth has been lost to time. However, much gossip has filled in these discrepancies over the years. Most people, as I am sure you men already know, believe that Máire was rescued by Belenus, the God of fire.

"Some say the burns she had suffered were not from the fire, but rather from giving her hand to Belenus in exchange for her life. Since Gods are not subject to the same temptations as man, it is believed that the marriage of flesh took on a ghastly appearance, and it was Máire's supple skin that showed the result of the fire God's love rather than her womb."

***

With the storm's end, the small voices of children could be heard outside the tavern. Splish-splash laughs sang sonorously as they played in puddles and pitter-pattered around the wet grounds. But inside, like a tomb's hush, the men waited quietly for the blacksmith to finish the tale.

"So death spared Máire because she gave herself to the God of fire?" Fionn asked.

"Remember to not seek truth in rumor." The blacksmith feigned a smile. "As I said, these stories were already hearsay before my birth. Fact cannot be attributed to such tales, but this next part I can speak of with certainty, as I witnessed the events with these two eyes of mine." The blacksmith pointed to his gray sea storm eyes.

"It was a cold day. Rainy. A kind of sadness hung in the air." The blacksmith paused, lost in thought. "I did not know much of the world then, being so young, but I knew what I felt that day. Something was wrong. You could see it on the faces of the villagers.

"You see, a child had gone missing the week prior, and the search party had not turned up anything. That was until a lone hunter rushed through Aslen like a whirlwind. 'The boy, the boy!' he shouted. 'In the bog!'

"At the entrance of this very tavern, which was the humble law building in those days, my mother and I watched as the hunter collapsed from exhaustion. 'It was the Bog Hag. It was the Bog Hag,' he repeated over and over in a feverish state.

"As I was only a child, I had to stay back while a posse of brave men took to the bog. Anger flushed the men's faces as the boy's father led the charge, hollering and riling them up as they set to go down the lonely road toward the wetlands. 'She may have escaped death long ago, but if she hurt my boy, she will not escape the noose,' he said to the crowd of onlookers before leaving.

"I feared the worst. For the boy as well as Máire. At the time, rumor had far surpassed the truths of Máire's past, and so she was thought of as a witch, a hag. This was mostly because of her age and because she no longer left the safety of her home. Few in Aslen had ever seen her, at least not the folk born after her assault. But the occasional hunter who caught a glimpse of the old leather-faced woman of the bog would always spin a yarn. If they saw her collecting water, she was making potions. If she was gathering herbs, she was concocting poisons. You fellows know how talk gets around. A mound becomes a mountain; a brook a river; an old woman living on a bog becomes an evil spell-casting hag. There is no end of faerie stories when fear overruns common sense.

"Anyway, as I said, the men took to the bog. They were not gone but a few hours when a tremendous shriek rose from over the hill. My mother bade me to stay in the house as she hurried outside to see what all the commotion was about. It embarrasses me to confess this, but I did not heed my mother's command. Instead, I crept outside like a field mouse and hid behind a woodpile.

"As the shriek neared, it turned into a melancholic wail the likes of keening funeral women. That was when I caught my first glimpse of the infamous Bog Hag. It started as blocky shadow figures blotted out by the sun, but soon the shapes escaped the horizon and entered Aslen."

All the laborers except for Fionn shifted uneasily in their seats as they knew the turn the story had taken.

The blacksmith downed the rest of his ale and then continued. "They had poor Máire's arms tied behind her and were shoving her along, threatening her neck with a rusted blade tip as they marched. She held her eyes closed, and the most piteous song emanated from deep within the woman. It was as if she knew the end was near and she was keening for her own forfeited life.

"They marched down the dusty road, and all the while the people of Aslen watched on in silence. Some looked grim, some sad, but most appeared to be in awe of Máire. For the witch of the bog, the hag, the stealer of children had been caught.

"From my hiding place, I could see the group walk by without them seeing me, or so I thought. As they neared, on their way to the village square, I noticed a young boy in his father's arms. The father that had led the charge hung back as another took command. I recognized the boy as an occasional playmate, and though tears streaked his face, he appeared unharmed. The same could not be said for Máire.

"When they walked past my woodpile, I got a good look at the old woman. Mud caked her humble garb, dried blood had crusted around her wrinkled mouth, and what was left of her wet, wiry white hair clung to her badly scarred face.

"Though spared from death in her youth, I think dying in that fire so many years before would have been a mercy. It certainly would have been better than becoming the marred monster Máire had transformed into. The monster that, as they walked by, suddenly opened its eyes and dropped its gaze upon my little face peeking out from behind the woodpile. Even now, I cannot unsee those blood-red eyes. Those crimson orbs threatening to steal my life force.

"I wish I could continue the tale, but so startled was I that I had bolted back into my home, so I did not witness what had occurred next. But if you wish to know," the blacksmith nodded to Fionn, "I believe Sean can finish what I cannot."

Sean tipped his mug toward the blacksmith. "A fine job you made of the tale, sir. A fine job." He then gave his attention to the young man seated in front of him. "I can only repeat the words of my mother and describe what she had seen that day."

***

As the men settled in for the long haul, listening with anticipation to a tale most of them already knew, the innocent laughter outside had ceased without notice. A slight commotion commenced, but the patrons of the tavern took no heed.

Sean continued the tale, adding what details the blacksmith had omitted. He mentioned how the young boy had been spotted by the hunter, walking hand-in-hand with the Bog Hag. The boy had told his father that Máire had lured him to her home and was planning to eat him, though he recanted the story later and admitted that the old woman had instead found him, lost and wandering through the dangerous bog alone. The reality was that she had saved the boy, but so ready to dole out punishment was his father that the boy felt compelled to lie to avoid a beating.

The history continued with Máire's capture, and how the posse marched her to the village square. It was there that she supposedly cursed Aslen as they set her up to hang in the great oak tree.

"My mother also spoke of Máire's red eyes," Sean said to the blacksmith. "Like fire, those eyes burned through the hearts of all who watched what they did to her that day. Before they pulled the rope tight around her frail neck, the father of the boy asked if Máire had any final words. She said, 'From here until the end of time, death shall come to all who enter my bog.' With that, she continued the sorrowful wailing you had mentioned," Sean said to the blacksmith. "I wish the tale ended there," he looked back at Fionn, "but history is never so kind.

"As soon as they pulled Máire up into that tree, one of the posse members, who had parted from the group upon entering Aslen, returned riding atop a black horse. My mother did not recognize the man, nor did anyone else. The way it was told to me, he had dark, predatory eyes and a long, hooked nose. Tall and lanky with flowing hair black as crow feathers, the man looked to be born not of Aslen, nor to a Roman mother. Also strange were the garments he wore, tight-fitted and oddly colorful like the setting sun.

ROSALIND
-Ashley Scheller-

One warm, fall evening, a gentleman of two and thirty, dressed in a humble tweed suit, walked through the iron gates of the lonely Saint Stars Graveyard on the outskirts of town carrying a bouquet of sweet daisies.

The foggy air did little to mask the scents of fresh earth and dying blooms from other visitors from that day. However, the gentleman kept going. Guided by the warm glow from his iron lantern, he ignored the slight discomfort from pebbles crunching under his worn leather shoes.

The echoes of the belltower back in town chimed and his heart thudded in his chest, knowing it was getting late. Picking up the pace, his hazel eyes behind his round glasses quickly scanned as he mentally counted the rows of mossy gravestones.

Twelve rows in, he turned left, passed four more sites, and halted in front of a tombstone which read:

Rosalind Steed
Our Dancing Angel

November 22nd, 1901 – December 21st, 1930

He closed his eyes and breathed in deeply, remembering the first time he had seen her twirling and spinning on stage. Young, talented, and full of promise.

"My pretty dancer," he whispered.

As if in response, a soft breeze blew through the graveyard, rustling the remaining orange and red leaves of the trees causing the candle within his lantern to flicker. The gentleman opened
his eyes, sensing a cool presence, a misty energy, enveloping him like a delicate hug.

Shrugging it off to simply the night air, he knelt before Ms. Steed's grave and placed the bouquet of flowers carefully on the damp ground alongside his lantern.

"Flowers?" a small voice asked. "For me?"

The gentleman looked up in surprise. "Rosalind?" he whispered.

A hand frosty to the touch slid across his right cheek. Frozen to the ground, his jaw dropped at the sight of her.

The *ghostly* her.

Dazzling and almost frighteningly beautiful in a romantic ballerina gown, his Rosalind came around from behind him, floated to the top of her tombstone with a hop where she held a perfect arabesque in her blue pointe shoes.

Gazing his way, her eyes glowed a morning glory hue while a smile formed on her faint lips. "Ta-da," she whispered.

The gentleman pushed up his glasses that had slipped down his nose with haste. "B-But how? You touched my—" He shook his head. "No. I-It doesn't matter I—" he took a quick breath
and blinked back his tears— "I've missed you."

The performer lowered her slender leg and remained up on her toes, balancing on the tippy top of the mossy surface.

"I've missed you, too," said Rosalind, her voice bell-like, echoing through the air. "Have you come to cry as well?"

The gentleman hesitated, unsure what to say. "I…no." He rubbed the back of his neck. "Forgive me for not coming sooner." He looked up at her pale face. "I came to wish you peace."

Rosalind tilted her head to the side, her ashen hair still in a bun decorated with a silver tiara. "Is that all?"

"Well. I-It's not as though I was expecting this."

Rosalind giggled and twirled around in place, showing off her dress. "Do you like it?"

"Very much. It's a miracle." The gentleman rose to his feet, patting his somewhat soaked knees, and a sudden chill ran down his spine. "B-But wait. Have you not seen Heaven?"

The dancer gave a wistful smile and hopped to the stone on his left, then the next, and the next, heading back toward the pebble path without a word.

"W-Wait!" he cried, picking up his lantern and leaving the daises in the dark.

But she didn't stop. Instead, with a grace only the wind could match she leaped from the ending stone on her row, flew over the pebble path, and landed atop the ending stone of the row across the way, finishing with a plié. From there, she continued hopping from stone to stone.

The gentleman kept on her trail until she halted at the tenth site, the furthest from the path.

"I don't understand!" he shouted, setting his lantern down. "W-Why did you bring me—"

Thomas Arrow
Our Broken Heart

November 25th, 1898 – January 10th, 1931

"'Our broken heart'?" Thomas repeated. "How did I☐"

"You're here, love." With a gentle caress, Rosalind settled her hands on both sides of Thomas' face. "You'll see how the 'why' rarely matters." She removed his glasses and let them fall. "And we're together again."

"But I need those—"

The spectacles disappeared the second they touched the ground.

"No, dear, you don't," the dancer giggled. "Though I imagine they'll reappear tomorrow."

"Tomorrow?"

"Or in Heaven." She spun in place. "Who knows?" She took his hands and stepped closer to him. "But I have been waiting." Her smile faltered. "You didn't 'lower the curtain' too soon, did you?"

Between the shock and awe of the evening, the speechless Thomas didn't reply, glancing quickly between his gravestone and her.

"Thomas?" she whispered, her smile fading into frown.

His vision blurred and all colors shifted from reality into a monochromatic blue, like a vision or a dream.

"Thomas?"

Rosalind's pretty face melted into that of a demon's, twisted with flecks of bone peeking through the rotted flesh.

The gentleman shook his head and looked again.

Pretty as a picture.

"Thomas, dear, are you alright?" She took his hands about her waist. "See? It's me, death isn't the end for us."

With no mortal heart left to beat, the gentleman took her into his arms. "I didn't lower the curtain, love, but it hurt missing you."

His graceful dancer smiled, placed her head on his chest, and both swayed in silence.

CAPRICORN

I'VE COME FOR THE MASTER
-A. S. C.-

I trod with care, each step gingerly touching the forest floor. Ancient trees surrounded me, their low-hanging branches a hairsbreadth from snagging at my diminutive frame. Had more light pierced through their crowns, would I have been visible? Or would I have remained as I was, a murky detail in someone else's painting?

I followed the narrow path as it wound along, seemingly without aim. I'd never been here before, none of my kind had. Not in person, at least. We knew to stay away. We allowed it to claim its tribute elsewhere, in the form of an oblivious backpacker whose joyful laughter reverberated through the stillness, rousing slumbering beings. Later in newspapers, we would learn about them - victims of unfortunate accidents, unprepared or underprepared, a sad case entirely their fault. As if the footpath peppered with slippery pebbles and stray roots didn't lay in wait for a moment's hesitation. As if the woods didn't revel in trapping intruders and breathing in their misery. As if it weren't alive. The news never said that. It would be mad.

As was I, I recognized, if not worse. I knew and had still come. I marched on, confused and wary yet determined, my feet heavy with effort and dread. I didn't want to be here; some things couldn't be helped. I attempted not to notice the surrounding movement, not to hear the leaves rustling behind, gaining on me, almost touching. Only leaves, I lied to myself. It helped some.

It had taken me a while to find the right entrance. It moved often. Our family records were of little use—why would they be, when all the others could dream themselves here? Walking, I wondered whether I wasn't the lucky one after all, despite everything. They say children find an abundance of monsters in the absence of light. I peered at the branches swinging unaided by the wind ahead of me and called bullshit. Adults are just pompous and blind.

Perhaps the forest recognized my determination to keep going despite the darkness, as the smells became more unpleasant. Stifling and humid braided with the sweet, nauseating aroma of decay enveloped me, coating my shoes, clinging to my worn carmine jacket, insinuating itself through the gap between my nape and my collar. It scratched imaginary lines with infuriating slowness. "I have you now," it seemed to whisper. I wanted to tear everything off and run back to the house, where there was soap and water and I could scrub the touch away. I almost went through with it; the sweat trickling down the patterns of my scars stayed me, reminding me why I was here. My heartbeat drummed away the whispers.

I slowed down to check for footprints. Despite the thick crowns above providing shade from the midday sun, I could still make out faint imprints in the soft, mulchy leaves below. Not there yet.

Retraining my gaze ahead, I frowned at the mound of earth now barring my way. Another trick of the light, I thought. Until I went and touched it: solid, really there. At least twice my height, so I couldn't jump over, and I didn't want to go around lest I be led astray. That left scaling it, with what little confidence I could muster. My tired, stiff limbs protested at the mere suggestion. I ignored them, much like everything else.

I felt it with my hands, attempting to find some hole to dig my fingers into. Something wriggled beneath my right palm. I removed it and discovered the maggot: yellow-white, fat to the point of popping. My breath hitched. How did this place know? It wasn't supposed to. I was hidden from it. It couldn't reach me no matter what, it couldn't see. How did it know? In the corners of my eyes, I noticed the black cockroaches scurrying to me.

I will not scream. I refuse to scream. I repeated my mantra, paying no mind to the assault, until I regained some semblance of composure. Gradually, my terror shifted to anger. I slammed my palm down, felt the maggot burst underneath. How dare they toy with me?

I dug my stunted fingers into the moist earth and kicked little holes for my feet as I went up, my stomach somersaulting from fear to disgust and back again. I fell twice; each time, I found the mound smooth as if I'd never touched it. I charged right back.

When I finally swung my leg over, a straight drop greeted me, taller than the ascent had indicated. There was no incline, no branch to hang on to, nothing to slow me down. I took a deep breath, lowering myself as far as my arms allowed, and let go. I saved my face from scraping against the earth, but my hands and front were filthy with mud and wet things I preferred not to explore.

Landing knocked the wind out of me. Despite my sturdy boots, pain exploded in my ankles, traveling up to my hips and lower back. My legs nearly gave out; I could barely feel them for a brief second and had to confront the very real possibility that this was the end of the road for me. All my old injuries awoke to groan their displeasure. I walked it off slowly, taking tentative steps so as not to further tax my ankles. I wished I had a stick for a cane. Glancing down, I noticed the lack of footprints. Close now. Good. I didn't know how much I had left in me.

I looked back. The barrier had vanished. The path glimmered in soft light, inviting me. All I had to do was turn around and return home. It wouldn't cost anything. I'd come, I'd seen, it would be alright now. No more pain, no more struggle. I would incur no more losses... An admission of defeat on its part or some new sinister trick? I shrugged, settled on the latter, and went on my way.

The rustling picked up again. Something rushed toward me. By muffled sound alone, I judged it big, many more times so than myself. I wondered what I would see. Father had told me all the stories, described all the monsters while I lay recovering in bed; he'd seen them all roam in his nightmares. I never had. We didn't know back then I couldn't. He'd attempted drawing them to prepare me for the inevitable encounters. A good storyteller, but a lousy artist. The recollection still had me giggling. He was gone now, expunged from everywhere save for that corner of my mind where his warm voice pleaded with me to give up this folly. No one ever listens to children and good men.

A sudden breeze brushed my cheek with nimble fingers. Its coolness conjured peculiar ideas. It unnerved me. It grew intense enough for me to hear what it was: a collection of cries and wails in countless voices, a memory of carnage in sound. A deafening concerto, for one. The little hairs on the back of my neck rose. For once, I was glad for my fear. It kept me from distinguishing the voices of my loved ones in the cacophony. I longed for a last listen… This was the lowest trick yet.

Focused on denying it victory, I nearly jumped out of my skin when something swished past, tearing a gash in my jacket. Thankfully, nowhere important, just my upper arm. I squinted at the long wiry body. A snake? I'd heard of this one. Beyond it, a coal-black patch of air marked the end of my journey. Finally! Nothing short of extreme caution would see me through to the end. I could waste nothing until I could touch that immaterial wall.

The serpent doubled back, halting inches from my face. All of me was smaller than its head. I had no idea what I was looking at: a being or a mere agglomeration of disconnected branches varying in shape and size, held together by a whim? It searched me with a malicious grin, wood creaking as it coiled itself around me once, twice, snug, too close for comfort; I protected my pockets. Having studied me all over, its face swung back to mine.

"Now," its sweet-toned hiss hit me with decaying breath, "what'sss an ugly little girl like you doing in a place like thisss? Ssshouldn't you be napping? Or playing with dollsss?"

I struggled to keep my words from trembling. "I've come for the Master."

"I am the Massster," it replied languidly.

"Of lies, perhaps," I identified it. A very minor player, not very clever, kept alive by its servile attitude; not someone I had to worry about, given my current circumstances. Something scuttled in the cavities he had for eyes. "Father told me about you. You're the trickster."

"The trickssster?" it bristled.

"That," I went on undeterred, nodding at the black patch that had surreptitiously approached us, "is the Master." Being rude might speed things up. I was tired of waiting.

"That?" the snake made a show of looking around. "I sssee nothing. Little girl, have you lossst your way?" it mocked, feigning concern. "A child ssshouldn't be out in the woodsss alone. Your parentsss mussst be worried sssick." It grinned.

"They're dead." I hadn't time for games. Besides, I already knew where it was going. No matter what grandfather or the death certificates said, their cause of death lived in this forest.

"A family tragedy? How—" it slightly inclined its head, eye sockets narrowing as it savored the air, "—deliciousss. The perfect tassste. Ssso ripe, ssso juisssy! I remember it well." It ceased its reverie to taunt me. "Do you know, little girl, what would tassste even better?"

"Me," I shrugged. The final morsel always tickled the taste buds with nostalgic regret. I was the last of my kind. "But I am not yours to do as you wish," I added. "I'm here for the Master." I persisted, barely aware of the terror and disgust ebbing at me.

"You insssolent child, I ought to–"

"Enough," a deep, rich growl arrested the coils tightening around me. Not a shout, a simple command with weight behind it.

The Master's revealed its silhouette in the near dark. As far as I could tell, it was similar to the serpent's, only on a scale of its own. I could make out disconnected roots and branches, and a powerful presence oozing my way. Sensing the bloated self-importance accompanying its age, I gave a bitter smile. I'd used to hold vestiges of lost things in fascination, never quite wrapping my mind around them disappearing until I became one. Greed builds, greed tears down. All grand things have an expiry date.

A pair of fiery-green eyes lit up and studied me. "Why are you here?"

I swallowed, nearly choking. The way it'd said you... I suppose it had no use for my name. It knew me, just like it'd known my family, my kin. I stood in front of my enemy, revenge in my grasp—how many would've killed for this opportunity? And how many would see themselves thwarted at the last moment, caught up in a petty, clumsy, fleeting attempt to settle the score? Not me. There was no score. I wasn't here for revenge.

"I came to bargain." Even I could hear the intimidation in my voice.

"Bargain?" the Master mused as the serpent blustered. "You possess nothing worthy of me. Would you have me bargain with a lesser one?"

A heavy weariness washed over me. I was fortunate that the serpent's grip kept me steady as my weak legs threatened to buckle. My backache intensified. I rubbed at my nape, tracing the scars that always anchored me to reality.

"A lesser one you couldn't kill," I pointed out.

It had taken me years to piece it together, years of bedridden reading, of pretending I was asleep while listening in on adult conversations. It had been slow, laborious, and I wasn't sure of anything. Once I could walk again, I perfected the art of invisibility. I kept my head down and did as I was told by a hateful grandfather who saw only shame and failure in me. I took the meaning behind his quiet rage—how dare I be less than expected? How dare I be a failure? In between, I also did what I wanted. The two are not mutually exclusive.

For years, Grandfather and the Master had disputed dominion over Father. Grandfather wanted someone who could communicate at will with the Master, who could call or dismiss it on a whim, who could bend it to do their bidding. He'd conveniently overlooked the Master's nature: proud, incandescent, independent. It wasn't a dog to house-train. Father had kept them both at bay for as long as possible. And then he'd tried running away.

I don't recall much about the Accident. Small blessing. I remember Father putting Mother and me in the car at the crack of dawn. I was in the backseat alone, no seatbelt on. He drove fast. I drifted in and out of sleep. I rolled around at turns. It was uncomfortable. I heard Mother cry. She was saying something, but I don't know what. She turned to me right before it happened; I saw her lips moving, saw her smile as she patted my shoulder. Felt her hand hold me in place. Try as I might, I can't remember the sound of her voice.

I woke up in a bed, tubes coming out of me. Grandfather had us again. He and his father made an agreement: Grandfather promised not to send me away, and Father agreed to confront the Master. On our own, we didn't have the means to keep me alive. I never let on I knew that.

Just like I never breathed a word about the silence in my head. I'd left the voices and the shadows in that car. I slept well because I didn't dream. At all. The Master had no access to me. Grandfather wouldn't have liked that—no value in an impotent pawn—so I kept mum. To Father as well; his joy would've seen it slip out. The freedom made me happy. Watching a black dog gnaw at Father from the inside made me less so.

"Couldn't?" the Master called me back from the flurry of memories. "A careless mistake." It glanced at the serpent, who withered and emitted hissed apologies. "One I ought to remedy."

The dark veil lifted fully. I stared in awe at the giant wolf sitting down. It stretched its neck lazily, working the stiffness out of its disused muscles. Where the serpent had been one being, the wolf was everyone and everything brought together. One creature containing armies, yet independent of them. Putrid birds flew out to surround me, scouting the tiny nuisance standing in their Master's way. Armed soldiers hung from its sides, awaiting command; their armors clanged and scraped noisily against whitened bone, their weapons partly consumed by rust. Between its front paws tiny creatures slithered, skittered, and padded, a barely discernible vanguard forged in countless battles. The Master was life and death holding hands, a wielder of terrible power, end to all hope. There would be no way for me to escape. My life was forfeit.

I snapped out of the induced fear. Given our disparity in size, his disproportionate display of force felt unnecessary, comedic even. Grandfather's image flitted briefly before my eyes. Oh, was that so? Interesting.

"If that is your wish, I won't stop you," I said. "You've led a long and fulfilling existence." Hunting people in their dreams. "Slaughtering a small person in a forest with no one to watch seems like a fitting end."

"Careful with your mockery," it growled. "My patience is hard earned and swiftly lost, child."

"Ssshall I kill her for you, Massster?" the serpent offered, a picture of servility.

Time to test my theory. I reached out to the nearest twig in the serpent's body and snapped it—easier than I'd imagined, so dry and brittle. It didn't notice, so I snapped another. And another. I methodically went through them one by one as the serpent wailed and thrashed us both about. Who knew they could hurt too? I worked harder, faster, without mercy. In a dying effort, the serpent moved to bite. The Master's paw swiped its head clean off and the whole thing collapsed. I hadn't expected it; perhaps neither had he. I found myself sitting in a pile of broken kindling, bleeding from a plethora of scratches yet alive.

The Master considered me. "That was a nasty trick. I shall not work on me, child. I am immortal." He rose and stared me down.

My neck hurt from the effort to return his gaze. "Immortality is less everlasting life and more undying memory."

"You presume to teach me? You, an insignificant sheep, cast yourself against my ages of might?"

"Goat," I blurted out, trying to buy time and get closer. Anything to get closer.

"Goat?" The Master burst into deafening laughter.

"My grandmother used to call me that. She said I used to jump everywhere, wouldn't stand still for a second." She'd said other things, too, about what it meant to be that, but I doubted the Master had time for stargazing and predictions. "I was always going off on my own in the forest before—" the Accident. Before I had to relearn to walk.

The wolf sat back down, closer to me, motioning for me to speak. His expression spoke of curious amusement at the tiny rambling human in front of him.

I'd pictured this countless times. I'd lure him in with some wild tale, anything my despair could conjure, and when he was close enough, I'd spray him with the lighter fluid and set him ablaze. I'd found the materials as I was packing the house up. Now I was alone. I couldn't live there until I came of age; Grandfather's careful provisions for me had neglected to appoint a legal guardian. No doubt he'd had no expectation of my outliving him so soon, if at all. The fortune was in a trust. I would be in foster care for a while, which meant being alone and defenseless.

I'd thought it all through, you see. I was small, ugly, scarred from top to bottom, and removed from any semblance of society. I didn't speak like my peers—I'd only had either adults or books for conversation partners. I'd been shut away from the world at large for so long catching up would present insurmountable difficulties.

Faced with the prospects of a life on the outside, the choice made itself. I'd come for the Master. Whatever I knew or thought I did about his nature and his power, I wasn't willing to risk him regaining a foothold in the world. Maybe my kind hadn't been wiped out. Maybe others would be born, all evidence to the contrary. That was why we had to die together. I never expected to come out of the forest that day. It was a freeing thought. Pain would cease. He would do no more harm. The cycle ended with me.

Now seeing his sharp face peering down at me, waiting for me to make a mistake… another way became clear. Possible. Seductive. Why destroy him when subduing was the superior option? I had the tools. Was the tool. Instead of wishing him gone, why not cause him to live every day with a hope that would never materialize? I'd been isolated and tormented for years; surely I'd picked up a thing or two. "Anything short of complete domination is an utter waste of time," grandfather used to spout after some wine. I'd thought it drunken folly. I stood corrected.

I carefully spun my tale, talked until my voice turned raspy. Most of it was nonsense, of course; I neither could nor was interested in reviving the race of slumber beasts. I had no plans of gather the Master followers to worship him back into power. And I certainly did not possess an amulet granting me immunity from his intrusions and a modicum of power over his servants—the serpent had been nothing more than a gamble.

It rarely matters if you believe your own lies. What matters is that your audience laps them up. Mine did, though they weren't particularly well crafted. I hopped higher and higher in my untruths, relentless as a mountain goat scaling a difficult rock face, and just as convinced of my successful ascent as I was aware of the perilous chasm of failure. I couldn't explain why I knew it would work. I just did.

"As such," I concluded, raw-throated, "I hereby make the following pledge: for as long as I live, my life shall be entwined with yours. I shall do my utmost to shield you from outside harm and combat any attempts to bring you down." I waited.

"The amulet?" the Master growled.

"It has no effect on you," I made a pretense of startlement. "Only on lesser beings like the serpent—"

"Of which none remain."

"For now. Once you have regained all that was lost, you can make more. I will need to protect myself from them. I trust in your promise, but it binds only the two of us."

He pondered. "Fine. Keep your toy, I've no use for it. But our deal…"

"Yes?"

"It binds you and your cubs in perpetuity."

"Sorry?" I frowned. Cubs? Did he… not know?

"As soon as your first turns six, you shall send him to live here with me. That is what your treacherous grandfather promised. He failed. You will not."

I tried grabbing hold of my spinning surroundings. That was why Father had had us run? Why Mother had died and I had been reduced to… this? My stomach filled with acid. I wished I'd pushed the old bastard down the stairs when I had the chance! Oh, but what golden opportunity now lay before me…

"If you don't like my terms—" he stretched.

"Seven!" I breathed erratically, clinging to my precious web. "At least give me seven years. That's not old enough to do you harm. I'm over twice that and can't do a single thing." Other than lie and make you mine. "Seven years. Then I will deliver you the fruits of my womb myself. Please, Master!"

"The fruits of your womb," he nodded, approving my wording. Poor bastard! "You humans and your silly words. Fine," he acquiesced. "I agree to your terms. After seven years, you shall deliver your first cub for me to use as I please. Should you fail, your life and his are forfeit."

I agreed. Our bargain was struck, breakable only by treachery or death, neither of which beckoned to me. Other ideas did. Cruel ones, though warranted in full.

The Master carried me out of the forest that day, my body too spent for the return trip. I clung to him as he padded along the path now wide enough to accommodate him, all the while thinking of my grandmother. She used to keep me company while the men argued, sneak me books I wasn't supposed to have, tell stories and peel fruit. She'd taught me to lie, clever grandma. She'd be proud of me now.

Perhaps I could come and peel the Master some oranges a few years down the road, when it was time to renew my lies. Apples, too, and maybe some watermelons or something. After all, that was the only fruit my body could give.

Later, much later. When the sensation of victory required renewal. For now, I had what I'd come for.

The Capricorn Man
-Lanie Mores-

He appears as if born of winter mist and moonless nights.
An ethereal man, mystical.
Bearing a countenance bursting with confidence, excites.
A form daunting while yet, irresistible.

Confused how one such as he should notice me,
When never have I drawn such favour.
But he sweeps into my space, gathers me up in his gaze,
Entranced in a moment paused, I savour.

Whispered, soft silken promises abound.
A sworn gift, stars plucked from the skies,
Enticing words spoken, the only sound.
Swirling constellations behind his eyes.

They mesmerize me. Enchant me. Bind me.
I know no more that I am me, and he is he.
Just that we are destined to be.
Together. Until the underlying truth I finally see.

A long, elegant hand extends, reaches smoothly for mine,
Beautifully formed fingertips stretch sharply.
"Come, my love," invites the silken voice, turned malign.
Words bearing seductive intention sensed darkly.

Despite warning bells shrilling, I lean in, all willing.
Take his cold, dark hand in mine.
Upon touch the full glamour peels back, the sight chilling.
Revealing corruption of what once was divine.

Pupils spread, elongate horizontally.
Majestic horns corkscrew to the heavens.
Eyes slide sideways, positioned monocularly.
Infatuation most swiftly deadens.

I ask, "Where's your fishtail, Capricorn Man?"
He throws his head back, laughing maniacally,
"You confuse me with another, for I am no man.
Nor am I beast, just a goat symbolically."

His taloned grip circling my hand starts to tighten,
And this evil touch steals my sweet breath,
Draws away my life essence, as I wither within.
The promise of stars, vanish. My gift only death.

A cloven hoof digs deep into my chest.
My body new leverage to climb,
On a staircase forged with gullible souls put to rest.
To reclaim what he lost in a distant time.

The celestial perch from whence he was cast down.
A punishment he chooses to ignore.
The collection of bodies arranged carefully in mounds,
To scale back to a realm he's allowed nevermore.

Fair Share
-Daphinie Cramsie-

Have you filed your taxes yet? I do hope you have, or else you'll have a visit from me. It's not so much a big deal; I'll make it a quick visit as I have many people to see, but I can't say it'll be pleasant.

As I pack my things for the journey ahead, I hear a commotion outside my cabin. It's a typical affair, so I brush it off. I have a pretty good record of taxes collected. One of the best among my peers, and I intend to keep it that way. Only one of my brethren has a better rate than me, but I'm not hungry enough to want to pass him. Likely, he doesn't even leave his quarters in the capital. He could stay there and never pass through the double padlocked doors for his whole life, and it would not bother him. But me, I'm all about personal growth, and part of that is to really stretch these legs and get out there.

The sounds outside grow louder and more intense. The Crown likes to see that I have an escort. I used to think it was because he didn't trust us, but now I know it's a gift. For doing all the collection for him. For keeping him in the Crown.

There's screaming and a howl coming from one voice now. It seems my guard has been selected. I don't know why they're so upset. It's an honor to travel with me. Did I mention they won't have to file taxes for five seasons? Yet they're carrying on like a newborn babe.

Gah, that's not proper. I take a deep breath to cleanse myself of any ill thoughts I might have let fester into preconceived notions of my travel companion. I take one more deep breath for good measure. It would make me a terrible person to take some silly bias with me and treat him poorly. That simply won't do. I've been told that my thoughts on this mean I have a strict moral code. I'm not sure about that, but I like the sound of it.

The man's screams are just now petering out and I hear him coughing and clearing his airway. I lean with force on the door, and it pops and slams open. I exit the cabin with a smirk and give a quick nod to Captain. He's a decent fellow. He always pays his taxes early.

Shit. Captain sees me staring, so I look away, but I've already seen his face drain of color. That's another thing. I can't look too long at anyone. I guess it gives them the creeps. I focus on my escort, who I notice is a satyr. He's being held up by his elbows by two of his comrades. So, he is a soldier. That's a nice feature. Always good to have someone with discipline. It's quiet for a moment and we all stand there, taking a moment of silence. It seems like they're waiting for me to say something, so I clear my throat and speak to the group of them.

"Well, onward and upward, eh? If we're all about ready, I'd like to leave momentarily." I put on my best, wide-stretched smile. The one that shows just the tips of my teeth. I find this most reassuring.

Captain nods and faces the guard. He steps closer and I turn away. I don't need to see this part. The satyr screams. Gah, I need him to have enough energy to make it at least to the first town. He can lose the voice, but those legs need to stay primed.

Captain finishes the Bonding and now that the guard can't leave my side... give or take a few yards, of course... It's time to travel! It'll only take a few hours and then we'll stop for the first collection. I'll let the satyr gentleman sleep and then we'll start again.

I must finish collecting before the season ends and I'm not one to risk not getting the job done. Not doing so would risk an audit. The last thing I need is Him poking around and asking detailed questions about my work. No, thank you.

I used to request a mule or horse for my guard to help through this adjustment period, but sometimes, their steed would startle and run off with my guard. They'd get more than a few yards... and, well, the horse would eventually return or be found covered in viscera and scorch marks. Or sometimes the horse would end up being a little Brighter than it should be and would try all sorts of ways to interfere with my tax collection. I can't have that, so I'd have to put it down, sell it, or eat it, and all that time add up.

So, the guard will have to manage. He trails behind me, but of course not too far. They usually act like this. They judge how close they can get without their initial revulsion of me sending them into a panic and how far they can get before the Binding begins to burn its eager warning of pending immolation.

Our first stop is in the next town. After a few hours of walking, the satyr finally stopped sobbing, and now only echoes of him clearing his snot-filled sinuses reach my ears. I'll attempt to talk to him a little later. I haven't yet yearned for companionship, and I'm also not yet hungry.

Fields and fields of dandelions greet us first. The town's main export, and I admit, I love to see them. I'm thankful they have already started turning from that sickening yellow petal nonsense to delicate skeletal husks. It makes coming to this town first a special little treat just for me. If I arrived too late or started at the other side of my route, they'd already be harvested, bagged, and sent on their way to spell reagent shops.

I run the man's name through my mind as I smooth the tongue over my teeth. This is his first violation. A nice, easy collection to start with. We'll collect first and then check into a lodge. I will give the guard time to process and more time for me to eat. I'm not hungry yet but will be soon, and no one likes to work on an empty stomach.

The man, Elias Reed, lives in a modest single building, noted on past taxes, and keeps up the yard and outside very well. I look behind me to my companion before knocking and see him wringing his hands. His eyes are full of sorrow, and he refuses to look up at me and meet my gaze. That's fine with me. I don't need his gaze to do my job, but he needs to learn to keep watch.

I knock and there's a shuffle inside and some hushed voices. A small elvish child peeks through the curtains and stares at me with curiosity. I smile and wave my fingers at it. The child laughs and climbs down. The door creaks open and there's Elias. He's tall even for an elf of this region and I notice worry on his face, the dark circles, the skin that was loose from skipping too many meals. His child... children look still well, and I watch them run to his side. He smirks quickly to be polite and backs away, holding the door open.

"Ah, yes, please come in. Welcome to our home." Elias's voice cracks.

I smile broadly, maybe a bit too wide since the children's eyes widen when I do; I adjust it again and they ease back to their carefree auras. It's always exciting for me to see the inside of someone's home. It's fascinating. What trinkets do they display, do they keep up the interior or do they have other priorities? I never hold anything against anyone; there's no judgment for that in my eyes.

"Thank you, Mr. Reed. Such a pleasure to be invited in. And hello to you, Dario and Selicio." I smile again. I know them from them being claimed on previous taxes. They beam at me, and Mr. Reed grins as he looks down at them. See, it pays to pay attention and memorize these things ahead of time. It's important. It's not just about money and taxes. It's about people at the end of the day.

We exchange the usual pleasantries, and we are offered some tea. I usually abstain. I don't want to take up too much of their time and I want to mind that not everyone has food or drink to spare. Also, I hate to dirty a dish because that means even after I leave, there is yet another task my host must complete. It isn't just about washing a dish; it is about the time they must devote to it. They should be spending that time doing what they wish, not more labor and unpaid at that.

There's always a pause in the conversation when you can tell that everyone is ready for business. My guard, who took the tea but now just holds it as best he can while balancing on a child's stool, seems like he's on the verge of being sick at any moment. He'll learn to swallow that feeling soon enough. I look back towards Mr. Reed and dig out of my pocket a silver dunspiece. "Perhaps the children wouldn't mind fetching me a bushel of those fine dandelions while we talk?"

There's a sense of relief that passes across the man's face and he nods to me, "Yes, would you boys please get our fine Collector some from the Dapplewoods?"

Eager to please, the boys nearly trip over one another before accepting the coin and running out of the home. The door's left open and I clear my throat to my guard, who amply stands and closes it softly. He places the teacup on the table and threads his fingers together. Clearly, he has no idea what he is to do at this moment.

"Mr. Reed, I believe you are aware I'm here for collecting and it has come to my attention that your taxes for this season have not been sent. I wish to confirm that this is correct information."

"It is, sir." The air is tense.

"Oh, no sirs, quite fine with just Collector." I smile again, careful to keep it at an appropriate size. "Now, we recognize this is the first time you've not sent. Two seasons ago you applied and received aid while last season you paid in full... was there a reason you did not apply for aid this year?"

"No, it just got away from me. I was saving up to pay as I didn't think I'd need aid, but then I had an incident that required the savings...." He's about to explain more, but I do not need to hear it. It's none of my business and I have no right to know anyone's reasons. They do not owe that to me.

"I see. This happens from time to time, Mr. Reed." I smile again. I bring my bag out and open my tax tome with its creaky spine. I keep the leather well moisturized and oiled, but it's so old and so full that it still groans when laid open.

My records indicate a rather large amount was due. He must have had a good season, but of course not good enough to make up for what had happened.

The elf stands quietly and looks around his home, eyes settling on the various pictures his children have drawn and on the signs of the life of a family well loved. This is when I notice two matching satchels packed and waiting near the front door.

"My sister will be here in the morning to get them..." He looks wrought, but ready. The poor dear has overestimated his tax collection.

"Mr. Reed..."

"Then I have paperwork ready to be sent in about everything else..." He turns and gazes around the room, not hearing me.

"Mr. Reed." I smile gently. "If you could just take a seat, I'll collect and then get out of your hair."

Reed is confused, but he takes his seat, nervously picks at a hangnail, and waits for me to continue. "Mr. Collector, sir, what do you mean?"

"Well, Mr. Reed, I suggest you not send any of those papers in, and as far as your sister goes... I cannot say if you should dismiss her visit, but I wouldn't want you to miss it." I reach my hand out to him, which he gingerly takes as tears fill his eyes and cascade down his face. He squeezes my hand and nods quietly. I squeeze his hand back, but don't release it. "Let's get started then, mmm?"

The children are oh so polite. They knock before entering, in their own home now, mind you. How sweet is it for them to wait until our business finishes? My guard, only slightly greenish on the edges, opens the door. The children hurriedly deposit my requested dandelions and begin to hand me the change.

I shake my head and hand my satchel to the guard. "The rest is a tip for such great service. Thank you, Dario and Selicio. I appreciate your hard work and attention to detail." Their eyes go wide, for it is likely they have never seen this much coin in person, let alone as change. It is important to tip. Service is work, and it is not a game. A person's time should be worth the world; egos and stinginess should not cheapen their work.

He drops to his knees and holds them with one arm while keeping the other behind his back. I duck my head and usher the guard out of the home. We don't need to stay any longer. I have finished my business here and, as my stomach growls, I put the money into my bag.

The sight of the children has touched the guard and doesn't hear my stomach rumbling, but he'll have to address it soon enough. I'll allow the time to be after we check into our room.

After a few days of travel, the guard seems to have found a way to ground himself. There are no sniffles and no sobs. With each stop, I see his training as he stands closer to me and more protective. He keeps to himself mostly. I think that perhaps he'll make it out of this tax season yet.

A few days later, past the halfway mark of collecting, we come to a rather imposing home. People are bustling to and fro and there seems to be a rather large party planned, as there are people in various states of dress. Nonetheless, we approach, and I knock, knock, knock.

The door opens and I see the manor's butler holding a large vase overstuffed with fresh blooms. He sees me and pales, but only for a moment. He stands aside and invites us in. As we wait in the foyer, the Guard shuffles nervously and speaks to me for the first time outside of our time in lodging.

"Seems an odd time for a shindig... you know, considering the season and all." His awareness is impressive.

"Mmmm, yes, I agree. But the world must continue on. Life is more than death and taxes, yes?" At the balcony, I see the very person we are here to visit, a human man named Latving Dunhimier.

He's dressed in rather expensive taste and as he descends the stairs, I can smell the tartness of a freshly dressed wound. I narrow down at one of his hands and see a finger missing, his left pinky, and I count the stitches out of habit.

He seems very joyous—so much so that it's infectious and I, too, begin to match his laissez-faire attitude when exchanging pleasantries. I notice my guard hasn't shaken the man's hand and keeps a stony expression. He's learning well. I'll have to make a report to honor such behavior when I return at the end of the season.

"Mr. Dunhimier, should we find a place to have a private conversation?" As I say this, I dodge out of the way of several staff who are bustling around.

"No bother, I can do that all from right here." He puts on an impressive grin, and I do my best to replicate it. I mirror it and make minor adjustments in real time. It's a good smile. It feels large... welcoming.

"Very well; according to my records," I pull out my tome and the man interrupts with a snap of his fingers for a staffer to appear. The aide hands him a jar and the lord whisks the man away with a flourished hand.

"Yes, yes... and here you go. Your collection." He holds out the jar to me and floating in it is a severed finger. It is the left pinky he is missing.

I don't take the jar and my guard doesn't move to take it either. Good on him. "Mr. Dunhimier, I have not issued that collection..."

"Yes, well, my brother-in-law Elias Reed owes more than I, and you took his finger, so I went ahead and had it removed early for you. I know you are one for efficiency."

If I could still feel the heat rise in my cheeks, this would be the moment. But I do seethe with anger. "Mr. Reed's business is confidential and although I appreciate... your admiration for efficiency, this is neither efficient nor appropriate."

The lord looks confused, and he palms the jar to the other hand before wincing, clearly already forgetting the missing finger. "He owed more than I; how can you say that this isn't sufficient?"

"Quite easily. Listen, I'll say it slower. This. Isn't. Sufficient. For your amount, I require more, Mr. Dunhimier. Mr. Reed paid his in good faith and you must realize..." I glance around all the extravagance and gaudy decorations. "...this is less than your fair share."

He begins to stutter, and his face loses its warmth as the color drains from his face. He looks back and forth between me and the guard. He drops the jar on the ground before sprinting up the stairs.

I sigh and jut my head in Mr. Dunhimier's direction, to which my guard starts off, easily taking two stairs at a time. As I hear doors slamming, Dr. Dunhimier yelling and the sounds of a struggle, I spend my time picking up the glass shards and the remains of the finger. It has popped under the weight of my guard's heavy, lumbering chase of a step.

The butler appears again, and I greet him warmly by name. He already has a bag ready to collect the shards and I place them all gently within. I thank him for his attentiveness with a dunspiece coin, and I wait for him to leave before I take a pinch of dandelion seeds and cast a cleansing spell. No need to waste someone's time cleaning up. Although Mr. Dunhimier's mistake, it was still a result of my visit.

I hear the ruckus has stilled, so I climb the stairs.

Guard shoulders my collection bag as we walk off the property and he has a spring to his step. He must have been able to let out some pent-up aggression, and if this was spent safely and appropriately, it was fine with me. He must also be pleased not to have to serve me up dinner tonight since our tax collection has been so significant.

We have one last stop. One I admit I have been putting off. The man owes back taxes and I'm ashamed to say I haven't been able to collect. It's time for another try. It will take some time to get there. So much in fact that I forestay my decision to walk and take a carriage. I'll write the cost off as an expense, but that doesn't make me feel any better.

Our carriage ride is decent, and no one seems to want to share it with us, so my guard and I are the single occupants the entire way. I pay the driver extra to drop us off further back so we can stretch our legs and discuss this last stop. Guard struggles to get off the carriage with only one arm now, but he takes my offered hand and leaps down. He motions a thank you and I nod back. The ride was too long, and I grew hungry. We don't have enough collections in my bag to keep me sated.

The large castle is looming in the distance. It mocks me. The elf inside has warded against me and my means. But if I can just wrap up this season with this collection, it will be good luck to bring in the next. I've been forgetting to blink and am only reminded to do so when yet another fly skitters across my eye. They've been more insistent lately and blinking is a must to keep them out of my vision, but this damn castle distracts me so.

I break my pattern of keeping tax information to myself as I say aloud the details of Sergio's situation. My guard dips his head at the appropriate places but doesn't comment. He's so good at this. I'm going to miss him when this season is over. As I begin to list the dependents listed in his file, I pause and repeat them. Sergio married a few years ago and his wife had paid her taxes early. However, perhaps there is an in; last year there was a birth declared in the local doctor's population reports. It seems Sergio and his wife have welcomed a new dependent. How fascinating.

We walk with renewed strength and a vigor that I was not expecting one day ago. I walk through the surrounding village... which Sergio has not bothered to ward. They are all well kept up on their taxes, most even pay early and receive reimbursement. It speaks of Sergio's character that he hides in his castle day and night, takes dues from those around him, but does not give back.

I ask around and tip regardless of getting the answer I want, and finally a little birdy tells me about a kitchen door of the keep. It's warded of course, but I can get up to it. I dare not touch the handle and I advise my guard not to, either. These wards also accompany those with a Binding mark, and I'd hate to have something happen to Guard on the job. I knock and call for help. I know the lord won't answer, but I request his wife by name.

The kitchen staff halts. They want to comply, but they stall out of loyalty. I insist it is only words that I would like with her and one of them breaks rank. It is a reasonable amount of time considering the size of the keep before a soft, unsettled voice beseeches me.

"Ah, Lady Greenshadow. I'd like to discuss the issue of your husband's taxes." I speak calmly and reassuringly.

"I file separately, Collector, and I'm sure I am paid in full. His taxes are not mine." She practiced this line, I can tell, but there is no strength in her voice.

"I am aware, and I thank you, but I wanted to let you know of another facet of my occupation. I not only collect, but I also inform." I dangle the thought.

"And what is it you wish to inform me of?" She's curious.

"Your offspring with Sergio." I'm careful in my word choice.

"She is a child, and she owes no taxes, dependent or otherwise." There's her strength.

"This is true, but if you'd entertain an old soul like me with a scenario..."

"...Go on, Collector."

"Your husband has not paid his taxes... in some time, and I note that you have paid yours and are not responsible for his... but I also know that keeping within these castle walls has likely not done well for your husband's health."

She says nothing, so I continue.

"And should his health fail him..." I stifled a cough. My throat is raw, and it stretches too much, causing gaps within the lining. "Any debts owed to the Crown upon one's death are not forgiven but transferred..."

We speak this part together. "....to the next of kin."

"That, legally speaking, is your child. Although your child will not owe taxes regardless until adulthood, there will be a significant accruement of interest and back-taxes on that account."

There's a pause, and for a moment I hear nothing, but then I smell her. Her skin, hair, and the blood circulating her right down to the capillaries and their glorious exchange. That gives me the warm and fuzzies just thinking about it.

The door unlocks and creaks open. The sigils on the ground are tarnished with dark lines of coal and cracked portions of runes, hinting at a history of wear and neglect. I was too distracted by her blood to hear the commotion she must have caused.

I nod my head to her and she gives me a slight one back, but keeps her chin high.

"Thank you, Lady Greenshadow, you do me, the Crown, and yours a great kindness. I shall speak with the Crown about a familial tax break..."

Guard enters behind me and refuses to look at her. He's focused on his mission and not looking at her seems like an unspoken promise that he sees nothing, hears nothing.

I bustle inside and know my way. Building plans are sent in for approval and I have obsessed about this keep. I've thought about all the ways I could enter.

He'd likely be in his study. I can smell the sweetness of a body uncared for. I also take note it is indeed far from the sour smell of a child's breaths. Hopefully this collection will do better for the mother and child than simply leveling their accounts.

I stop at the doorway. I'm usually silent when moving, but the sloshing of skin and entrails barely held within my skin gives its own noise. Perhaps the guard's steel greaves lend more sound than I do, but whatever the case, it's enough, and Sergio stands from his desk. His face. He knows. It's time. He doesn't run, and I give him that. If only it were sooner.

His eyes flood and drip and I'm finding my stomach growling. He is frozen in place, so I sit at a chair pulled up near his desk. He can take his time unlocking from fear. The tax season ends tonight, but I'll give him until the moon casts no shadow.

He releases and cries out for me; he throws himself to the floor and grovels at my feet. I'm barely listening to his offers of money (more than he owes, by the way) and I would roll my eyes if not for the fear they'll loosen from the sockets and land on the ground. He offers more. His staff, his wife, his child, everything. But it's time for me to collect. It would have been easy to prevent this entire situation. As he cries, burying his face into my robe, seeking comfort. He's laid his head on my lap and I stroke his hair, tucking it behind his ear, careful to avoid snagging the crescent moon earring there.

I nod to Guard, who closes the door for me, and I rub Sergio's back a bit. It's always tough for the elves. They live such a long life and it's clear Sergio wants to live longer, forever even. "Sergio, Sergio. I could perhaps offer you a tax break. One substantial enough where your accounts would be cleared up and," I chuckle, but it comes out more of a death rattle, "even cover some seasons after."

He stills under my attention and snorts to control the phlegm invading his face. "Really? You'd do that for me? You'd give me time to figure it out?" He's beginning to smile.

"Yes, yes. Of course, I would. I can offer this tax break only once every century or so and it's about time."

He goes to sit up, to thank me I think, but I hold his head against my lap, his cheek pressing into my leg, and I stroke his hair again, adjusting it around that damn earring again.

I close the kitchen door behind me, and I stride quickly through the town, which is quieter than ever, and look up to the glorious moon.

"Does it look closer? Does it look bigger?" I say this aloud to Guard and forget he's not here. He almost made it through the season. I say it a few times in my mind, so I don't forget again, and I adjust my blond, flowing hair. It catches on the earring and my fingers fly up to it and snap it off. I put it in my tax collection bag. The hole will close in some time.

I find myself walking too fast and I have to slow down. This body has its issues, that's for sure, but it still has so much elasticity. This is a body that will aid in so much work. This is a body that remembers to blink. It's a well-fed body, thanks to Guard, and I'll have more than enough energy to get back to the Crown. I find my lips whistling softly.

This next tax season is going to be a good one, I just know it. But don't worry, you'll all be fine as long as you remember your fair share.

AQUARIUS

Underwater
-AP Vrdoljak-

Beneath the air
Where giants sing,
In hidden worlds
'For time's begin.

Where the light doesn't shine,
Where our world doesn't exist,
Where dust settles among claws,
Where our curiosity can't resist.

What swims, what crawls,
What waits and stings,
And grabs and feeds,
You'll never know such things.

Unclose your eyes
And keep in your breath.
We move like ghosts
Within the depth.

PALE SISTER
- Skye Myers -

"Wow. Juliet Jacobs."

Shit. I sigh, and disappointment makes my shoulders droop. So close. I almost made it through the entirety of the wedding without being caught in the awkward hell that is small talk. If only I hadn't gone back to grab that bottle of wine I'd spied during the bride and groom's first dance...

"Hello," I say, shoving the bottle into my purse before turning around. I wave and hate myself for it.

"I did *not* expect to see you back here." The woman before me is my age, plump and excited and dressed in an unflattering fuchsia pantsuit. She smiles like she knows me, like we're old friends. I have no idea who she is. The only thing I can focus on is the smear of pearly pink lipstick on her slightly crooked front tooth. I twitch my mouth in a grimace of a smile.

"You and me both," I mutter, and try to keep my face from showing the mounting desperation I feel as my eyes dart around the stuffy hall. In the corners and empty spaces, shadows cling, trapped by the twinkling lights and paper lanterns that fill the room. Even though we have tried to improve ventilation by propping open the front and side doors, it has made no difference. I take a deep breath of the thick, moist air and tug at the suddenly constricting collar of my shirt. I hate finding myself alone like this. Where the hell is—

"Was that your little band? Lovely that you're still playing folk music. And that voice of yours. Truly a siren." The woman lets out a bray that reminds me of Goofy's laugh, *ah-hyuck*! She smells of beer and pickled onions. "I'm surprised you came back so soon after your sister...Anyway. I'm sure Mallory appreciates you being here." She splays a small, puffy hand across her chest. "The ties of friendship are so strong."

I make an effort to avoid rolling my eyes, even though she is partly right. There are many reasons for my being back in Harthwaite, the most relevant being that the band was taking a hiatus, and Mallory and her new husband, Nigel, had asked for the privilege of being our last show. Despite everything, it still feels like being stabbed slowly in the guts with a letter opener.

"Where are your bandmates?" the lady is asking, and I slam back into the present, into this cringe-worthy conversation.

"Where indeed," I say, and offer her another tight smile I hope isn't as awkward as it feels. "If you'll excuse me." I grab a flute of champagne from a passing caterer and duck away. Determined not to get caught like that again, I gulp the bubbly elixir and avoid eye contact as I weave my way around the maze of tables and chairs in search of—

There you are. I find them near the coat check, standing too close together, tucked into the shadows with their heads bowed toward each other. Conveniently, I'm partially hidden behind the velvet curtain partitioning the main hall from the front entryway. Her hair is unbound and tumbles like gold over her shoulders. He is just reaching to touch a strand when they seem to sense me and disentangle. I leave the empty flute behind and stumble forward.

"Juliet! There you are! Where have you *been*?" Jovie cries, and bounds over like a retriever. I stare at Sawyer as I walk past, catch the panic that crosses his face before he cranks up the wattage of his smile. He follows after us.

Outside it is the indigo blue of near-dark and damp, but blessedly cool. I forgot how quiet small towns are after 8 p.m. The street seems deserted, with the mild, warm glow of the streetlights and the mostly dark surrounding houses.

"Oh, hon, before I forget, the bride was looking for you," Sawyer says, and kisses my cheek when we stop. My eyes sweep over him, take in his tousled, ashy hair and fox-like features. He reeks of Belmont cigarettes and Jovie's perfume and I feel my stomach hollow out. His shoes are far too pointy.

"The bride?" I pull away from him, frowning, and bump into Jovie, as usual, oblivious to personal space. She grins at me and lights the joint she has pulled from her purse. She takes a toke before passing it to Sawyer. I can't tear my eyes away from the strand of long, straw-coloured hair clinging to the front of his shirt.

"And here she is," he says, voice heavy with smoke, and he hurriedly passes the joint back to Jovie. He exhales out the side of his mouth, waving the vapour away as if afraid of being caught. His Prince Charming smile is in place when he looks past me. I turn around.

"Mallory, hey." Seeing her turns my brain into a bag full of tumbled stones, my tongue into a glue trap. "You were so beautiful, during…" Words escape me, and I motion toward the hall. I watch as Jovie offers her the joint. Mallory takes a drag and lays a cool hand on my arm.

"I'm glad you could make it." Smoke leaks from her nostrils like ectoplasm, spilling drowsily from her mouth when she speaks. "You sounded downright haunting on stage." Her eyes flit to Jovie, over to Sawyer, and back to me. "You all did." She offers me the joint and I take it. The filter feels moist and acrid against my lips, so I take a deep breath in.

Despite not changing much, there's something about her now that makes her almost unrecognizable. Lost whatever puppy fat she had and so is less linebacker, more European model. Her raw, dark eyes and milky skin were accentuated by the way her wavy, shoulder-length ebon bob and blunt bangs framed her face. She wears a leather jacket over her garnet red after-party dress.

I meet her gaze and take another slow toke. The smoke is thick and spicy, and I half-close my eyes. One side of her mouth hitches into a smile, and Mallory reaches for the joint. Our fingers brush when I pass it back and I watch her put it to her lips. I wonder if she can she taste me.

"Juliet's told me so much about you," Jovie butts in, stepping forward. She goes to slide her arm through mine and I press my elbow against my ribs so she can't. I imagine I can feel the heat from Sawyer's hands on her. Is the small patch of red rash on her neck from the cheap metal of her necklace, or is it whisker burn from Sawyer's beard? Jovie beams. "It feels like all of us are already friends."

I grimace. She means well, but that self-involved obliviousness gets old quickly. Mallory's gaze once again sweeps over Jovie, taking in her gently crooked incisors, the tie-dye t-shirt that has *Aquarius* written across the front in pink rhinestones, her bitten fingernails that are painted highlighter yellow, and then slides to Sawyer and his ridiculous shoes—to the strand of hair still clinging to his shirt—before coming back to me. I want to turn away from her clairvoyant eyes, but I don't.

"Mmm," Mallory hums, and turns back to Jovie. "January or February?"

Jovie frowns. We all frown.

"Your shirt." Mallory's hands are graceful birds as she accepts the joint once more, inhales its essence, passes it back.

"Oh! Uh. January."

"February, myself." A smile touches Mallory's lips and she says, "*Water bearers*. Almost like we have a duty to protect our more fragile comrades, in our way. Right? Like a ribcage is to the heart." She glances at me before turning. "Sawyer. I've heard some things." She raises her brows a fraction. "Is it your first time visiting Harthwaite?"

"Yeah." Sawyer clears his throat but makes sure to keep a broad smile plastered on. "I knew someone who was from here, though. It seems like a nice place."

"Indeed." Mallory turns back to me. "I thought we could go for a little jaunt on the lake. Like old times."

I blink at her. "What?" I know perfectly well what she said. I'm just panicking inside. I stuff my hands in my pockets.

"Oh, fun!" Jovie grins and looks between me and Sawyer. "Let's go!"

Sawyer's smile finally falters. "Like…on a boat?"

"Yes. It's a big lake, but we would likely be some of the only ones out there at this hour. It's optimal stargazing, and there will be fireworks. What do you think?" Mallory asks us. I forgot how intense she could be, with her low voice and big, unblinking eyes.

Jovie claps excitedly. Usually I find her easy joy endearing, but at other times, like just then, it makes me grind my teeth.

"You don't want to go out there with your husband, just the two of you?" Sawyer rubs the back of his neck, not bothering to hide his discomfort. I let him squirm. "I mean, you just got married…We wouldn't want to impose on your first night as a married couple."

"You can't swim, I take it." Mallory casts him a wry smile and heartily claps him on the back. He jumps in surprise. "Nigel's getting a migraine and has gone to lie down, unfortunately. A common occurrence. But not to worry, we've got water wings on the boat." A lie. I'll be surprised if she even has life jackets.

High as fuck, I shrug, watching as my anxiety flutters away on wings fashioned from smoke. "I'm in."

***

The boat, larger than I remember, floats gracefully on the water, guided by Mallory, who proves to be an amiable captain. All of us are quiet on the ride out, tucked in the cockpit, and I duck my head against the wind as we fly smoothly over the water. It doesn't take long before Mallory cuts the engine. We coast to a stop at the mouth of a small inlet—*the* inlet, *ours*, where Mallory, Emry, myself, and a few others would spend summer afternoons after school, lazing around like cats on the anchored dock—and I raise my eyebrows at her. She pretends not to see me as she flips a switch and poison green strip lights come to life along the outer edge of the deck, just below the gunwale. Jovie makes a sound of delight.

"Here," I say, pulling the stolen wine from my bag. I take a swig and then pass it to Sawyer, who mutters "Cheers" before gulping greedily from the bottle. I watch as he passes it to Jovie. The liquor sours in my stomach when his fingers brush hers.

The inlet is exactly as I remember, bracketed by rushes, cattails, and purple loosestrife. Red maple, oak, and willow trees, which make it just that much more private, cradled it. The lake is empty and still, and both the water and the sky sparkle as though millions of tiny diamonds have been spilled across their surfaces. But down here, beneath the calm metallic façade, that water is *black*, yawning and hungry as any cavernous mouth, and I've never been one for it. The idea of what could hide down in the depths knots my stomach with dread. I focus on the moon, waxing gibbous from her perch above; on Mallory, whose eyes finally find mine.

On one side of me, Sawyer bobs his head and drums his fingers against his seat to the beat of the jazz song that's playing softly. I pretend not to notice the way he glances at Jovie, who sits across from me. Her head is tilted back, hair spilled over her shoulders. In a bad English accent, she begins to name the constellations.

I reach across and take the stolen wine from her. There's only a few swallows left, so I drink deeply, letting the sweet elixir flood my mouth and warm my belly.

"How long have you been seeing each other?" Mallory asks no one in particular. Her eyes glitter. It's bait, that question, and she'll have made up a rule like *whoever bites first has the most to hid*e. I look away.

"Oh, what's it been, babe?" Sawyer says to me as he reaches for my hand. "Almost a year—"

"I meant you two, actually." Mallory raises her eyebrows as she looks pointedly between he and Jovie.

"Oh, no. We're not—" They offer differently worded objections in the same hurried, desperate tones. Something out on the lake makes a sad, eerie cry, similar to a loon.

"Oh. My eyes must have deceived me." Mallory is so convincing, I can't tell if she's being sarcastic. My cheeks blaze with second-hand embarrassment anyway and I stare at the empty bottle in my hands.

She turns to Sawyer. "Do you know what lake this is?"

"What...lake?" Thrown by the sudden turn in conversation, Sawyer frowns. "No. I mean—"

"Surely Juliet has told you about her sister." Mallory's gaze does not waver from my unfortunate companion. Another cry pierces the night, closer now. The hair on the back of my neck prickles. *Bit late in the season for loons*, I catch myself thinking, as their haunting calls echo closer to the shore.

"What?" Sawyer's brow furrows. I can practically hear the gears in his head, sluggish from the pot and the wine, attempting to catch up. Jovie pulls her denim jacket tighter around herself but says nothing. I stand and make my way carefully over to the stern. The obsidian water laps at the hull, asking for entry, and I shiver.

"The one who disappeared last year?" Mallory taps her temple. "Ringing any bells?"

"Oh," he says. "*Oh*." I glance at him, see that Sawyer's mouth has fallen open. I turn back to the water, but I can feel the weight of his eyes on me. "Oh, my god. Babe. That…that wasn't *this* lake?"

Something splashes a few feet away and I flinch, startled. That sounded big. I squint, scanning the murky surface of the lake, but all seems calm.

"What was that?" Sawyer asks. I shake my head. He rises to his feet and takes hesitant steps to join me at the stern. We peer into the water just as something glides past, slightly breaking the surface.

"That was huge," Sawyer blurts. His Adam's apple bobs as he swallows. "Probably just a gator." He grips the seat behind him to steady himself, knuckles white. His eyes meet mine and I see that he's afraid. "Right?"

I can't help but wince. *When your teeth are the brightest thing about you.*

"A gator." We turn at the sound of a tongue clucking to face Mallory, who stands port side. She haughtily raises her brows and we see that she, at least, does not share our fear. "Is that what you think you saw?"

"No gators in Canada," Jovie provides with a smirk.

Confusion flickers over Sawyer's features just before something hits the side of the boat hard enough to make it sway. I gasp. My heart stutters in my chest, uncertain whether to settle on panic or confusion, and I find myself wishing for a life jacket.

"What the *hell* was that?" Jovie cries, leaping to her feet. She stumbles closer, wild-eyed. The breeze rustles her hair, parts her jacket.

Sawyer reaches for me. I pull away from him just as something hits the boat again. It knocks me off balance, and with a surprised yelp, I topple backwards. I hear Jovie scream my name just before I hit the water, and then all sound is muffled as I am swallowed by the lake.

The cold shocks me, and I force my eyes open as I sink into those murky depths. Mallory must have turned on the underwater boat lights; the water is suddenly magenta for a good six feet around. I violently flutter my limbs, but my jacket is too heavy and drags me down. I struggle out of the garment with my lungs threatening to collapse as a sudden primal fear grips me.

There comes a low moan, followed by a series of clicks, and something big swims by above me, interrupting the boat's light like a cloud drifting in front of the sun. I freeze when I catch a glimpse of a thick, pallid tail before it glides out of sight. The rest of my air escapes in a bubbly wail as I let go of my jacket, kicking and thrashing my way to the surface.

"Juliet! Juliet! Oh, my god!" Jovie cries as I gasp and cough and gulp air. How did I get so far away from the boat? The twelve or so feet I'll have to swim may as well be a thousand. Sawyer stands with his arm around Jovie's waist, holding her back.

"Mallory," I choke out, splashing like an animal in its death throes, desperate to keep my head above the surface. I know my panic will drown me as fast as anything, but I can't quiet it. "There's something in—"

I feel the current as that something swims past me. It bumps my leg and I launch myself toward the boat. Over the turbulence of my frenzied splashing, I hear my companions calling to me. Fear makes their voices high and shrill, and I cling to the sound like it is a lifeline. I am almost to the boat when what feels like a hand wrap around my ankle and pulls me back down.

I scream until my lungs burn. The grip releases me, but I am too stunned to swim to the surface. I wrench my eyes open. Through the cloudy water I see a long, waxen mass of lithe muscle, glimpse unblinking eyes that are liquid-dark, a mouth crammed full of jagged teeth, red hair.

Like Ariel, I think wildly as the creature glides into the black water, out of view. From the darkness, the hand of a woman reaches toward me, but it's wrong. The skin is corpse-pale, the nails more like talons, long and tapered. A translucent membrane connects the fingers. But what really makes my heart nearly leap into my mouth is seeing that small, familiar black heart tattoo on her pointer finger.

The burning in my lungs intensifies, and I kick my legs, making for the surface once more. The magenta lighting is a blessing and a curse, showing me that there isn't just one toothy swimmer in the water with me, but three. I know that it's not that they can't get hold of me again, it's merely that they don't want to. The knowledge doesn't provide any comfort.

When I break the surface, I hear Jovie cry, "Come on, grab my hand!" She and Mallory are braced and ready. I blindly reach upward, eyes blurry. Hands grab me from above, wrapping around my upper arms, and I nearly sob in relief. They haul me out of the lake and I am dumped unceremoniously on deck. Sawyer, who had been cowering near the console, steps toward me. I roll to my stomach and cough up lake water onto his elf shoes.

"Not this." I push the words through the tightness in my chest and sit up. My teeth chatter. Jovie drapes her jacket over my shoulders and I stare at Mallory, who leans against one of the seats with her arms crossed. "I didn't want this for her."

"I know," Mallory says softly. Her voice echoes my own sadness, and my eyes fill. Now that I am out of the water, it is grief that threatens to drown me.

"Have you all lost your goddamn minds?" Sawyer snaps, voice nasally and serrated. He jabs a finger toward the water. "What the hell are those things?"

The three of us turn as one to look at him, and my lip curls. I appreciate the heat that accompanies the fury rising in me as I take him in. It envelopes, pushes away the sorrow, replaces it with red-hot titanium. I notice Jovie's strand of hair still clings to the front of his shirt and I dash my tears away. We're not finished.

None of us speak. The boat rocks gently, soothingly, as if nothing has happened. Soft jazz is still gently playing from the radio. Shaking, I lean against Jovie, and she rubs my back. The breeze carries the sweet smell of rotting autumn vegetation. A cry like the one from earlier pierces the quiet. It's close and somehow sounds impatient.

"*Seriously*," Sawyer practically yells. His lips are red and wet and he pants. Swiping at the string of snot that hangs from his nose, he looks back at the water. "What the *fuck*—"

"Undines," Mallory says simply.

Jovie makes a small sound of surprise. "*Those* are undines?" Her gaze is more owl-like than usual when she looks at me. I nod once, squeezing her hand. There is a pause as the music changes to a more upbeat tune.

Sawyer motions with his hands, jerky and impatient. "*Well*? What are undines?" He glowers at me with narrowed eyes. His fear has stolen his tolerance, and I almost like him better this way, prickly and stripped of his oily charm. At least it's honest.

"Shh. It's all right," Mallory croons, taking slow steps toward him. She gently touches his arm, and he softens. He is spellbound by her, by the situation. "You'll see. I know they seem scary, but they won't hurt us. Look." She smiles, looking toward the water, and Sawyer peeks over the side of the boat. "They're dancing."

I can't see from where I'm sitting, but I can imagine the creatures swimming and circling beneath that garish light, their long, alabaster bodies, movements as smooth and fluid as the water they glide through.

"Yeah, right." Sawyer licks his lips again. Shifts his weight uneasily. Looks back at me, as if I'm the danger, before his gaze moves to the water once more. "I saw those teeth."

"Nigel and I have been feeding them. They're strange and lovely creatures, very shy. Be brave and you can hear them singing," Mallory says. The wind flirts with her hair, lifts it to show a glimpse of her diamond drop earrings. She offers him an encouraging smile. "Get closer to the water."

"For real?" Sawyer glances at her, brows furrowed, and I imagine the dull ache of the railing pressing into his hip bones as he obeys. "I don't hear anything."

Putting a hand on his back, Mallory urges, "You have to get *closer*."

Sawyer swallows hard and leans even farther forward. His nose must be grazing the water by now.

"There, I hear it!" He sucks in a breath. "That's not…You call *that* singing? They sound like they're in pain." His back muscles flex, but still, he leans.

"They're hungry." Mallory steps away from him.

"Hey, I think they're getting closer," Sawyer says excitedly. He grips the railing. "You sure they won't hurt us?"

"Oh, no, sweetheart," Mallory says, looking over at Jovie and me with a small, private smile. "I said they won't hurt *us*. I didn't mean *you*."

"What—" He lets out a squeal as something massive rises from the water before him, bloodless and glistening. Sawyer rears back, but not fast enough. Two webbed hands grab him by the head, and suddenly time seems to freeze.

She is Frankenstein's pet fish, a woman's torso attached to a scaly tail, all jutting ribs and a too-wide mouth. Her skin is so fair I can see the blue rivers of her veins. My eyes greedily take in her long, water-damaged red hair, the heart tattoo on her finger, and suddenly I feel such an intense longing it is almost painful. I miss her. I haven't seen her outside of my dreams in over a year, and I know I probably won't again, but here she is, transformed, grotesque, and as beautiful as ever.

Sawyer breathes, "Emry?"

Her onyx eyes find me and she flashes her many pointed teeth in a grin, making throaty clicks of glee, before she wraps her arms around Sawyer and pulls him overboard. The boat tips alarmingly, and the resounding splash sounds final. None of us move or make a sound. I remind myself that he is at fault for literally everything. That even if there was something I could do to lessen his suffering, I wouldn't. Satisfaction joins the rage in my heart, and I exhale.

"So *that* was your sister?" Jovie asks softly. She pulls me to my feet and we stand together at the railing. Sawyer's pleas for help harmonize with the light jazz.

I nod. "Yeah." Clear my throat, touch my neck with icy fingers. "She wasn't as…as scary, before. Had less teeth, you know?" I smile grimly.

We fall silent as Sawyer resurfaces, begging and hollering, before being pulled under again.

Jovie loops her arm through mine and rests her head on my shoulder. "She's stunning."

"Always and forever," says Mallory, joining us. "To Emry, and those who came before, and those who are still to come, inevitably." We join hands. I feel Mallory's warmth against my side. The leather of her jacket creaks.

I watch proudly as the undines play with their catch, wearing him out, letting him scream himself hoarse, filling the meat with terror so it tastes better.

"I didn't think you were serious, you know," Jovie tells me, motioning toward the water. "About the undine thing."

"I don't know that I did, either," I admit. Growing up, I'd heard the stories of how the women born in Harthwaite needed to diligently protect their hearts, lest it be broken so badly they waded into the lake and became a monster. Everyone chalked it up to a town curse, one that had supposedly gotten my mom, and then Mallory's. I'd never seen a real undine, though, so I'd always assumed the stories were just that made up.

"Who were the other two undines?" Jovie asks.

Mallory shakes her head. "Don't know."

"I can't believe Emry fell for that asshole. And how did he not know you were her sister?" Jovie grimaces. "He deserved what he got. You know that, don't you, Juliet?" She squeezes my arm.

"Absolutely," I reply. "We were estranged for years, which could explain how he didn't know. He was charming, and she always did love things quickly." I glance over the railing and shiver. The moon shines down, adding a touch of silver to the roiling pink water below us. "I don't want to be what they are. Not ever."

"We won't," Mallory says.

I pull Jovie's jacket tighter around myself and frown. "How do you know?"

"I just do." Her smile is haunted when she meets my eyes. "Can't become a monster if you never actually fall in love." The diamonds on her wedding ring proudly reflect the moon's light.

"I'm glad Emry got her retribution," Jovie says, and we all nod. Emry knew it, too, judging by that last look she'd given me. I wanted her to know we did this for her. Estranged or not, there was always love there. With a heavy heart, I choke down more tears. I feel as if the wound in the shape of my sister has been torn open again.

"Thank you. Both of you." I say. "For everything. I couldn't have done it without you." And I mean that. Shortly after Emry had given herself to the lake, Mallory had approached me and we'd hatched the plan to avenge her. Jovie, who started out as my roommate, had overheard me on the phone and wanted in on it. She'd been invaluable, and had put on a performance worthy of an Oscar, pretending to be interested so Sawyer would cheat on me with her and thus condemn himself further, talking him into taking the gig at Mallory's wedding (he'd really dug his heels in for that one, knowing Emry had grown up in Harthwaite). I couldn't express the depth of my gratitude.

"Wait," I say after a moment, quirking an eyebrow. "You didn't believe us about the undines, but you went along with everything, anyway?"

"Well, yeah. You're my best friend." Jovie grins at me and shrugs. "I thought we were just going to drown him."

We cackle like feral things and stand with our arms around each other until Sawyer is pulled under one last time. The water blossoms with blood, dark as octopus ink.

"And that's our cue." Mallory winks. "Have a seat, ladies. I have an after-party to attend." The engine starts up with a rumble and we pull away from the grisly scene, letting my sister and her companions feast in the dark. I exhale, weary but content, and let them whisk me back to the shore, my water bearers.

An Unusual Agreement
-Brianna Malotke-

the maiden ship creaked as she sailed
across the inky black waters
strong-minded and self-reliant

the gently lapping of the waves
hitting the cedar wooden sides
a soothing lullaby, mystical

the wind whistled, the saltiness
of the air lingered on her skin,
the blood had dried days ago,
embedded in every crack

sailing alone now, no other
crew to help steer, the ocean's
uncharted waters and expectant
storms would cause her trouble,
but she was free, she'd find a way

no more monsters lurking in the shadows
no more witch hunts for independent women
no more hanging trees to teach a lesson
for those all who spoke freely

most crewmen had succumbed
to the sultry tones of sirens,
the wicked mystical beauties
were all too keen to feast,

and the only logical way to
survive, was for her to
take care of the rest of the crew

a blood bath all around

no second thoughts, just a smile as she sails
freedom finally in her blood-stained hands

PISCES

THIS IS MY WEIGHT TO BEAR
-Caitlin Marceau-

Her limbs are heavy and her movements slow, as if she's sculpted out of marble, but Cordelia pushes herself forward. For a moment she considers letting the pain go but stops herself.

No, she thinks. *This is my weight to bear.*

Purple and gold lights dance and shimmer beneath her, and she peers down into the dream, hoping to catch a glimpse of what's unfolding. The child's pool of consciousness is calm, the waters composed of memories and felt emotions are mostly still, and so she lets herself rest for just a moment. She relaxes her body and sighs with relief as she lets herself drift.

Below, the dream's narrative unfolds without structure or sense. She smiles at the brightly coloured animals, the spiralling forest floors, and the nonsensical cartoon people the boy imagines. She's happy to see ripples of camellia pink and cotton candy blue emanating from the dream, a telltale sign that the boy's feeling loved and safe in his world of make-believe. She watches his dream and the gentle waves of his joy wash over her. She wishes she could stay like this forever.

Focus, she tells herself. *Carter is near.*

She pictures their face—the skin wrinkling around their green eyes when they smile, their honey-coloured hair cascading down their back, the way they laugh with their entire body—and despite her exhaustion, Cordelia forces herself to swim onwards.

Once she gets to the edge of the child's consciousness, she stops, waiting patiently for another stream to appear. After a few moments, the subconscious of an older woman beckons her, and she falls into it, inhaling sharply as the bracing cold of the emotions, dreams, and memories hit her all at once.

Although she's lived this way for centuries, Cordelia has never gotten used to travelling between minds. Everyone's consciousness is made of the same fluid thoughts, but they all feel so different from one another.

She takes a moment to adjust and notices with sadness that some of the woman's thoughts trail off in wisps of white; the memories eroded by the passage of time. Others, she notes, end in murky tendrils as her failing neurons distort happy moments into imagined nightmares. She can feel the woman's sadness and confusion as she fights to remember both her loved ones and herself.

Cordelia wishes she could take on some of the woman's pain, that she could alleviate her anxiety for even just a moment, but she knows she can't.

If she takes on any more pain than she already has, she'll sink and be lost in the woman's consciousness forever. She knows she's too heavy as it is, but she can't bear to let go of the pain she carries.

It brings her closer to Carter.

She runs a hand through the nearby current. The liquid is dark like the skin of an over-ripe plum. It smells sweet and sour.

Fear.

She lets it wash over her, the tide pushing and pulling at Cordelia's body in the woman's—Joanne's—pool of thought, but she doesn't let herself take on any of the pain. She can't afford to, not when she's so close.

Cordelia keeps swimming, each gesture made slow and laboured from the weight of the emotions she carries. Flashes of memory play around her as she propels herself forward. She lets herself get lost in them, an impossible future stretching out in front of her as she makes her way to the edge of the woman's mind.

She curls up in Carter's arms as they sit by the fire.

They hold hands, walking down a stormy pier.

Carter's lips soft against her own as they taste each other between whispered *I love you*s.

As vivid as her imagination is, she knows it's just that. Imagination.

The dream folk only exist in the recesses of people's minds.

Besides, they only have eyes for Amber *now.*

The name is bitter in her mouth, like rotten fruit, but she swallows it down anyway.

Carter's partner is tender and loving and kind and *real*.

As she waits at the edge of the old woman's mind for the new stream of consciousness to draw near, her jealousy begins to gnaw at her. She tries to imagine her arms wrapped around Carter, but she can only picture Amber's. She shakes her head and tries to recall the taste of Carter's lips, but she can only picture them pressed against Amber's supple ones.

She doesn't realize the surrounding water has turned emerald, the dark green seeping from Cordelia's skin and infecting the older woman's subconscious. She feels lighter from the release, but quickly pulls the green water back into her body.

No, she thinks. *This is my weight to bear.*

The new stream approaches, its familiar current drawing her in, and Cordelia lets herself be swept up by it.

But what meets her isn't what she's expecting.

She imagined Carter's subconscious would be streaked with waves of pink and red and lilac; their love for Amber seeping into every corner of their mind. She imagined Carter would be reliving every second with their partner, their most intimate moments ready to drown Cordelia in.

Instead, the water of Carter's mind is choppy and violent, tendrils of black and gunmetal grey cutting through the once clear surface. The darkened waters grab at Cordelia, sweeping her up and dragging her down into the pain that shapes them. Beneath the surface of her consciousness, she watches Carter beg Amber to stay. The memory looks as if it's playing on a loop, but she realizes that Carter's words and Amber's responses change each time.

In some of them, Carter imagines convincing Amber not to leave, the waters darkening with the grey of their regret for words unsaid. In others, Amber tells Carter that she never loved them, the waters rippling with the midnight blue of their deepest insecurities.

Cordelia clutches her chest, the pain threatening to swallow both her and Carter whole.

Part of her is happy knowing that Amber's gone.

Part of her is furious.

"How am I supposed to move on?"

Cordelia looks around for the source of the voice and finds the memory shimmering deep in the blackened pool. In it, Carter stands in front of their mirror and whispers the question to their reflection. As expected, their reflection never answers back.

"How am I supposed to move on?" they ask the nothingness again.

Cordelia moves towards them. It's just a memory, but she knows it's the closest she's ever going to come to touching the real Carter.

"How am I supposed to move on?"

This time when Carter asks the question, their eyes find Cordelia's in the darkness.

"How am I supposed to move on?"

Cordelia wraps her arms around the imitation of Carter, pulling them close against her bare chest and pearlescent skin. Cordelia opens herself up to the memory, drawing as much pain and anguish into herself as she can.

"How am ... How am I ..."

The memory begins to quiet, the words fading away and the figure of Carter going still. Around them, the black water turns navy, then turquoise, then sky blue. The pain in Carter fades as it finds a new home in Cordelia, the waters of her subconscious slowly growing calm.

Cordelia tries to keep her arms wrapped around the memory of Carter, but her limbs become impossibly heavy and eventually she's forced to let go. She tries to swim but it's pointless, the weight of Carter's emotions dragging her down and pulling her under. The only way up is to let the pain go, to release the suffering back into Carter, but she can't.

She won't.

Not if it means hurting Carter.

No, she thinks. *This is my weight to bear.*

A Gift of Pearls
-S. C. Fisher-

When the child was orphaned, her prospects scattered on a northerly wind; one by one, delicate seeds of a dandelion clock, blown away by an unfortunate gust of fate. Irene's papa died suddenly, leaving behind great debt and few possessions, save for a chamber pot and a bereft little girl. At the behest of the village elders, Papa's brother received both bedpan and child into his keeping, where he found far more use for the former than the latter.

Despite such fettered roots, Irene flourished with each turn of the tide. By five and ten, she was mild-mannered, sweet-tempered, and – most important - soft in all the places a woman ought to be. It was unsurprising, then, that Irene attracted her share of suitors, though it was a fisherman by the name of Philip who cast the net to snare her. Philip's mastery of trade spoke in favour of his suitability and, without better options before or behind her, Irene acquiesced to the match. Secretly, however, she determined Philip to be peculiar. The siren song of the sea had beckoned him for most of his days. It flowed through every part of him in a wild wave of desire that could be neither quelled nor equalled by any other earthly delight. The ocean was his first love - his true love – and Irene was apprehensive that nothing beneath Andromeda's patch of sky could be deemed more powerful than that.

They married within a month. Poor as she was, Irene's dowry was simple: a few piles of middling stone, with which Philip could build a house. Irene would never know what possessed him to select the cliff jutting over the beach as the spot upon which to lay the foundations, but he was adamant that it should be so. The next morning, as construction on the cottage began, the gulls swooped and soared above, their calls echoing through the air. The newlyweds would be caught in the middle in their two-roomed stone palace, which Philip boldly determined would outlast all the stars in the sky. He sealed his promise with a kiss beneath the milky moonlight, and thus, the most important part of Irene's story began.

Winter gales orbited the cottage, rattling the unshuttered windows. They were too close to the sea to experience snow. Instead, there was frigid rain, which Irene collected in jugs to boil over the fire. The harsh curve of her belly gave the fisherman's wife away before the season's end. Despite the miserable cold that attacked the cliff each morning, Irene found some measure of joy in the promise of new life.

Where the pregnancy had not, the labouring near killed her. In the raw hours of a Sunday morning, Philip trudged down to the village to raise the midwife. Irene's hair was plastered to her forehead, and her eyes were tightly shut, unable to bear the excruciating pain. She waited, her heart sinking as hope slipped away. When the crone arrived, limping into the house behind Philip, she appraised her patient before ushering the father-to-be back to the yard. There, he smoked his pipe until the first tinges of orange leaked from sea to sky, and Irene's screams were absorbed by the caw of the osprey.

They buried the babe at the foot of the yard. When the shovel broke, Philip was forced to finish the chore with his bare hands whilst Irene looked on, weeping into the fringe of her shawl. All that remained was to mark the plot, and to once more shroud the redundant cradle.

"Shame," the fisherman remarked, crushing a stray spider beneath his boot. "But I shall have my son, when the time is right."

With no suitable response forthcoming, Irene turned away to shuffle back to the hollow cottage.

A second stone took up residence beside the first soon enough. Another boy, who lived to puff half a breath against his mother's breast. The third grave sprang from the earth within twelve more months; another unwelcome weed in an intended rose garden. Two years lapsed with nothing to show for them, aside from an herb patch that had been fertilised by Irene's own flesh and blood. Philip extended the cottage, adding rooms he swore into the neck of a bottle would sleep his sons. When the fourth was ripped from between Irene's legs – mottled, too tiny, and unnaturally limp – Philip beat his fists bloody on the outside wall.

"Fuck you! Fuck all of this! Just give me the child I fucking deserve!"

Bedbound - her face etched with lines drawn by their collective misery - Irene listened through the window as her husband unleashed his wrath. The door creaked moments after the night had quieted and, fearing the worst from Philip's state of mind, Irene slid down the mattress to feign sleep. Hardly breathing, she waited for her husband to make his move - whatever that might be. Irene could feel him nearby; feel the warmth of his shadow looming over the bedframe; feel his eyes burning into her shrivelled body with something akin to resentment.

Their hapless child had been swaddled in linens, then laid to rest temporarily in the cradle. This struck Philip as some form of a gruesome joke by the midwife - to lay a corpse in the crib he had so painstakingly carved; to discard a broken, dead thing where it might wound him most to see it. His latest son. His chance at some legacy beyond a dank cottage and a boat that could barely withstand the roll of the tide.

Drunk on wine and fury – oft a deadly combination - Philip snatched the bundle, and hurried to the garden. At once Irene sat upright, heart thrumming in her chest. Though her mind cautioned against it, Irene's aching breasts and gut implored her. On legs still streaked with blood, she stumbled from the house as the herring gulls cackled amongst themselves over her grave misfortunes.

Haste and alcohol made him sloppy, and Philip almost fell headlong over the fence. However, somewhere between the gate and the cliff, he recovered his footing. He managed to approach the ledge at a breakneck run, then. Helpless to prevent it, Irene could only bear witness as her husband pitched forward to offer his sacrifice to the ravenous waves.

The sound of the corpse breaking the water was swallowed by the rush of her pulse in her ears, and Irene heaved a cry that caused her womb to seize. For Philip, there was no remorse. It had felt right, somehow, to gift this one to the sea. After all, what did it matter if fish rather than worms gorged themselves on baby cheeks and toes?

Voice a cinched growl, Philip echoed the sentiment that had by now lived longer than the babe.

"The child I *deserve*."

Long days passed, consumed by a recovery process more difficult than those that had come before. Irene shied further away from her husband, whose touch grew crueller as alcohol bloated his stomach. With nothing to be done about it all, Irene took refuge in the shadows of her personal graveyard, where a fourth stone – distinctly lopsided – completed the row.

It was one night soon after, when Irene's cheeks stung with tears and violence, that a great storm swept in. It raged louder and longer than any inclement weather she had known, and Irene almost forgot that her fear of the cliff crumbling beneath the weight of the downpour could be eclipsed only by her fear of the man she had wed.

Outside, clouds skewered by lightning skimmed the roof. Inside, Philip threw back the bottle. Irene hunkered under the sheets and prayed for Aphrodite's protection. *She* had been reticent to provide it before, however, Irene's faith was the last life preserver left to cling to, and so she hung on as hard as she had to the bedposts during her labours. That was, until - despite the thick and misted pane - a whisper reached her ears. A feminine voice, inflected with a tenderness that Irene had all but forgotten.

"*Irene? Irene? Come down to the shore.*"

The fisherman's wife stilled, fingers tightening around the blanket, and cocked her head as she listened to the melody that beckoned her into the eye of the storm.

"*Irene, come to the shore. We have a gift.*"

She did not think on it long before Irene swung her legs over the side of the bed. Inexplicably, her fear lifted as the chill seeped from the tiles into her toes. Philip sat by the fire, warming himself and supping, but he was distracted enough that Irene made it to the door without notice. Sheets of lightning lit up the sky, dyeing it shades of white and pale yellow, and the rain fell in spears that plastered Irene's hair to her cheeks. Despite it all, she made a beeline for the path that meandered to the beach, sure of her destination already in the marrow of her bones. When she reached the sand, muck and mud caked her feet and ankles, browning her skin and the hem of her nightgown. The tide crashed against the rocks, birthing waves that plucked at the constellations, yet Irene persisted, unperturbed by the danger. Somehow, in the middle of the beach, a solitary rock pool had survived the carnage and, like a moth drawn to the pull of the lamplight, Irene hastened on.

And there, within the shallows of the pool, snuggled inside a nest of seaweed - much to her amazement - Irene found an egg.

It was not at all like the eggs the chickens laid daily, nor the small speckled offerings that the sparrows sequestered in their nests. Instead, Irene's egg resembled the mermaid's purse that Philip had once shown her, tangled in his net - only this was bigger, at least the size of a dinner plate, and twice as swollen. When she lifted it into her arms, the weight of it struck Irene, made greater by whatever creature wiggled away inside the jet-black membrane. Smiling, Irene cradled the egg, then rocked it gently. The wind caressed her face, pleased that she had accepted the gift, and the deluge receded to a patter that resembled a mother's lullaby. With the prize secured, Irene made her way back to the cottage.

For several weeks, the egg never left her side. Irene wore it close to her chest in a makeshift sling, then took to bed with it tucked into her stomach. Existing in a state of near constant inebriation, Philip questioned none of it – not the egg's mysterious appearance nor his wife's obsession with it - and Irene found herself more benevolent towards him for his apathy.

It hatched at the end of a fortnight, when the couple was preparing for bed. A sudden wet tearing sound was all the warning they received. Together, shoulder to shoulder, Irene and Philip gathered around to watch as a tiny, human hand emerged to swat the air. At once, Irene was in motion, tearing the slimy casing apart with her nails until the babe was free. Naked and newborn, the perfect little girl lay upon soiled sheets, sucking her fist and staring at her new parents through eyes as grey as the clouds that overhung the cottage.

"Margalo," Irene breathed as she stroked the infant's hair. Such a precious discovery. A treasure. A pearl.

"A girl," was all Philip saw fit to remark in a tone coloured vividly by his disappointment. Regardless, that night, the cradle he had fashioned with his own kin in mind was given over to its first living occupant.

Margalo grew like any other child in the village. She crawled, then walked, then made her mother's heart pound when she eventually ran without care. She wailed all night as she cut teeth, then lost them one by one a handful of years later to the apples Irene brought home from market. She sang, and she danced, and she played, and she learned to cook under her mother's patient tutelage. It came as no real surprise, however, that what she did best, above all other things, was swimming. Margalo had mastered the art as a toddler, whilst Irene clapped from the sand and shouted praise that almost gave Philip cause to lift his head from his nets. Margalo had a knack for holding her breath, too, and whenever her golden head disappeared beneath the foam, her mother knew without any sense of concern that it might well be minutes before she broke the surface in search of air. Margalo was not simply connected to the water, she was an extension of it; as enduringly beautiful as the clearest ocean and, unbeknownst to the one who loved her most, as deadly.

For a while, Irene was almost content, and she bore her burdens with a forced cheerfulness that saw her through the worst of days. It was Margalo's eighteenth birthday that changed it all.

To his credit, Philip held off organising a match for their daughter longer than Irene's uncle had. Unfortunately, the prospect of marriage was an inevitability that could not be avoided forever. As was his way, Philip broke the news without preamble when they sat down to supper on a calm evening.

"You are to be wed." Philip reached for the bread, freshly baked in the fire that morning, and tore off more than his fair share. "The arrangements will be final within the month."

Margalo looked down at her plate, setting aside her fork as hunger deserted her. In truth, she did not wish to wed, ever. Men were brash and coarse and cruel in her experience, and trading a father who treated her as an inconvenience for a husband who would likely do the same - whilst demanding so much more - was not the way she wished to spend the remainder of her years.

Irene sat straighter in her seat, shock galvanising her spine. "Wed? She is a child!"

The protest drew a hard look from Philip, who had never liked to be questioned, even on his best days.

"She is ten and eight. Old enough, unless you would have your only daughter for a spinster?"

Irene pushed away her meal, jaw locked by barely restrained anger. Sensing the impending eruption, Margalo clasped her hands in her lap and looked away, gaze straying to the window where she could watch the sea ripple, stirred by fingers of moonlight.

"Eight and ten is hardly grown, and…"

Philip's fist met the table, upsetting the jug. Whilst Irene startled, Margalo at once scrambled to right the wrong. Using the hem of her apron, she mopped the spreading pool of water, almost frantic in her approach to the task. Her breaths came in gasps of exertion that did not match the effort of the labour, but Irene scarcely noticed her daughter's distress over the focussed roar of her own fury.

"Not another word on it." Philip swallowed a mouthful of fish and potato. Grease wet his lips, and he licked at them with his caustic tongue to savour the taste. Made brave by an outpouring of maternal outrage, Irene was undeterred.

"You have sold our daughter as though she were the daily catch! I have many words."

The silence settled inside and outside the cottage, creating an eerie stillness. Margalo fixed frightened eyes upon her mother. In her experience, Irene had always been mindful of Philip; obedient and observant to a fault, in fact. Margalo was certain that this reckless defiance would not be allowed to pass unchecked - it was simply too bold. Whilst the fisherman had never raised more than his voice to her directly, time and experience had given Margalo the measure of the man. She knew that the bruises that regularly adorned her mother's wrists like jewels were a product of more than a maladroit manner. Perhaps it was this, in the end, which spurred her into action.

"Away to your room, girl," Philip barked, his voice filled with authority. His narrowed eyes did not stray from his wife's face, which paled in the lamplight suddenly. Margalo, for the first time, disobeyed the instruction as if she hadn't heard it.

"I did not mean to question…" Irene struggled through a trembling bottom lip that heralded tears. "It is only that…"

In no mood for contrition, Philip reacted before Irene could: the fisherman's fist plunged across the table, driven by the full weight of his body. Irene's chair rocked back, displacing her, and she immediately scuttled crablike across the floor to cower against the wall. Philip stalked forward, reaching out with meaty fingers that clamped around the base of his wife's neck. He lifted and she stumbled to her feet, both hands grasping at his wrist. She felt dainty bones shift beneath the force of his grip and panic blew her pupils wide.

"Learn your place." Philip's thumb found the divot in her clavicle, and Irene clawed at his arm as darkness invaded the edges of her vision. "You bring shame upon yourself. Shame upon me!"

A sudden blur of movement was all that Irene was aware of before the pressure at her throat abruptly eased. Margalo's fingers were equally strong, fastened around Philip's arm so that her nails pressed crescents into his skin. Philip barely felt the discomfort of it; the outrage was another matter entirely.

"Get off me, girl," he roared, attempting in vain to shake Margalo free. She held on, lips pressed into a solid line of determination.

"You will not touch her again."

Foolish and arrogant, Philip refused to heed the warning. Raising his free hand, palm open, he swung for his daughter without hesitation.

Margalo was a Black Marlin, speeding for a shoal without a backward glance to the open water as she committed to the act: an act that set her apart from the other girls in the village far more than the ability to swim without breathing. The scream was unholy as teeth clamped down on Philip's index and middle fingers.

"What have you done?" Irene croaked, aghast, as her hand fluttered to her bruised neck.

Blood spurted from the nubs that were all that remained of Philip's fingers when Margalo drew back – cheeks bulging and jaw working as she chewed. Philip fell to his knees, wailing, with his ruined hand held adjacent to his face. Irene balked. Her husband crumpled and her daughter opened her mouth wide enough to allow two bones – picked meticulously clean - to tumble from her lips. Irene's eyes flashed to Margalo's crimson-smeared face long enough to catch sight of the rows upon rows of wicked curved teeth that now filled her pretty mouth. Without a word, the girl bolted for the door.

Margalo was a streak of emerald skirts, and though Irene tried to follow, it was hard to keep her feet under her with the growing puddle of blood ebbing across the floor.

"I will gut her! Wicked little bitch!"

Although paled and quivering, Philip was not to be silenced. He flopped on the ground, a giant fish out of water, clutching his hand and issuing threats that seemed feather-light when interspersed with his sobs. Irene had time for one final glance at her husband - pitiful creature that he was – before she gave in to the call of the ocean.

The door thumped against stone as Irene flung it open and a gust took it. One of the hinges, rusted with age, gave way and the frame sagged with a squeal that went unnoticed by the fisherman's wife, who had already reached the path beyond the gate. She could see Margalo in the distance; a speck with streaming blonde locks, moving at speeds that could surely be defined as otherworldly. She cut across the beach with singular focus, and Irene tried not to dwell on what might be lost to her if her daughter reached the water first.

"Margalo! Margalo, wait!" Her voice slipped into the pockets of the breeze and Irene wailed as she watched the child glide across the sand.

Margalo shed her skirts as she ran, tossing them to the air, upon which they ballooned like sails. Next, she moved onto her bodice. She clawed at the laces, fastened that morning by her mother's weathered hands, but gave in when the strings refused to loose. Instead, she ripped the garment in half and discarded both pieces in the sand, which was already littered by the many footprints that tracked her progress. It was as Margalo stood in the shallows - naked and with the tide kissing the backs of her thighs - that Irene finally caught up. Laboured breathing gave her presence away and, fearing reproach more than anything, Margalo's back straightened. Irene tried not to notice how the knots of her spine had melted away beneath the surface of suddenly grey and leathery skin.

"I am sorry," Irene rasped, her breath failing her. "Never again. I swear it to you now: never again."

Margalo wheeled around, surprise a tiny light in her eyes, which had clouded into silver pools shaped like almonds. She had not expected the apology. The gills that had opened at her throat flared, tasting the salt in the air with longing, and something in her core urged her to sink back beneath the waves from which she had been born. She did not have long. As though sensing as much, Irene stepped into the water so that her dress pooled around her waist, where tendrils of yellow hair already floated.

"I did not mean to choose him over you. Never again," Irene repeated, swallowing past the regret. "Can you forgive me?"

Blinking with eyelids that closed from cheekbone to brow, Margalo nodded. Her mouth opened, revealing the teeth that had wrought damage and deliverance, yet not a word passed her lips. She keened in frustration and Irene reached out to rest a hand against her cheek.

"I know," Irene murmured, thumb smoothing away a mixture of spray and tears. "Go now, child. You have nothing to fear."

With as much of a smile as she could muster, Margalo turned towards the horizon and ducked beneath the foam until the sea had swallowed the crest of her head. A single, triangular fin sliced through the water, heading at speed for the freedom of the wide ocean, whilst the fisherman's wife watched from the sand - a peculiar sort of grief drawing her features.

It was dawn before Irene returned to the cottage. She found things much as she had left them, save for the snoring lump with the bandaged hand that dominated her bed. A gust of wind surged through the open window, carrying the scents of salt and change. Resolved to keep the promise she should have made years ago, Irene closed the bedroom door behind her without waking her husband from his stupor.

The final grave to appear in the garden bore neither name nor date nor likeness. A patch of forget-me-knots circled its base, and the string of pearls draped over its apex never failed to catch the sunlight on fine mornings.

Faithful as the tide, Irene remained to tend to the little stone cottage that might outlast all the stars in the sky, although she had come to doubt that this would be the case. Some things - like the gods and the ocean - were eternal, but houses and wooden boats and men were not.

The fisherman's widow knew this better than most and - for such a gift - she rejoiced until her end.

LADY FISH
-LaShane Arnett-

My name is Marianne Rain. I never put much stock in old wives' tales. I assumed they were made-up stories; like fairy tales told to children before they fall asleep—or drift off to the land of dreams, where pink skies have cotton candy clouds, and beautiful goddesses rule the sea.

There was an old wives' tale mother used to tell me on repeat. Lady Fish, the Great Mother of the sea, was known for her iridescent skin that shimmered with beautiful colors and her long marginal lappets that flowed like cascading hair. With a single touch, she transformed the corals into a vibrant display of blues, purples, and pinks, and brought life to the once dull algae with shades of red and green.

Mother also used to tell me I could be anything I wanted to be. "Your thoughts will change your world," she'd say. "Do your duty and leave the rest to the gods," always with a smile and two thumbs up. And my favorite, "Don't let anything stand in your way." Which was motivational kevlar—permission to walk steadfast towards my dreams. Her words serenaded me with hope. As a child, I clung to the dreams she laid out for me. And there was absolutely no reason to doubt they would ever come true. That is…

Until I found her hanging off the side of her bed. The empty pill bottle lax in her hand; eyes opened wide.

Soul vacancy.

Empty vessel.

Void of dreams.

Until she became an empty shell, and her words, her laughter, her hopes for my future fell,

down,

down,

down,

tumbled into the puddle of blood and vomit on the floor.

It made me question, is it truly possible to be anything I desire? Or was it a lie, like her laughter?

Or was it truth, like her pain?

***

Mother's death changed everything. Aunt Jane came and scooped me and most of mother's things up in a frenzied blur; inhaling and exhaling our family secrets between sobs and pleas I didn't understand.

"We were raised in a house of pain, destined to die!" she cried. "It's so fucked up, up, up!" echoed in the semi-empty house. "This is fucked up! Mother told us…no!" First her eyes were wide and filled with sorrow, then anger crept in and with narrowed eyes, she disciplined her dead sister.

"You were so stupid! Look what happened to Ma! I told her." she whispered the last part; grabbing toys and toiletries; wiping tears, shoving clothes in trash bags haphazardly.

"She shouldn't have even had yo—" she pulled me close. "I'm sorry. Soo…sorry Pisces Child. No need to dwell." With a sigh and a slight push toward the door, she continued her lament. "Lady Fish. That fucking bitch!" Her hand went fast to her mouth as though someone was listening. "Well, she… she…" The vomit started.

I smelled the rancid fear bubbling up.

She bolted to the bathroom and all her worries poured down, down, down into the toilet.

Six-year-old me stood in the doorway crying.

"She came to collect. Pisces child." She choked out. "You mustn't be like my sister. Promise me!" She took my shoulders and shook the answer out of me.

"M'hmm." I promised with a vigorous nod.

Her eyes were far away when I agreed. They looked right through me — through my innocence, my despair, my trust, my need.

A quick mouth rinse and we were out the door.

"I'll protect you." She returned the promise. "I will. But I can't protect you here. We gotta go. Don't look back, my little Pisces Child. Don't look back."

I was too young and too hurt to comprehend what she was talking about. She forcefully dragged me out of there as I kicked and screamed.

That day, I left behind happy memories wrapped in relentless tickles; motherly hugs that lasted through the night; bedtime stories and chocolate syrup topped sundaes on Friday nights. We left the family home as it stood — stained with the embitterment of sudden death, and what Aunt Jane feared the most: the pursuit of Lady Fish.

***

We made an empty, lonely life for ourselves—far, far away. But not far enough, we couldn't see the sea. Maybe Auntie Jane wanted to keep a watchful eye on its foaming waves.

When I was 10 years old, I discovered that Lady Fish had placed a curse on our family. After years of beautifying the sea, she was rewarded with a beautiful child of her own. But after only six blissful years, watching her child learn and grow, one drunken night, one of our ancestors, a fisherman named Milton Bledsoe, ended her child's life with a harpoon through the heart—killing her instantly.

Heartbroken and full of rage, Lady Fish tore through the sea, cursing and transfiguring creatures; like the once timid jellyfish to whom she gave a sting. She created lampreys, and piranha, and electric eels that lit her way. Everything in the ocean became either icy vengeance or blackening ire. And the once beautiful goddess grew hideous polyps and welts all over. Her iridescent skin turned slimy and gray. The marginal lappets that once looked like cascading, flowing hair turned into life sucking tentacles that ensnared her prey; and if these tentacles didn't submerge you under water, their suckers drained you of your blood.

She searched for Mr. Bledsoe for weeks; causing cyclones that devoured towns and mile wide tsunamis, which plunged even the bravest men undersea to die painfully drowning. All coastal towns were destroyed. Then, after she was done drowning Milton in her sorrow and rage, she didn't stop there. She vowed to the gods above and the devils below to kill the firstborn in his bloodline—for all eternity.

"Your mother wasn't sup'pose to have you." Aunt Jane confessed. "I told her ta stay away from men, but she fell hard for your dad who left…" she scoffed. "As soon as you started growing inside. And she refused to get rid of you. Such a selfish, selfish bitch." Jane slurred into her bottle of gin.

She went on to say, until she heard my daring screams that challenged the world, she had despised what I was for their family.

A burden.

An obstacle.

A harsh reality, meant to make life harder for her and her sister. "

You hated me?" My 10 year old self questioned.

She didn't answer; she continued, with slovenly words sputtering sweet apologies. "Then I saw your rou…wound wittle cheeks. Pisces Chil'. And your ten chubby toes and I…yep…I was still angry."

The tears fell.

She gently shook them away.

"But I understood the power of love. Your mother got six good years to love you." She smiled in remembrance, then hiccuped loudly. "They were six good years, weren't they?"

"Yes." I said, remembering as well.

"She followed in our mother's footsteps and appeased Lady Fish by choosing to end her own life. A brave thing to do. For mother, it was Marni. And for Marni it was you."

Twelve-year-old me made a vow to Aunt Jane to never fall in love. "No men. No children. Ever!" she made me swear.

"I swear." I said and went back to singing an old melody that played in my head on repeat.

"Where'd you hear that song?" She asked, crazed. She grabbed me up from the table, stared deep into my eyes, then shook me so hard my head ached. "T'ell me!" She hiccuped. The sweet sting of gin slapped my face.

"I don't know." I cried. "I hear it in my dreams!"

She let me go. Pushed me away. After a hard stare and a long swig from her bottle, she made me swear again. "Don't sing that fucking song no more! No more singing! No more fucking curses! You hear!" and I agreed.

Four years later…

The day I believed old wives' tales were true was a few days before my sweet sixteenth.

Sweet sixteen.

Wasn't that what they called it?

Aunt Jane leaned against the doorframe of my bedroom. She bit the tips of her fingers, a little nibble here and there. So nervous and fidgety. I was used to it, for her nervousness started as soon as I turned 15.

She would sit with heavy lidded stares that made me uncomfortable. And some days they were vacant, empty of focus, as if she wasn't truly there. Her mind was far off in the distance, as though some memory or longing held her hostage. Or a voice I couldn't hear lulled her, and she'd sway back and forth to an inaudible beat.

"Auntie Jane, you're biting." I had to remind her to stop sometime.

"Such an annoying habit." She laughed.

There was something else on her mind. A meaning behind her stutters and awkward stares. I knew she loved me and feared me all the same. But that fear made her distant—it changed our relationship.

But that day she stood in my doorway, for no reason at all. Her fingers looked like prunes, like they'd been marinating in water. I must have been staring at them strangely, because she clasped her hands behind her back so they couldn't be seen.

"Are you okay?" I asked.

She carried her emotions like a baby; cradled them in her arms, tightly wound around her insecurities. She rubbed her elbows, searching for something to say.

"I'm fine." She chuckled. "Don't worry about me, Pisces Child."

"Wow… Pisces child? You haven't called me that in a long time."

She turned her head down the darkened hall, as if someone called her name. I couldn't see from the bed, but I lifted to my elbows and listened. The house's silence was thick and tangible.

"What's up Auntie? Do you hear something? Is someone here?"

"Huh?" Her sweat caused her hair to stick to her forehead. "Huh? Oh, no. Just us." She grinned.

"Are you sure you're okay?" I had become quite curious and wondered if she would answer and tell me truthfully what was wrong.

Her arm fell to her sides. She stood up straight and smiled. "I'm okay. I'm sorry I…I haven't been sleeping very well."

"Me neither." It was time to come clean, and with one question, I opened the gates. "Soo, are you hearing her too?"

"What? What do you mean? Who?"

"Lady Fish."

Her jaw dropped, but she held firm to her ignorance.

"About three days ago, I started hearing a woman's voice calling to me in the night. At first, I thought it was mother." I searched her widened eyes. "But I don't really remember what she sounded like." I looked down at my feet dangling from the bed. I reached back for mother's voice. I knew it to be soft and sweet, pained and distant at the end, like Aunt Jane's had become.

"But now," I continued, "I know this woman's voice isn't mother's." She shook her head no with me.

"But it sounds so familiar. Have you heard it Auntie?"

Auntie Jane went pale, but she didn't speak.

"This woman sang the most saccharin melody. It was as calming as soft waves ebbing and flowing. Truly mesmerizing."

I closed my eyes and listened to Lady Fish sing to me.

My true mother.

She beckoned me.

Although I vowed to never sing again. I began humming the haunting melody.

Auntie Jane was visibly nervous, so I knew she had heard the siren's song. I hopped off the bed, feeling invigorated, ready to be vindicated, for my auntie was a snake. That's what Lady Fish told me.

I glided to the window, my feet barely touched the ground. I stopped singing and could hear Auntie's breathing quicken.

"She has been telling me tales of old. And some new ones, too." I began. "She had very interesting things to say about you, Auntie."

I turned on my heels, pointing an accusatory finger at Auntie Jane. The nervousness that made her head twitch and chest convulse traveled down to her knees.

"What? Me?"

One step back.

Two steps.

Three.

"Pisces Child," she laughed, "What are you talking about?"

"Lady Fish! Surely you remember her? She said it was you who was supposed to die the night mother killed herself. You!" I felt the skin on my left leg grow taut as it stretched—my head inched closer to the ceiling. "She said it was your pill bottle in mother's hand."

Taller still. Hips opening wide.

"That you made a vicious, desperate deal to keep yourself safe."

"What?" she eked out through tightly pursed lips. "Lies!" she shook her head.

I saw the fear swimming. I heard her heart pounding, pounding. "It isn't true. She's warped your mind. That's what she does! Pisces chil'—"

"Don't call me that! That was mother's name for me. You don't ever get to call me that again! She said you talked mother into killing herself. That it was your words, like venom injected through soft sentences disguised as care and concern. All night long, you poisoned her mind. Blaming her for having me. Liquoring her up and handing her pills at the end."

I felt my right leg bulge and pulse, stretch and elongate. I couldn't hold back the moans of agony. They echoed a terrible sound through the house as my skin ripped and my body morphed into a creature of the sea. A long continuous wail, like a bated call for revenge—the pain was buried beneath so much anger. My once smooth skin erupted with diamond shaped dorsal scales. My legs were no longer legs, they were giant muscular tentacles.

"She said you were destined to die. You! That you and mother were close in age, but you were the oldest in the family. You made the deal to save your own life, in exchange for mothers and mine!"

The room grew dark. All the rage that pumped through my veins made me want to throw-up; instead, I screamed.

"Me!"

Auntie Jane backed into the hall.

"The day I turned sixteen, you were going to give me up. You were going to kill me!" Driven by anger, I screeched and wailed and rushed her. And oh, it felt so good, the way the wall split when I pinned her against it. My anger seethed.

"I loved you Auntie! I thought you loved me!" My tears fell. "I dooo!" She quivered.

"I thought you loved my mother. Your only sister!" I laughed. "I don't even care. I was destined to die! I can accept my duty. Mother taught me that! But you! You're a coward! And a liar!" A deep, guttural voice came through from my mouth. "It should have been you! I could have had ten more years with her!"

Like fire through my brain, the blackening pain of death and loss seared through my reasoning.

I was sorrow.

I was vengeance.

"It should have been you!" My voice was deep and unrecognizable. "How could you?"

All I saw was red. My fists pounded the wall.

"Coward!" Boom.

"Coward!" Boom.

"Coward!" By her head.

"Die!" Boom.

"Die!" Boom.

"Die!" through her head.

Rage.

As I thrust my hand forward, it pierced through her skull, slicing through her brain, and finally coming to a halt as it embedded itself in the wall. As I pulled my hand away from her face, she crumpled onto the floor. Empty vessel.

Void of dreams.

As I stared at Auntie lifeless on the floor, the image of my mother's dead body burned through my mind. I blinked. My eyes were transformed, big bulging eyes that saw through the hideous monster she used to be. I lifted her and held her gently, then took her out to sea. In the middle of the ocean, bright and glowing, was a beautiful goddess restored—Lady Fish—waiting for me.

I threw Auntie Jane to the sharks. Lady Fish smiled at my offering. She rode an enormous wave, glistening in the moonlight. I bowed when she came to me. "Get up! Get up!" She kissed my cheek. "My beautiful child!" She cried.

"Mother?" I asked. Happiness overwhelmed me. All the rage and anger I felt slid off and fell deep, deep, deep into the ocean.

"Yes, my Pisces Child," said Lady Fish. "I've waited so long for you. What took you so long?"

ACKNOWLEDGEMENTS

About The Editor

There was always something a little off about Harriet...she was the only who lived and adored the dark and macabre...as well as the spooky. So, she decided, why not write horror stories with supernatural elements to them? Growing up in the middle of a cornfield in northeast Iowa, what else is there for an imaginative little girl to do? Harriet is the author of several published works, including "Cursed Legacy", "Aborted Justice", "The Summoning" as well as several submissions in anthologies. Her first published anthology, 'HorrorScope: A Zodiac Anthology' was released this past February.

She lives in Cedar Rapids, Iowa with her husband and their four fur-children. And she doesn't see that changing anytime soon (unless you wanna donate to her Ko-Fi to help her move to Europe).

Lylith & Herne

Lylith Nyx is a pansexual witch that loves nothing more than to push the boundaries between sex, death and monsters. She is the Mistress of Monsters at The Cult of Horrotica, where she shares tales of macabre eroticism to the mortal world, told to her by the supernatural creatures that reside within. She is also the Co-Founder of Infernal Gates Press, and Editor and Curator of Cult Horrotica Magazine. It is her desire to raise more awareness to the overlooked, and sometimes unfairly judged, genre of erotic horror and to give a voice to all authors who write in this exquisite style. You can find her being unashamedly depraved and fearlessly kinky at www.infernalgatespress.co.uk and on Instagram @lylithnyx

Herne The Horned is a child of the moonlight and a worshiper of the earth. For many years he lived someone else's life, but is now fulfilling the destiny he always knew was written for him. Herne is proud to be a part of The Cult of Horrotica, Sub-Editor and Curator for Cult Horrotica Magazine, and Co-Founder of Infernal Gates Press. You can find him fulfilling his role as Keeper of The Damned at www.infernalgatespress.co.uk and on Instagram @hernethehorned

Rose Whittaker

Rose is a writer and game designer based in the UK who loves creating fantasy adventures. Alongside writing for tabletop games, she is an illustrator, graphic designer and avid DnD player.

A.D. Jones

A.D Jones lives in the North of England; where he spends his time favoring books over people and can be found writing or devouring said books to review online. He loves Coca-Cola and cult movies and dislikes the movie 'The Karate Kid' with a passion that burns brighter than the sun. He recently released his debut novel, 'Umbrate,' a gritty urban fantasy crime thriller. You can find him on Instagram - the_evergrowing_library

Alex Penuelas

Alex is just an aspiring writer trying to make a name for himself. He has written various short stories and poetry – check them out on vocal.media/authors/alex-penuelas and on his IG: @penuelasalex for more shenanigans.

Alyssa Milani

I'm a Canadian mom of two who studied at Concordia University obtaining a Major in Creative Writing and a Minor in English Literature. I independently published my first novel in 2014 of all the works I wrote at University. I now have eleven independently published novels under my belt . My anthology Asylum of Diction has received many awards; The BookFest Spring 2023 Third Place Award for Anthologies, Silver Award Winner 2021-2022 Reviewer's Choice Awards, Five-Star Reader Views Review, Award-Winning Indie Brag Medallion Honoree 2021. I've received positive reviews for my independently published works and did a book signing at Indigo in 2020 for A Truth Be Told.

Jena Glover

Jena Glover is a life-long reader and writer with a passion for telling stories about strong, independent women just like the ones in her family. She enjoys exploring the twists and turns of what makes us all tick as human beings and prefers to create characters who are innately flawed. She lives in Ohio with her husband, two cats, and dog.

Kerry E.B. Black

Kerry E.B. Black writes from an over-stuffed little house situated along a fog-enshrouded river in the land where Romero's Dead roamed. Her children think she's dull, and their dogs agree, but the family cats, Poe and Hemingway, feel differently. The felines find a kinship with their nocturnal buddy and encourage Kerry to write. She is included in several anthologies and has a handful of books of her own.

Jenna Dietzer

Jenna Dietzer is the author of **Fear Her**, a female-centric horror short story collection, and **Dark Offerings**, a horror novella set for release in 2024. She resides in Tampa, Florida with her husband and their fur-kids. Her short stories have been published in Scare Street's Night Terrors Vol. 21, New Gothic Review, the Executive Dread anthology by Jolly Horror Press, and Coffin Bell. You can find her on Instagram @jenna.dietzer.

Alyssa Stadnyk

I have a degree in English Literature from Concordia University. I've been writing novels and short stories since I was five years old. I have a few written works on the writing platform, Wattpad. I also have a submission in HorrorScope: Volume 3, titled 'Compatibility Kills!' I currently live in Montreal, Canada where I spend most of my time daydreaming.

Alexander Michael

Alexander Michael is a dark fiction author based in Australia, and a member of the Australasian Horror Writers Association. 2023 has been a great year, seeing the release of a new novella, titled Home, a haunted house story with a cosmic twist, and several selections from publishing presses and magazines. Books, nature, and music are his biggest loves, so he will often combine the three out walking national parks, using the time as a source of inspiration.

Ashe Woodward

Ashe Woodward is an English teacher and author of horror and dark fiction who sneaks bits and pieces of spooky stories into her classroom every chance she gets. Her original work includes the pandemic novella, *A Cemetery for Zooey* and the YA horror series, *Blackrock High*. She is also the host of the podcast, *That's So Morbid*. She lives, writes and records surrounded by her menagerie of pets and poisonous plants in northern Ontario, Canada. More of Ashe's work is available at ashewoodward.com.

Anthony Taylor

Anthony Carl Taylor was born and raised in Canton, Ohio in 1989, the third child of Donald Ray Taylor, and the second child of Carla Jo Taylor. He is the grandson of veteran William Workman and MaryAnn Workman. As a child, Anthony always enjoyed writing, which started in the 3rd grade and progressed then after. Throughout his childhood and into adolescence, Anthony carried a notebook wherever he went just in case inspiration would occur.

Hayden Robinson

Hayden Robinson is an English writer and poet. He writes about neurodivergence, overcoming trauma, and surviving in a dark and terrible world. His works have been published in various outlets, including Re-Route Art Magazine, HNDL Magazine, Diverse Verse 3, and Poetic Vision, as well as HorrorScope: Volume 3 and other anthologies. He currently resides in Georgia, USA with his wife and two cats.

Emma Jamieson

'Growing up in a haunted house in the middle of a forest which was an infamous spot for burning those accused of witchcraft.....all things morbid, spooky and dark were in Emma's destiny. She has always found comfort and beauty in things others may find terrifying and frequently seek solitude in graveyards. Embracing her creative streak, Emma has performed in the Edinburgh Festival Fringe several times and loves to write, in any capacity. She is an enormous horror movie geek, has an abnormal fascination with serial killers, reads like a women possessed and can be found sharing her bookish ramblings on Instagram @book_nooks_spooks'

Lucy Grainger

I don't consider myself a writer, but always wanted to try my hand at it, and I'm thankful for my friend, Harriet, for giving me the opportunity to submit my first attempt at a poem. I live in Colorado with my husband and cat, Milly. Also, I enjoy a good board game night or video gaming with friends.

Jack Finn

Jack Finn is a folk horror author and member of the Horror Writers Association living in the wilds of the Pacific Northwest. He is a lifelong believer that the Tooth Fairy proves you can trade body parts for cold, hard cash. Jack's debut horror novel, The Seven Deaths of Prince Vlad, was released in February 2023, and he is the author of two folk horror anthologies, Hell Shall Make You Fear Again and Legend of the Deer Woman. His short story, They Come When You Sleep, was recently included in Terrorcore Publishing's Doors of Darkness anthology. Jack is on Instagram and Twitter @TheRealJackFinn.

Allison Hillier

Allison Hillier lives in Montreal and spends her time drinking iced coffee, reading too many books and is always looking for a new world to fall into.

Elliot Ason

First and foremost, I'm a lover of all things romance, especially if there's a monster sprinkled in there somewhere.
I write steamy (and sometimes quirky) bite sized insta-love tales of monsters and magical creatures that are on a journey to find their one true match.
I work full time and am also a wife and mom - always outnumbered by two boys!

Kassidy VanGundy

Kassidy VanGundy was born and raised in South Bend, IN, a city juxtaposed between Chicago and a sea of cornfields. Built with a set of wings, she set out to see as many parts of the world as she could, from Athens to Sao Paulo. Although, she admits that heat lightning and driving on dirt roads occasionally tempts her to come back home. Right now, she's nesting in Chicago with her beautiful husband, Douglas, who is constantly subjected to chapter reviews of her writing, especially during the development of her first book, Cursed Fate.

Sabrina Voerman

Sabrina Voerman is a West Coaster with a penchant for visiting the numerous cemeteries across Vancouver Island. With a profound love of fairy tales and all things witchy, she draws her inspiration from the nature around her, allowing it to bleed into her storytelling. She is always seeking new adventures and places to explore, either in life or in her writing. When she isn't traversing all Vancouver Island has to offer, she can be found with a cup of coffee either reading a book or writing one.

Byron Griffin

Byron Griffin, author of Anastasia's Putrefaction and The Lilithian Verses, is a UK based writer of gothic literature and occult poetry, with a penchant for archaic language. Alongside their self published books, they have had their writing included in Curious Corvid's Magpie Messenger.

Alex Tilley

Although I don't consider myself a writer of horror, or am even any kind of connoisseur on the genre, my writing tends to draw on a dark intensity as an act of cathartic creativity. I am overly fond of researching matters of the occult, and spend lots of my time studying world religions, mythological constructs, and supernatural concepts/creatures. To have an opportunity to explore the Zodiac through a horror lens was one I could not pass up, and I took full advantage to loop in my undying appreciation for Anne Rice and Edgar Allen Poe into this short story that explores my own conflictual Gemini sign.

I'm a Canadian from Toronto, Ontario. I published my first novel of a fiction/folk horror/anti-colonial/magical realism series called Meshkwadoon December 2021, where the second novel of four is due for publishing early 2023. Meshkwadoon: Book 1 won the 5-star gold award through Literary Titan. I avidly write poetry, and have an unpublished collection that I will likely eventually share. I am also working on a literary fiction novella and a steam punk action-adventure story. For more information on my works, please visit www.alextilleyauthor.com or connect with me through Instagram at @alexander_tilley.

Morgan Chalfant

Morgan Chalfant is a writer, poet, gamer, and an instructor of writing at Fort Hays State University. He is a native of Hill City, Kansas. He received his Bachelor's degree in writing and his Master's degree in literature from Fort Hays State University. He is the author of the horror/thriller novella, Focused Insanity, and the urban fantasy novels, Ghosts of Glory and Infernal Glory. You can find him at his author page on Amazon.com and on Instagram: @eyesonly34. In his free time, he likes delving into horror movies, collecting ancient weapons, and playing with his cat, Reb Reginald "Danger Close" Brown.

Jelena Vuksanović

Academic flutist, awarded with International awards, improving and traveling the world as a soloist, member of orchestras and various chamber ensembles. She worked at the City Library in Novi Sad where by playing flute in the workplace she would attract users of all ages. Jelena is now the Head of the Music Collection at the oldest National Library in Serbia, Matica Srpska Library, and a member of the New Professionals SIG. She has assisted the people, like Senior Pastor of one of the inc.org.au/about/churches, and she is the founder of the non-profit organization https://sr-rs.facebook.com/udruzenje.restart/. Here, she has carried out projects, organized events and managed accounts on social networks in cooperation with international organizations and European Parliament. Jelena applies her eclectic experience in the field of librarianship & Music. She thinks globally and only "try" to acts locally. She quit role of social Media Manager for International and National Organizations in various fields of management. Working as a motivational speaker for years. She is also a professional singer, singing worldwide, also actively working in the field of Music Therapy.

Caleb James K.

Caleb James K. hails from Washington Pennsylvania where he lives with his wonderful wife. He is currently working on his first novel as well as several other projects. Some of his recent work has been featured in SPANK the CARP literary journal, Coalitionworks, and Literally Stories.

Ashley Scheller

Ashley Scheller lives with her family in Iowa. She is the author behind *The Wielder Diaries* fantasy adventure series, and Scheller enjoys making art of all kinds. Volume four is her first anthology, and she is excited for her debut: *Rosalind*.

A.S.C.

Avid reader and chronic pantser, ASC lives somewhere between the Internet and real life and enjoys setting stories free to fend for themselves. So far, none of them have come back.

Lanie Mores

Lanie Mores is the award-winning author of the four-part fantasy series, Father of Contention, and the horror novel spin-off to the series, Code of Reanimation. She has an Honours Bachelor of Science degree, an MA in Clinical Psychology, and is a member of the Canadian Authors Association. In her spare time, you'll find Lanie writing poetry and short stories, reading, gaming, binge-watching Netflix, or baking. She lives in Ontario with her family, and forever barking fur babies, Batman and Petri.

Daphinie Cramsie

Rumor is Daphinie (she/her/they/them) is really just three kobolds in a trench coat. They live in the SW United States with two spawnlings and a husband that is also likely to be yet another three kobolds in a slightly longer trench coat. Somehow they all live with a cat, and three dogs. You'll find that most of their work swings within the genres of fantasy, horror, and occasionally sci-fi.

A P Vrdoljak

A South African author of comics and poetry, mostly within the horror genre. Vrdoljak's writing often weaves the ordinary with the otherworldly. Take a journey into the darkness with a spark of lighthearted humor along the way. Follow @badspellcomics

Skye Myers

Skye Myers is a writer and photographer based in Alberta, Canada. She is a Hallowe'en, horror movie, and tattoo enthusiast, a tea drinker, a book lover, and a reader of people. She lives outside Edmonton in the boondocks with her partner and their fur babies. Her sun, moon, and ascendant signs are all Scorpio.

Brianna Malotke

Brianna Malotke is a freelance writer and member of the Horror Writers Association based in Washington. Her most recent work can be found in *Out of Time* from Timber Ghost Press and *Their Ghoulish Reputation* from Dark Lake Publishing LLP. You can find her horror poetry in *The Spectre Review* and *The Nottingham Horror Collective*. She also has horror work in the anthologies *Beneath, Cosmos, The Deep, Beautiful Tragedies 2, The Dire Circle, Under Her Skin,* and *Holiday Leftovers*. In 2023 her debut horror poetry collection will be released by Green Avenue Books as well as *Fashion Trends, Deadly Ends*. For more malotkewrites.com

Caitlin Marceau

Caitlin Marceau is a queer author and lecturer based in Montreal. She holds a Bachelor of Arts in Creative Writing, is an Active Member of the Horror Writers Association, and has spoken about genre literature at several Canadian conventions. She spends most of her time writing horror and experimental fiction, but has also been published for poetry as well as creative non-fiction. Her work includes *Palimpsest, Magnum Opus, A Blackness Absolute,* and her debut novella, *This Is Where We Talk Things Out.* Her second novella, *I'm Having Regrets*, and her debut novel, *It Wasn't Supposed To Go Like This*, are set for publication in 2023. For more, visit CaitlinMarceau.ca or find her on social media.

S.C. Fisher

'British horror author S. C. Fisher lives wherever His Majesty's Royal Air Force tell her to at that moment in time, usually with her husband, four children, and an impressive menagerie of pets. Fisher's debut YA horror series, Base Fear, explores the trials of military family life on a number of supernaturally troubled bases, (which is absolutely *not* a metaphor for the colourful array of fellow wives and girlfriends she has met over the years!) You can find examples of her other work in anthologies such as This Old House: The Bathroom, and Sinister Stories by the Ten, as well as on the Crystal Lake Publishing Patreon page and the Trembling With Fear website. When she is not writing, Fisher can usually be found gaming, cooking, or drinking far too much iced coffee.

LaShane Arnett

LaShane Arnett is a poet and author living in Southern California. She is a weaver of words and a lover of the imagination. She loves all things, dark and twisted that make people question their reality and their connection to it. She loves diving deep into the beauty of reality, exploring the depths of the human condition, and she does it through both prose and poetry. She is an indie author advocate. Her first book is a book of poetry Go Ask LaShane Decades of Ramblings. She has also published two paranormal thrillers, The Pain Eater and The Magic Man, books one and two in The Sadie Reed Series. When she isn't writing she enjoys reading and spending time with her family, especially her grandchildren, and her dog Buddy.

Printed in Great Britain
by Amazon